PRAISE FOR *MURDER TOWN*

'Darkly gripping from its first pages . . . The cast of characters are so well described I felt like I'd met them . . . Startling, filmic and haunting' **ALLIE REYNOLDS**

'Unveiling one richly layered character after another, *MURDER TOWN* has plenty of tricks up its sleeve and crackles with tension throughout. Shelley Burr walks the mystery tightrope with ease, making every character as sympathetic as they are suspicious, and bringing the town of Rainier to life with a knowing flick of her pen' **JACK HEATH**

'Shelley Burr's legion of fans are sure to enjoy the twists and turns of this small-town Australia murder thriller' **SALLY BOTHROYD**

PRAISE FOR *WAKE*

'Boasts all the energy of a true-crime podcast with a cast of wounded characters you desperately want to protect. A complex and tightly wrought plot pulsates with intrigue. The starkness of Shelley's prose echoes the parched land, while her atmospheric descriptions draw you in to a town that quickly feels so familiar you could walk into the pub, pull up a stool and order a beer' *THE AUSTRALIAN WOMEN'S WEEKLY*

'The tension builds, and the revelations keep coming, right until the final page where a thrilling climax combines horror, relief and hope. If I wore an Akubra I'd doff it' *THE TIMES*

'Offers readers something more than merely a page-turning rush, although there is plenty of that to be found too . . . A cracker of a story and some surprising twists to the tale' *BOOKS+PUBLISHING*

'Politically savvy, cleverly plotted . . . the kind of book that invites the ravenous language of binge reading: compulsive, propulsive, addictive' *NEW YORK TIMES BOOK REVIEW*

'An absorbing cold case crime story with a strong sense of place and a good set of characters' **CANBERRA WEEKLY**

'A nerve-jangling thriller with a brilliantly twisty plot . . . A haunting exploration of trauma in the age of celebrity victimhood. Shelley Burr's true-to-life characters, beautifully evoked landscapes and breakneck pacing make for compulsive reading. A triumphant debut' **ROSE CARLYLE**

'An effortlessly accomplished, astonishing debut set against the heat and isolation of the Australian outback, deftly unpicking the layered repercussions of a decades-old crime. This is a sharply observed unravelling of trauma and survival, exploring which crimes get to make the headlines and stay in the public's consciousness. Gripping rural noir at its tense and atmospheric best, which will hook you from the very first paragraph. *WAKE* is a standout debut and Shelley Burr's a voice that will make you sit up and take notice' **DINUKA McKENZIE**

'If you love Jane Harper's books, you will love this even more. Compelling characters, an intriguing plot and so well written' **KAYTE NUNN**

Shelley Burr

Murder Town

HODDER &
STOUGHTON

First published in Great Britain in 2023 by Hodder & Stoughton
An Hachette UK company

1

Copyright © Shelley Burr 2023

A CIP catalogue record for this title is available from the British Library

Hardback ISBN 978 1 529 39488 7
Trade Paperback ISBN 978 1 529 39489 4

Printed and bound in Great Britain by Clays Ltd, Elcograf S.p.A.

Hodder & Stoughton policy is to use papers that are natural, renewable
and recyclable products and made from wood grown in sustainable
forests. The logging and manufacturing processes are expected to
conform to the environmental regulations of the country of origin.

Hodder & Stoughton Ltd
Carmelite House
50 Victoria Embankment
London EC4Y 0DZ

www.hodder.co.uk

Because after all, what can we hope for in life and death but to be buried under a stone carrying our own name?

Dr Colleen Fitzpatrick

PROLOGUE

THE LOCKED SHOP door rattled, startling Gemma out of her focus. She'd closed up hours ago, but had the light on so she could count skeins of wool for the taxman. That didn't mean she was trying to invite midnight visitors. It was a man, huddled inside a large black jacket. For an awful moment she thought it was Vincent, until she remembered, as she had so many times in the past weeks, that Vincent would never knock at her door again.

'We're closed!' she hollered. What kind of absolute twit expected a town like Rainier to have a twenty-four-hour teashop? She felt bad for him, with no sign of a scarf or hat in this cold, but she wasn't opening the door in the middle of the night.

It was amazing how much things had changed in only a handful of months. Back in April, she'd have gone up to the door and told him to jog on. But after the police found the second body, that poor woman, Gemma's mother had sat her down and told

1

her to forget polite. Forget kind. Forget helpful. The only rule that mattered now was to stay safe. She'd given her a copy of Ann Rule's book on Ted Bundy, with passages highlighted about how he'd lured victims with plays for sympathy and requests for help.

The man pounded on the glass with his open palm. He swayed, and leaned against the window with one shoulder. He was three sheets to the wind, and she hoped it was only booze affecting his balance. He kept slapping the glass with his other hand.

Her irritation inched closer to fear.

He stepped back and then stumbled forwards, hitting the door with his full weight so it shook in the frame.

She dropped her clipboard and backed as far into the shop as she could, terrified he was going to smash the glass. Scuttling sideways to the kitchen door, she slipped inside. She secured the door behind her, but it was just a hollow sliding door with a little hook and eye latch at the top, so that would do nothing. She grabbed the cordless phone from the wall and dialled with one hand, resting the other on the handle of her grandmother's cast-iron teapot. She knew she could swing that, if it came to it.

To her relief Constable Hugh Guillory answered the station phone. Detective Mick Seabrooke, the shit-hot arsehole transferred from Sydney when the murders started, made her nervous. Besides, she'd heard he barely answered the phone on night shifts, and brushed off everything short of murder as 'hardly police business'.

'Are you there alone?' Guillory asked. The genuine worry in his voice did nothing to help her anxiety.

The banging had faded to a meek tapping, which was more unnerving in a way. The man didn't sound angry anymore, but he hadn't given up.

'Yeah, it's just me,' she said. 'My parents had to take Nan to the hospital again. I'm nineteen.' She added the last part a little more sharply than she'd intended. Even when Nan was at home, it was usually just Gemma downstairs in the shop. Her grandmother's health was failing rapidly, and her parents were exhausted from her care. Somewhere along the way they had stopped asking Gemma to help out running the business and just started assuming she would take care of it. That was fine by her, but it meant she wasn't going to stand for Guillory, who was barely a few years older than her, treating her like a frightened kid left home alone.

'Yeah, I know who you are, mate. Can you get upstairs and lock the door?'

She peered through the kitchen window at the dark of the walled back courtyard. Getting upstairs meant unbolting the back door, running up the back steps, using her key to open the house door and then locking it behind her again. A long time to be out there and exposed.

The courtyard gate stood open, and she could swear she saw a flicker of movement in the alley beyond. But it could be her racing mind playing with her.

'No.'

'One of Christian's customers probably had a few too many,' Guillory said, but there was nothing dismissive in his voice. He was

3

calm, and soothing, and warm. 'I'll do a drive-by and move him along if he's still there.'

'Thank you,' Gemma said. 'You could stop in for a cuppa. I'll put the kettle on.'

'Yeah, ta,' Guillory said.

It only took a few minutes for the police cruiser to pull up, the engine distinct on the otherwise silent street. The man stopped his banging, and Gemma felt like she could breathe again.

'Gemma!' Guillory shouted, and the tone of his voice knocked the calm right back out of her. He wasn't calling her because he wanted his cup of tea. 'Gemma, open the door!'

She ran for the door and unlocked it, pulling up the bolt at the bottom. The door struck her shoulder as Guillory pushed it open. The man was draped against him, one arm over his shoulders. Gemma had no idea who he was – if he was a Rainier local, he hadn't been for long.

'I've called an ambulance,' Guillory said.

Guillory half-dragged, half-walked the man to the chair in the craft section, the one Nan had put out for husbands to sit in while her customers chatted and pawed through the displays. The man leaned back into it and his unbuttoned jacket gaped open, revealing the shreds of his once-white tank top, now soaked with red.

'You're okay,' Guillory said. 'We've got you, mate. The ambos are coming, they'll have you right as rain.' He seemed to be talking to himself more than the man, blathering clichés as he wadded up a handful of crocheted tea towels and pressed them to the man's chest.

Gemma hovered behind him, trying to remember what the St John's Ambulance volunteer had said about stab wounds when she and Aubrey took a one-day first-aid course. She'd got one hundred per cent on the quiz, but she was good at tests. She couldn't remember if they had given any advice on what to do if you knew all the right steps but couldn't make yourself move from a spot two feet away from the victim.

The man blinked woozily at her.

'I'm Hugh, and the pretty lady you're eyeing is Gemma,' Guillory said with forced jolliness. 'Can you give us a name, mate?'

'Dean,' he whispered, sounding sad.

Gemma glanced at the open door. She wanted to race over and lock it, but the ambulance crew would be on site at any moment – they were only coming from the station on Edgeworth Street – and she didn't want to slow them down.

It wouldn't have mattered, as it turned out. No matter how many tea towels Guillory pressed into service, Dean's blood continued to escape. Less than thirty seconds after she opened the door, and two minutes before the whoop of the ambulance sounded in the street, Dean took his last breath.

And Earl Grey's Yarn and Teashop became the last stop on the Rainier Ripper walking tour.

RAINIER RIPPER TRIAL TOUR - VIP LIST

POLICE
Detective Mick Seabrook (arresting officer)
Sergeant Hugh Guillory (young constable at the time, worked on the case)

VICTIM FAMILIES
Jaylene and Antoine Tjibaou (parents of Vincent): Jaylene only confirmed as attending
Marcus Shadwell (brother of Dean): not local, unconfirmed if attending

SURVIVOR
Tamara Fleischer: unconfirmed if attending

LOCAL RESIDENTS AND BUSINESS OWNERS
Gemma Guillory (nee Grey) - Earl Grey's Yarn and Teashop owner
Aubrey Seabrook (nee Dillon) - local farming family
Christian Holst - Pub Owner, engaged to Ruth Tanner, also a long-time local
Dr Tim Nicholls - town GP, married to Magistrate Lotte Nicholls - both on council!

ONE

'SO, UH, AS you would have seen from the map provided ahead of time, our planned route is circular. We would start and end here at the fountain. Part of what makes this such a, uh, compelling site for a tour, in my opinion, is that all of the points of interest are close together.'

Lochlan Lewis was a small man trying to look bigger, with his shoulders drawn back and his head up in a way that really just drew attention to how rapidly he was breathing. He wore a brand-new blue polo fleece, with the name of his tour company, *Lewis and Co.*, embroidered in gold across his chest.

The group was gathered beside the stone fountain that marked the precise midpoint between Melbourne and Sydney. Rainier was built around two parallel roads, both leading back to the old highway. One road took drivers south, to the on-ramp for Albury and Melbourne. The other took them north, to the on-ramp for Gundagai, Canberra and Sydney. On maps, both roads were labelled *Federation Road*, but for as long as Gemma could remember they had always referred to them as Melbourne Road and Sydney Road.

In between the two roads was the long, narrow Fountain Park. In Rainier's heyday it had been a busy picnic spot, shielded from the traffic by a curtain of pine trees. Now people avoided the area, and it was little more than an oversized pedestrian island.

'So you plan to start the tour with Vincent, not Eva?' Mick Seabrooke asked.

Hearing Mick speak their names so plainly made this whole idea suddenly, terribly real. Gemma sucked in a breath. Hugh grabbed her hand, and she resisted the impulse to pull away.

'We're, uh, still workshopping how best to begin the story, given that the first victim to be found was in fact the second to be killed, or at least the second of the known victims. We could kick off from the parkland beside the church, where police found the body of the first victim, the unidentified female –'

'Woman.'

Gemma didn't recognise the voice of the speaker, meaning that she must have been one of the 'interested parties' who had come from out of town to see the tour demonstration. Gemma resisted the urge to turn around and look. She could feel the tension in the gathered group, and didn't want any sidelong glances to be misinterpreted.

'Right. The unidentified woman now referred to as Eva Nováková.'

Gemma felt a little sorry for Lochlan. He was obviously nervous, slipping back and forth between stilted, clearly scripted lines and more off-the-cuff statements. Even if you set aside the open hostility from some quarters, it had to be painfully awkward to stand in front of an audience and recite the details of their own lives to them.

'If we start from Eva's burial site, we could then proceed to the other side of the church and the tour could follow the likely path Vincent Tjibaou took from his home to the fountain where his body was discov– '

'You are not going to include our home in this monstrosity,' Jaylene Tjibaou interrupted. She was nearly invisible under a slouchy knitted hat and high-collared coat, but there was still no mistaking her. Jaylene was the mother of Vincent Tjibaou, the first victim to be found.

'I assure you, the script would be extremely cautious and would certainly never point out your specific house or the fact that you still live there. But our research has found that the ability to walk in the path of the victims, to see what they saw, imagine feeling what they felt, is a major draw for potential tour customers. That opportunity for empathy.'

'Empathy,' Jaylene muttered under her breath, and a few people around her tittered uncomfortably.

'But the, uh, because the discovery of Eva's body was a result of the investigation into Vincent's murder, starting with Eva creates quite a confusing narrative. We're leaning towards a Vincent–Eva–Dean sequence. Beginning and ending here, which also emphasises how closely linked the murder sites are, their positioning right in the centre of town. One of the many unsolved mysteries surrounding the Ripper slayings is what drew the Ripper to this precise site. Tour customers will be invited to ask themselves that question as they view the area.'

'What about the service centre?' Mick asked. 'The story actually ends there, right?'

Of course Mick wanted the site of the Rainier Ripper's capture included in the tour. As soon as Hugh had called in the murder of Dean Shadwell, the police closed the roads in and out of Rainier. Within an hour and a half, a handful of officers, led by Mick, closed in on the Ripper at the service centre on the highway. The Ripper, a trucker named Jan Henning-Klosner, had a woman named Tamara Fleischer bailed up against a wall. The CCTV footage of Mick tackling the Ripper became one of the defining images of the case.

'That is true,' Lochlan said. 'It would be fantastic to include the dramatic end of the story in the tour.'

Beside her Hugh huffed, almost inaudibly. Gemma squeezed his hand.

'However,' Lochlan continued, 'the service centre is privately owned land, and the owners have declined to be involved. Not to mention the service centre isn't within walking distance, so we would need to change from a walking tour to a bus tour to include it, which would significantly increase our costs.'

'I had a question about that, actually,' Lotte Nicholls piped up. 'I'm not sure I understand how you expect to attract enough tour customers to cover your expenses. Your primary business runs in Melbourne, correct? So to run this tour you would need to cover six hours of travel and at least one night's accommodation. At thirty dollars a ticket you're not breaking even with less than twenty guests.'

Lochlan blinked rapidly, but smiled. 'That's a really great question, thank you. Obviously at the end of the day the, er, business and profits aspect are our concern, as we're not seeking any financial input from the town –'

'But you are asking us to risk our reputation,' Dr Nicholls, Lotte's husband, put in. 'The tour needs to be successful to make it worth the trade-off. You want to put up posters in Sydney and Melbourne advertising a tour that links our town name to its most terrible events.'

'It's already linked. Most people only know this town exists because of the Ripper murders,' Christian pointed out.

'It will fade away with time, if we let it,' Dr Nicholls said, his voice soft. 'This only gives it more oxygen.'

'The town will fade first,' Christian snapped.

This was the central argument the town had been having for months, since Lewis and Co. had first brought their proposal to the town council.

Rainier had once made a comfortable living as a pretty lunch stop for travellers on their way between Melbourne and Sydney. A few cute little restaurants, an art gallery, the teashop, the pub and even a winery and farm-to-table spot. Then the Rainier Ripper had arrived, and nobody heard the word 'Rainier' and thought of cute little restaurants and a lovely park for a picnic. They thought of bodies, and blood, and terror. A few years later a bypass shaved half an hour off the Melbourne–Sydney drive and cut Rainier off entirely, and now the only people who bothered with the Rainier exit did it for one reason: to take a selfie in front of one of the infamous places where someone lost their life.

Why not make it formal? Why not scrape a little bit of a living back from the horror they'd all endured?

The uncomfortable truth was that the town couldn't actually stop the tour from going ahead, if Lewis and Co. were determined to run it as planned. All the spots of interest were public parks and footpaths, and they didn't need permission to bring people through. However, the town could make life difficult for them if they wanted to. They could drag Lewis and Co.'s reputation through the mud, they could protest against the tours, they could refuse to serve any customers the tour brought to town. But there were a lot of businesses in town that wanted those customers.

To end the impasse, Lewis and Co. had offered a deal: they would present their tour to the community, the survivors, and the friends and family of the victims, and the council would then put it to a vote.

'To circle back to your question, which was two questions really, we are confident that we can get the interest we need to make this tour a go. Traffic into town may have slowed in recent years, but thousands of cars pass by every day, travelling between Sydney and Melbourne.' Lochlan pointed east, to the distant freeway. 'We don't need to convince them to drive all the way here – we just have to offer them something interesting enough to make a detour. And once they're here, they'll need fuel. A pub lunch. A cup of tea.'

He flashed a smile at Gemma, which she found faintly insulting.

'Interest in true crime is growing constantly. But it's always been a human fascination. There were tourists at the site of the Villisca axe murders within days. Whitechapel has dined out on interest in Jack the Ripper for more than a century. My tours in Sydney and Melbourne consistently book out. And Rainier offers something that I can't give tour-goers there – immediacy. In Sydney I can take a tour to the precise spot of a razor gang killing, but half the time the site has been knocked down and rebuilt a dozen times over. I have to give my spiel outside a Liquorland. Here, the park, the church, the fountain, the teashop are all perfectly preserved, almost exactly as they looked at the time.'

That got him a mix of murmured agreement and scoffing. Gemma found it unsettling, the idea that the same stagnation that made them willing to consider this was the only reason it was even possible.

'As for the costs, once the tour is up and running I plan to step back. My company can take bookings and do the admin from Melbourne, and we'll train someone local to run the tour. Which generates employment here.'

'If the tour runs monthly, you're talking about twelve hours of work a year,' Lotte said.

'That would make it perfect for a young person,' Lochlan said, swiftly enough that he had probably jotted this argument down ahead of time. 'It's flexible enough to fit around school-work, while also offering valuable experience. They'd have a leg-up applying for tour work if they went to university in one of the major cities. And of course, Lewis and Co. would gladly transfer them to a position in any of the cities we operate in.'

Smart, Gemma thought, considering how many of the people in attendance had teenage children, herself included. But of course, the Nicholls' daughter, Fawn, would never have to worry about getting her foot in the door for a job. As the daughter of the town's magistrate and its only general practitioner, she was destined for a university career filled with prestige internships and prepaid meal plans.

Not that Gemma was bitter about it; that was just a fact.

And, of course, Jac Tjibaou, as the child of one of the victims, could never take a job like that.

She wondered briefly if she was the target of this particular inducement – her daughter, Violet, was the right age, but even if Gemma was willing to let her take the job, which she wasn't, Hugh would hit the roof.

Still, those three were far from the only young people in town.

'Are we ready to begin?' Lochlan asked. He cleared his throat. 'While the area has been inhabited since the mid-nineteenth century –'

'It was inhabited long before that,' the same woman as before interrupted. This time Gemma did turn and look. With a start, she realised the speaker was Tamara Fleischer. The survivor.

'Are you going to open with an acknowledgement of country?' Tamara continued.

Gemma noticed that Christian and Ruth both sighed and rolled their eyes. She expected Mick to as well, but he remained stoic.

'Ah, yes. Thank you. That's an excellent suggestion. We'll work on that for the final version. Uh, the majority of homes and businesses were built in 1952, when the Bennett Dam was expanded, flooding the town now called Old Rainier. This gave the town a distinctive, mid-century feel that made it an attractive lunch spot for travellers on their way between the capitals. Rainier was the kind of town where everyone knew everyone. A friendly town. A safe town. Until . . .'

Again, Gemma felt a pang of sympathy for him. The idea of talking about people like that, when they were right in front of you, made her cringe.

She deliberately tuned out as he described Christian Holst's discovery of Vincent's body in the fountain early one morning. She looked down at her boots, focusing on the spot where the leather was starting to wear away over her left big toe. The world had fallen off its axis that day. There had been murders dotted through Rainier's history, but they had been domestic tragedies, bar fights that got out of hand or robberies gone wrong. At first, everyone had assumed that Vincent had met one of those three ends too. Secretly, Gemma had wondered if Aubrey's cousins were to blame, perhaps taking 'if you hurt her, we'll kill you' too literally.

The idea that they were all being stalked by a psychopath was the last thing anyone considered.

'Then a crime scene technician decided to take her lunch break in the beautiful gardens beside the church,' Lochlan said, gesturing with his arm for them to follow him across the park.

The spot where Eva Nováková's body had first been buried was not marked in any way, but Gemma knew exactly where to go. She suspected most people in town did. Even after the barriers had been removed, the tape cleared away, the surface relevelled and seeded with grass, she always looked at it every time she passed. How many times had she unknowingly passed it in those weeks Eva was down there? Perhaps she had even walked over it, cutting through the church gardens on her way to pop in at the Tjibaou house.

'The tech, a keen gardener in her spare time, noticed a patch where the shrubs and flowers seemed to be struggling more than those around them, and an unusual amount of weeds – the sort that flourish in disturbed soil.'

Lochlan hesitated, piquing Gemma's interest. This was a tricky spot in the retelling – the local Rainier police, already out of their depth with Vincent's murder investigation, hadn't been quick to respond to the tech's report. They just hadn't had the resources to follow up on something so tenuous.

But explaining that meant criticising the local police – including Hugh.

'To confirm her suspicion, the tech asked a friend on scene with the dog unit to take a look, and the dog's reaction kicked everyone into high alert.'

Ah. So the plan was to skim right over it. Smart.

'When the area was excavated, police found the remains of a young woman wrapped in a yellow knitted blanket. Inside the blanket was her severed right hand, placed over her heart. The post-mortem concluded two things: that Eva's hand was cut off prior to her death and that she had been heavily pregnant. The baby's remains have never been found, despite extensive searches of the area.'

Beside her, Hugh let out a shuddering breath. At the time he had been a newbie police officer and had escorted a number of people into the morgue to view Eva's body in hopes of identifying her. Gemma knew that he still had nightmares about it.

'This gruesome discovery changed everything. There was a psychopath on the loose, one who had killed two people within the space of a few months and who could strike again at any time. Overnight, the friendly town of Rainier became a fortress. Within hours, the local hardware store sold out of deadbolts. Shops closed early so employees wouldn't have to walk home in the dark. The streets were empty by sundown – ironically, making conditions perfect for the Ripper's third and final murder.'

'Is that all you're going to say about Eva?' Tamara asked. 'You're just going to narrow her down to nothing more than the moment of her death?'

'Steady on,' Christian said. 'We don't know anything about her, and you get pretty damn mad when anyone speculates.'

'You could find out more,' Tamara said, ignoring this last barb. 'Investigation techniques have changed a lot in the last fifteen, twenty years. We can learn incredible things from DNA samples now. We could know more about her race, her ethnicity, maybe even find living relatives. If someone is willing to foot the bill.' She gave Lochlan a significant look. 'You're looking to make money from Eva's pain, why not pay something back?'

That obviously hadn't been on any of Lochlan's prep notes. 'Uh,' he said, then cleared his throat. 'I mean, that's an interesting idea, but that sort of DNA analysis can be prohibitively expensive, and any remaining samples are with the police.'

'You'd find us very cooperative,' Mick said. 'It's something we've looked into, but the backlog is long and, with limited funding, priority has to go to unsolved murders.'

'Oh.' Lochlan put his salesman smile back on. 'Thank you, Ms Fleischer – that's something we hadn't considered, but I'd love to discuss it with you at a later date.'

Gemma's heart fluttered painfully. If Tamara now had a reason to vote in favour of the tour, then this might really be happening.

'Uh, if we're ready to proceed, then we'll walk from here back to the fountain.' Lochlan shifted back into his 'reading from a script' voice. 'It's not known precisely where the Ripper attacked his final victim, but the blood trail shows that the victim was in the park, then crossed the road and sought help at Earl Grey's Yarn and Teashop.'

Gemma felt sick, and found she could barely hear him over the ringing in her ears. Hugh tried to pull her closer to him, but she stepped away, following the group towards her home. Hugh trailed after her.

'The victim was identified by Constable Hugh Guillory as Mr Dean Shadwell, based on a driver's licence and Medicare card found in his pockets that matched the first name he had introduced himself with. The identification was later confirmed by Mr Shadwell's brother.'

'Are you going to call him that?' a man's voice interrupted. He was leaning against a parked BMW, his arms crossed over his chest.

Gemma's chest leapt like she'd seen a ghost. He had the same dark hair and sharp nose as the man who had died in her shop, a distinct family resemblance.

'It's his name,' Lochlan said, smirking in a way that Gemma assumed was a result of discomfort rather than genuine smarm.

'His name was Dean. If you'll forgive the cliché, Mr Shadwell was our father.'

That made him Dean's older brother, Marcus Shadwell. She'd seen his name on the email list. Gemma relaxed, although the effects of the adrenaline spike hadn't faded, especially when she'd already felt off.

'Of course,' Lochlan said. 'I'll make a note of that. It's important to us that the wishes of the families are taken into account.'

'Ha!' Jaylene muttered.

Marcus opened the car door and pulled out a smart canvas satchel. He unzipped the top and pulled out a pair of expensive-looking leather gloves and a black beanie.

The group waited politely as he rugged up against the nippy evening weather, and then Christian approached with a broad smile.

'We're so glad you could make it,' he said, holding out a hand for the other man to shake. 'We weren't sure you were coming.'

Marcus looked down at his hand for an odd beat before grasping it firmly. Christian tried to give him the usual posturing mid-handshake back slap he did, but the satchel was in the way and he ended up just fumbling awkwardly. He stepped away, looking abashed.

Lochlan resumed his spiel. 'While Dean had no opportunity to identify his killer, the fact that he made it to the shop to summon help meant the police were on the scene within minutes. They were able to close the roads leading in and out of Rainier, and Jan Henning-Klosner was captured at the truck stop at the edge of town a little more than an hour and a half after Mr — after Dean's death.'

'Is that the end, then?' Christian asked. 'What about the trial? You could wind it up at the courthouse.'

'And deposit them all in front of your pub in time for lunch, right, Holst?' Dr Nicholls retorted.

'It's across the street,' Christian snapped back. 'It's not going to make any difference to anyone's lunch plans.'

'Gentlemen,' Hugh said mildly. His tone of voice was enough to convey a head tilt in the direction of the victims' family members.

The two men fell silent.

'Er, there was discussion on the subject of delving into those aspects,' Lochlan said. 'But we've found that, in our research into where people stop when guiding themselves through Rainier, the courthouse is of little interest. Most are interested in the, uh . . .'

'The juicy bits,' Jaylene said. 'A fountain full of blood. Dismembered limbs and a stolen baby.'

'We stick to the facts,' Lochlan said. 'You've heard the script. There's no embroidering.'

'We've heard the script you want us to vote on,' Jaylene retorted. 'You think there isn't going to be any editorialising once the money starts flowing, and you don't have to look into our eyes while you tell it? Are you going to tell them how much pain my son would have been in? Will you tell them how, according to that man, he called out for me when –'

'Okay.' Hugh dropped Gemma's hand to squeeze Jaylene's shoulder. 'We've all seen the presentation now and have a lot to think about. Gemma has been working hard on a spread in the teashop, which Lewis and Co. have provided free of charge. It's Saturday night, you can take your time, have something to eat, talk it out, and then we can all go away and make our own decisions.'

The street was quiet, as the shops had closed for the day, and the pub had closed early to allow Christian and his fiancée Ruth Tanner to attend the tour run-through. As a result, the group didn't have to worry too much about cars as they drifted across the street towards the Earl Grey.

Gemma tipped her head to the side to accept a ritual cheek kiss from Hugh before she turned to lead the group across the road. It had been decided a few weeks ago that Hugh would be the one on shift today, so that Mick Seabrooke, who had always been more comfortable playing the role of Rainier hero cop, could attend the dinner.

It wasn't the way Gemma would have preferred it. Of the two officers, Hugh was better at smoothing ruffled feathers and calming people down. But she understood, and kept her worries to herself.

TWO

GEMMA SCANNED THE QR code beside the door with her phone, then fumbled with the keys to unlock the door. She usually came in and out through the back, unlocking the shop door from the inside, so it was an unfamiliar motion to open it from here.

'Don't forget to check in,' Dr Nicholls called out to the others from behind her.

Gemma was grateful. If she'd had to stand there reminding people there would have been grumbling, but nobody was going to get snippy with the town's only GP.

That caused something of a bottleneck, as people formed a loose queue.

The inside of the shop was warm and familiar, and filled with the rich smell of the homemade meat pies and sausage rolls she'd put in the oven before the tour started.

Jaylene came in first, and stood in the doorway while she shrugged out of her overcoat and hung it up, then shoved her gloves and hat into the pockets, without any concern for the people stuck in the cold behind her.

'Would you rather be closest to the fireplace, or the first table to get served?' Gemma asked.

Both tables were the furthest possible from the one in the bay window, where Christian and Ruth always sat when they came in. The rest of the guests, who were a little less staunch in their views on the tour, would flow in and form a buffer between them. It wouldn't prevent spats breaking out, but hopefully it would stop anyone throwing chairs.

'Oh, I hate to be too warm,' Jaylene said, and took herself to the table nearest to the counter and cake display case.

'Is Antoine joining us tonight?' Gemma asked hopefully.

'I'm flying solo, I'm afraid. Would you like to sit with me?'

'Sure,' Gemma said, although she doubted she would actually get a chance to sit down.

In the doorway, Dr Nicholls helped his wife, Lotte, out of her vintage Collette Dinnigan coat. He hung it up as she fixed her hair in the mirror Gemma kept behind the rack, combing her silver-streaked white-blonde hair back into a perfect bob with her fingers.

Jaylene put a hand out and touched Gemma's forearm. 'Are you holding up okay, sweetheart?'

'Shouldn't I be asking you that?' Gemma asked, putting a hand over Jaylene's.

Jaylene sniffed a little, but smiled. 'I'm fine. This is a whole lot of noise and nonsense. I know people will do the right thing and shut it down when it comes time for the vote.'

Gemma made a reassuring noise, which Jaylene appeared to take as enthusiastic agreement. When Gemma went to pull away, Jaylene squeezed her forearm.

'Is Jac here?' she asked, her voice low.

Gemma hesitated, then nodded. 'The three of them are upstairs,' she said, referring to her daughter, Violet, and Violet's two friends, Jac Tjibaou and Fawn Nicholls. 'Please don't go up there, Jaylene; things are tense enough tonight.'

'It's never me that causes the trouble,' Jaylene said, but withdrew her hand.

Gemma said nothing. Aubrey gave birth to Vincent's child, Jac, only a few months after the Ripper's arrest. All she knew was that Jaylene and Antoine ended up with custody sometime between Jac's first and second birthdays, and raised Jac until Aubrey married Mick Seabrooke. Gemma hadn't been around when it all went to hell, and had tried to stay out of it as much as possible.

Gemma ducked into the kitchen to fill the teapots. By the time they were steeping, Aubrey and Mick had seated themselves at the table closest to the banked fireplace and, as she expected, Ruth was getting comfortable next to the window.

The next arrival was Tamara Fleischer. She took her coat off and hung it on the rack beside the door, then took off her pink knitted beanie to reveal short cropped hair in the same shade.

It suited her remarkably well for a woman who was closer to retirement than her teens, and Gemma felt a brief moment of envy. She would have to bleach her own thick, dark hair until it fell out to get colour that bright. Then she felt awful, remembering that Tamara deserved any scrap of good fortune she could come by.

Tamara hovered in the doorway, looking not uncertain – Gemma doubted she was capable of it – but merely expectant. Gemma quickly scanned the tables, weighing the risks of various vacant seats. The Seabrookes, she decided. Maybe Tamara and Mick could talk further about DNA testing for Eva.

'Follow me,' Gemma said to Tamara, who flashed a grateful smile that faded to something politely neutral as they came to the table. 'I'm sure you remember Mick, and this is his wife, Aubrey.'

Gemma probably would have missed Tamara's brief look of surprise if she hadn't been expecting it. Mick had just turned sixty, and looked every year of it after a long and harrowing police career. Aubrey was the same age as Gemma – thirty-six – and was frequently mistaken for her husband's daughter.

'Nice to meet you,' Aubrey said. She gave Tamara a long look, from the pink hair down to her black boots and then up again, and pushed her chair back. 'I'll help you bring the food out, Gemma.'

'You don't need to –' Gemma started, but Aubrey walked past her into the kitchen. On the way she swept past Jaylene, pointedly not looking at her.

By the time Gemma reached the kitchen, Aubrey was incorrectly plating a tray of mini quiches. She turned and hissed, 'Did you see what she was wearing?'

'Who?' Gemma asked. Her mind had jumped tracks to Aubrey's beef with Jaylene, and she couldn't recall anything remarkable about Jaylene's outfit.

Aubrey rolled her eyes. 'The whore – I mean, the hooker.'

'Sex worker,' Gemma corrected, then corrected again, 'Tamara?'

She wasn't sure if Tamara considered herself a sex worker anymore. Gemma's understanding was that after her experience with the Ripper, Tamara had moved to Sydney and was now working for some kind of sex workers' rights non-profit. Her outfit didn't seem particularly striking either: a comfy-looking black wrap dress, black leggings and a denim jacket covered with bright badges and patches.

'Yes, Tamara. She's got a badge on her lapel that says: *No TERFs, No SWERFs, No Cops, No Problem.*'

Gemma bit back a sigh. 'She probably forgot it was on there. I doubt she carefully arranges the pins every time she goes out.'

'It doesn't matter if she did it on purpose. My husband saved her life! How could she be anti-cop?'

Gemma put out a new tray, and started arranging sausage rolls and ramekins for sauce. 'I doubt that was her only experience with the police, Aubrey.'

Aubrey muttered something under her breath that Gemma didn't catch, and stormed out with the tray of quiches.

Gemma still found it kind of funny how seriously Aubrey took her identity as a 'cop wife'. When they were at school together she would never have picked Aubrey Dillon as someone who would embrace law and order as her whole identity, given that it was an open secret in town what the Dillon family farm's real cash crop was.

But then, Aubrey had always been like human oobleck; she took the shape of whomever she spent the most time with.

Gemma's hospitality brain took over. Her feet could walk the paths between the tables without any need for higher thought. She rushed the food out, since Aubrey had upset the service order, then went back for the drinks. Twelve pots of tea, two for each table, trays of locally made mugs, deliberately thumb-printed and uneven. Six little pots of honey from Bob with the Bees, six etched-glass sugar jars. On the way back through, she gently touched Tamara's shoulder.

'You needed the gluten-free option, right? Can you come through to the kitchen with me to check I've made it right?' she asked.

Tamara looked puzzled at first, since she definitely hadn't requested a gluten-free meal, then understanding dawned. She put her napkin aside and followed Gemma back.

'Is everything okay?' she asked.

'I'm just trying to keep a lid on any unpleasantness,' Gemma said, starting on a replacement cup of tea for the one Tamara had left on the table. 'Tensions are running high tonight. Sorry,

I thought you and the Seabrookes would get along well. I forget sometimes that Aubrey has some serious teeth.'

'I could have handled it,' Tamara said. 'But thanks. I have to ask, though – she's Seabrooke's wife, but she was also dating Vincent back in the day, wasn't she? I remember the kerfuffle she caused at the trial.'

Aubrey barely left her family's farm in the months following Vincent's funeral. As a result, Jaylene and Antoine had no idea they were about to become grandparents until she showed up at the trial visibly very pregnant. They didn't take it calmly.

'That's her.'

'Talk about going from one extreme to the other. Vincent was so nice.'

'I know,' Gemma said with a sigh.

Tamara must have caught the edge of wistfulness, because she raised an eyebrow.

'Vincent and I were really close as kids. We dated for a bit, but it didn't work out. We were still best friends until he died, though.'

'And you and Aubrey are friends? Wasn't that weird?'

Gemma shrugged. 'We fell out briefly over it, but in a town like this there isn't really room for "girl code", or whatever you want to call it. There were three kinds of single boy when we were growing up – your brothers, your cousins and your friends' ex-boyfriends.'

Tamara laughed.

Gemma handed her the teacup. 'When you go back out, perhaps sit by the window with Christian Holst and Ruth Tanner. Christian owns the pub, he'll get along with anyone.'

Tamara pulled a face. 'Uh, maybe not. I'm sure Christian is great, but I knew Ruth back in the day. She worked at the service centre.'

Gemma's eyes widened. 'She worked there? As in . . .'

'No! Sorry, not my line of work. She ran the cash register in the petrol station. But I don't want to go from the frying pan to the fire. She might not be pleased to have me sit down with her and her man for a chat about the good old days.'

Gemma got it. Rainier town proper had always had a complicated relationship with the Rainier service centre, where the truckers stopped for food, fuel and showers, even before it became infamous as the site of the Rainier Ripper's capture. The people and business owners of Rainier thought they were a cut above the service centre, in a way that Gemma had always thought had shades of Hyacinth Bucket delusions.

'Okay. Well, I'm sure Jaylene Tjibaou would love it if you sat and chatted with her about how nice you thought Vincent was, but Jaylene will definitely read a lot into you moving from Aubrey's table to hers; there's friction there.'

'Oh god.' Tamara shook her head. 'Maybe we should suggest Lewis and Co.'s tour pamphlets include a chart of all the weird ways everyone here is tangled up with everyone else.'

'That's small towns,' Gemma said. 'Everyone is connected to everyone else in six different ways. Now, if you want a neutral table, that just leaves the Nicholls. Doctor Tim Nicholls has been the town GP for as long as anyone can remember, and his wife Lotte is the local magistrate and coroner. They're here because they take turns holding a seat on the local council – they weren't related to any of the victims.'

'Thanks,' Tamara said, offering her a genuine smile before slipping back into the dining room.

Gemma went back to serving food, keeping one ear out for the conversations swirling around the room. Nobody seemed to be getting particularly heated, just rehashing the same arguments that had been splitting Rainier for the months since the tour was proposed.

'Good on you, Gemma,' Christian said, as Gemma put their food down on the table.

Ruth looked out the window, biting her bottom lip. 'Did you notice that there's ice in the fountain tonight?'

'Is there?' Gemma followed her gaze over to the fountain, which sat kitty-corner to the teashop. Of course, she couldn't see any ice or water from here, but considering the biting chill outside she believed it.

The fountain wasn't run during the winter, and in particularly cold years the standing water froze over. For as long as anyone could remember, there had been a superstition that ice in the fountain was a bad omen.

The water had frozen the day Vincent died, starting their nightmare.

Out of the corner of her eye she noticed movement in the other half of the shop, the section that had once held yarn and other materials for sale, but was now screened off with a wooden room divider.

Marcus Shadwell stood looking at the small brass memorial plate screwed to the wall behind where the chair had once sat.

She wished that she'd had it replaced before he arrived. She polished it regularly, and sometimes put a single flower in a stem vase on the sideboard beneath it. But no amount of attention could make a seventeen-year-old plaque shine like new. She'd meant to get a new one the next time she had some cash to spare, but the hardware store had closed, taking the little engraving and shoe repair kiosk with it, so even when she had the money she would need to drive into Wagga to get it remade.

She slipped past the divider and approached Marcus cautiously. 'Would you like a cup of tea? Or some coffee?'

'Oh, I'm good.' He nodded to the plaque. 'This is nice. Thank you.'

He turned to look at her, and for a moment she was looking down at Dean, the wide desperation of his eyes, the heavy scent of his blood in her nose.

'It's nothing,' she whispered. She looked back at the tables, hoping someone would catch her eye looking for help. She didn't want to talk to Marcus, couldn't stand to answer any questions about his brother's final moments. She'd made a mistake coming over here.

'Will you open this part back up, if . . .'

'If the tour goes ahead? No, definitely not,' she said. 'Sometimes we get people who try to take pictures here,' she admitted. 'Once even a pair of teenagers who . . . the chair was part of a set, you see. The original was taken as evidence, but these kids dragged another one from another part of the shop so they could get better pictures. I got rid of all of them after that, then put up the divider.'

'Teenagers,' Marcus said, shaking his head with a little laugh. 'I suppose I did some dark shit at that age too.'

'I need to get back to the dining section,' she said. 'But stay as long as you need, okay?'

'Actually, I needed to talk to you about that,' he said. 'I am. Staying here, that is.'

'Staying here?' she repeated. 'You're the one who booked the Airbnb room?'

The booking definitely hadn't been under the name Marcus Shadwell. It had stuck out to her that the name – Mark Herald – wasn't anyone she'd heard of. She'd assumed it was one of the tour company's employees, or a journo looking to do a write-up, or maybe somebody's lawyer.

She'd debated for a long time before accepting the booking, worried it was someone looking for an early-bird ticket to the tour, but ultimately the red text on their electricity bill had won.

She wouldn't have accepted if she'd known it was Marcus.

'I took my wife's name when we got married,' he said.

'Oh,' she said. 'That's modern.'

He laughed, a joyless little huff. 'My grandfather, father, mother and brother all died far too young. I honestly thought there was some kind of curse on the Shadwell name and didn't want to saddle Gabby with it.' He looked down. 'Turns out it wasn't the name.'

'Oh, I'm sorry,' Gemma said.

'I appreciate it,' he said, and then, with the grace of someone used to extracting himself from that particular awkward moment, added, 'Anyway, Mark Herald, also known as Marcus Shadwell, makes me feel like a spy or something. It's kind of cool.'

She chuckled politely. 'Do you prefer Mark or Marcus?'

'Marcus is fine.'

That threw her for a moment – perhaps only friends called him Mark – but she pushed on. 'Do you need help with your bags?'

'No, I'm travelling light. Let me grab my bag from the coat rack, and you can lead the way.'

'Sorry to force you out into the cold, but the entrance to the flat is around the back.'

For some reason, Marcus brightened at that. 'Can you give me a few minutes and I'll meet you there?'

'Sure.'

Walking through the dining section to the kitchen, Gemma noticed that Tamara was now deep in conversation with Jaylene, and Christian had inserted himself next to Mick and Aubrey, in Tamara's empty chair. That had potential to turn bad, but for now the two tables were ignoring each other.

Gemma could see the rear courtyard through the window over the kitchen sink. The little outdoor space was enclosed on all sides by a high brick fence, but through the steel gate she could see Marcus standing on the footpath, lit by the glowing end of a cigarette.

That explained why he'd been happy for an excuse to pop outside.

She sent Hugh a quick text apprising him of the situation, then opened the back door. 'The gate's unlocked, come on through,' she called.

'Must be a bit of a nuisance, not having internal stairs,' he said, rubbing his hands together to warm them up as he crossed the courtyard.

'It's a real pain when it's raining,' she said, gesturing for him to go up. The stairs led to a back verandah that shaded the window to the teashop kitchen. There was a mirror carefully positioned inside so that from the stairs she could peek in and see the dining section. Everyone was where she had left them. No-one was smiling, but the room was calm.

'Now, we live here,' she said, gesturing to the first door at the top of the stairs. 'Your room is self-contained, and has its own entrance around the corner. I'm just going to pop in and let the kids know we're up here, so they don't get a fright hearing us moving around.'

'Sure,' he said, and went to lean on the railing to wait.

'Uh, I wouldn't do that,' she said, embarrassed. 'This place has some . . . eccentricities.' That was the euphemism they favoured, like it was quirky and charming, instead of calling it what it was: a money pit.

She stepped through the door and sang out, 'It's me, kids.'

'Hi, Mum!' Violet called back, echoed by shouts of 'Hello, Gemma!' and 'Hello, Mrs Guillory!' from Jac and Fawn.

'We've got a guest,' Gemma said, poking her head into Violet's room. The three teenagers were sprawled on the floor, looking at their phones. 'His name is Marcus, I'm just showing him to his room.'

''Kay,' Violet said. 'How's it going downstairs?'

'Nothing broken yet,' Gemma said.

'Mum and Mamy haven't got into it?' Jac asked, lifting their gaze from their phone. Jac was handsome, in the old-fashioned sense of the word that could be used for any gender. They had Vincent's eyes and cool-toned brown skin, but Aubrey's slim neck and sharp chin, complemented by short, almost buzzed, brown hair.

Jac had announced they were non-binary, identifying as neither a boy nor a girl, a year earlier. Gemma was still having trouble getting her head around it, but Violet and Fawn seemed to take to the idea as naturally as breathing.

Fawn had her feet in Jac's lap and her head in Violet's. She was pale all over – pale skin, pale blue eyes, and chin-length blonde hair that she'd dyed a silvery blue.

Violet was in her pyjamas already, and had her stick-straight red hair pulled back in the braid she always slept in. Gemma was struck, as always, by how young Violet seemed beside her friends. They'd sent her to school early, and at the end of Year Five she'd been skipped straight to high school. The local primary school was closing, and the other option was to drive her forty-five minutes every day to the next-closest one. Her teachers had been sure she would keep up, but Gemma hadn't really relaxed about the idea until Jac and Fawn took her under their wing.

She couldn't believe the three of them were in their final year of school already. Jac and Fawn were almost adults.

'They're behaving,' Gemma said.

Jac rolled their eyes. 'Give it time. And don't serve any wine.'

As if they were trying to make a liar of her, the low hum of conversation coming from downstairs abruptly hushed, and then Jaylene bellowed something. Gemma couldn't make out her actual words, but she sounded far from happy.

Even worse, the low amused voice that responded wasn't Aubrey's – it was Christian Holst. Gemma groaned.

She was torn between running downstairs to throw water on the brewing fight and getting Marcus settled in. She opted to focus on her guest, since she was sure Mick would have the situation in hand before she even made it down there.

Gemma went back onto the verandah, and gestured for Marcus to follow her around the corner to the other entrance.

The building had once been the town's pub. Her grandmother inherited it from her parents in the 1950s, and always said she didn't feel up to running a pub in a suddenly bigger town. She sold the licence to the Holst family – who built a new, modern (at the time) pub down the road – and renovated the old pub into a home and shop. The upstairs had been converted from rooms for rent to a single family residence, leaving it with a strange layout. A hallway ran down the centre of the house, which all of the rooms opened onto. Gemma's grandparents had changed two of the rooms into a small kitchen and an odd little lounge room, leaving three bedrooms. These days Gemma slept in one, and Violet was set up in the room beside it.

The third had been the original publican's residence, so it had its own door to the outside and an ensuite. Gemma had locked the door leading to the rest of the house, creating a private, separate space for Marcus.

She opened the door with a little 'ta-da' gesture, and quickly scanned the room to check for any signs Hugh might have left that the room was usually occupied. The room was simple and masculine – a king bed with a navy bedspread and matching pillows, a single bedside table and a locked built-in wardrobe.

'Nice picture,' Marcus said, dropping his bag on the bed.

Gemma cringed. Above the bed they had a framed picture of her and Hugh standing on the steps of the church on their wedding day, flanked by their parents. She should have taken it down; that was way too personal for an Airbnb room.

'Have you guys just got the one daughter?' Marcus asked. He was still examining the picture. Gemma had worn a white satin Caroline Kennedy-esque dress that made no secret of the five months pregnant bump behind her bouquet. She'd been trying to make it clear that she wasn't trying to hide, wasn't ashamed.

She looked at her parents' faces. Above their smiles for the camera, did their eyes look doubtful? Or was she rewriting history?

Hugh's father definitely looked worried, for a very different reason, his arm around his too-thin wife. Her smile was the most genuine one in the scene, thrilled to have made it to her son's big day.

'Just Violet, yeah,' she said. She wondered what jumped out at him about the picture. His face had taken on a look of barely suppressed yearning, and she remembered that he was a widower. 'Do you have kids?'

He shook his head with a sad smile. 'That wasn't on the cards for us. We had all the time in the world until we didn't.' He nodded at the picture. 'That was about six months after Dean died, right? I remember reading about it in the paper.'

'Five months, yeah,' she said. The papers *loved* that she and Hugh had ended up getting married. It made for the perfect closing paragraph of stories about the Rainier Ripper, a lighter side to the story to get readers ready to flip the page and read about a shoe sale or new movie.

'Hugh wanted to get it done before Violet arrived,' she blurted out. She wasn't usually the type to tell near strangers her business, but the conversation was skirting dangerously close to the subject of the night Dean died, and she didn't want to leave him an opening to ask her any details about it. 'I mean, it's the twenty-first century, neither of us really cared, but his dad was the town's minister at the time. Hugh didn't want to cause him any difficulties.'

'Son of a preacher man, hey? That must have been rough.'

'Nah, Eric's a good man.'

Her phone buzzed in her front pocket, derailing her thoughts as she tried to come up with a new safe topic. She ignored it at first, not wanting to be rude to Marcus. The phone went still for a beat, then began to buzz again. Whoever it was had redialled as soon as it rang out.

'Sorry,' she said, and pulled it out. It was Hugh, probably overreacting to her text about Marcus. She stepped out onto the verandah.

'Hugh, this isn't –'

'Are you in the tearoom?' Hugh interrupted. 'I need you to keep everyone inside and close the blinds.'

'What? No, I'm upstairs.'

'Gemma,' Hugh said, 'there's been an incident.'

'An incident?' she repeated. Vandalism, she supposed, or some kind of protest against the tour proposal. She stepped closer to the railing and saw Hugh standing in the street, his face lit by the glow of the phone pressed to his ear.

'I need you to go downstairs,' he said, and something in his voice made her stomach squeeze in on itself. 'I need you to close the blinds. Try to do it quickly and calmly. Don't let anyone go out the front.'

Every part of her screamed at herself to listen to him, not to look. But she looked.

A figure hung from the fountain. Their legs were in the water, their torso hanging out, chest facing up. Their arms were completely lax, long white fingers brushing against the pavement.

Their head dangled, the force of gravity tipping their chin up to expose the length of their throat.

What was left of it.

She turned, and came face to face with Marcus, who was standing in the doorway.

'Oh god – what *is* that?' Marcus said.

'There's been an incident,' she repeated and then, to her horror, she laughed. It was just such a ridiculous thing to say.

The scene didn't look entirely right. It all looked too peaceful, too clean. Shouldn't there be blood everywhere? Wouldn't they have heard a fight, a scream?

Could it be a mannequin? Maybe it was a tasteless stunt for the end of the tour. She and Vincent had once gone on a midnight ghost tour, during one of their whirlwind jaunts, and the tour had been capped off by a prank where a man in a ghost mask had come screaming out of an alley, making the already jittery tourists shriek and scatter. They'd been primed for a scare, and they'd got it, and it had all been very funny in the pub later.

Gemma relaxed. It had to be a fake-out.

Downstairs, a woman screamed.

* * *

Not again. Not again. Not again. Gemma forced herself to breathe as she sprinted towards the stairs.

'Mum?' Violet was standing on the back verandah, Jac and Fawn hovering behind her in the doorway. 'Is everything okay?'

Gemma had to stop herself from body-checking her daughter back inside, she was so desperate to stop her from coming around the corner. 'Go back inside. Lock the door. Stay up here until I come back for you, okay?'

'What?'

Gemma would never be able to unsee the body in the fountain. She could never forget Dean Shadwell's last moments. She couldn't use a tea towel to mop up a spill without remembering trying to staunch his blood. Christian Holst couldn't forget finding Vincent. No-one who was escorted through the morgue in a fruitless attempt to identify Eva Nováková could ever erase the image of what was left of her. No-one in town could ever fully move past three months of shared nightmares and constant anxiety.

She had worked so hard to shield Violet from that. She couldn't let her see the horror outside.

'Violet, if you never listen to anything else I tell you, listen to this. Lock your door. Stay here.'

THREE

THE TEASHOP WAS in chaos. Chairs lay tipped on their sides from when the guests scrambled out of their seats, and someone had shoved a table aside so the guests could huddle in the bay window. Gemma checked them one by one, a roll call of who the body wasn't.

Not Jaylene, who, to Gemma's shock, had one arm wrapped around Aubrey's shoulder, her fingers squeezing the meat of Aubrey's upper arm as she tried to turn her away from the window. Aubrey resisted the pull, staring out at the gory scene with an odd, serene look. Jaylene had her face turned towards the floor, her cheeks blotchy with tears.

Gemma couldn't see Mick anywhere, but surely he had gone to join Hugh out the front.

Lotte Nicholls, Fawn's mother, stood framed in the open doorway, hands pressed against the jamb as if holding herself up.

43

Her pale blonde hair hung around her face as she leaned forwards and dry-heaved into the street.

Dr Nicholls, her husband, was gone, no doubt to try to help whoever was in the fountain.

Christian and his fiancée Ruth huddled at the other end of the window. Ruth had her head tucked against Christian's chest, and he had his forearms locked around the back of her neck, elbows out and chest puffed like he was trying to look imposing to any would-be attacker.

'Oh Gemma,' Jaylene said. 'I'm glad to see you.'

'Is Jac still upstairs?' Aubrey interrupted.

With a lurch, Gemma realised she was the only one of the parents to know for sure the body wasn't one of the kids.

'They're all still upstairs,' she said, and Lotte let out a strangled half-laugh, half-gasp. Aubrey ducked out of Jaylene's grasp and sprinted for the back door, Jaylene right behind her.

'Is Dr Nicholls . . .?' Gemma asked.

'He's alright,' Lotte said, stepping aside so Gemma could go out the door.

It was so much more awful up close. But a guilty relief, too, because those staring eyes, the open mouth and blood-slicked hair were immediately recognisable. Lochlan Lewis, the tour guide. His wound was terrible, but that wasn't what frightened Gemma most about the scene.

That was Hugh, standing beside the fountain, looking straight through the body with a thousand-yard stare. His face was blank, but his hands were clenched into fists at his sides, white-knuckled and trembling.

* * *

'Nothing to see here,' Mick called to her, retreating to soothing cliché. He ushered her back inside, and closed the door behind them.

'I need everyone to take a seat,' he said. He scrubbed a hand over his face. 'Guillory and Dr Nicholls have the scene secured. We've called this in, and an additional unit is on the way from Wagga. I'm going to do a sweep of the area for the assailant. They won't get far.'

Gemma wanted to believe that. With the wound she'd seen on Lochlan, the killer had to be a walking blood spatter. But there were a lot of directions in which to run, and the Rainier police didn't have the resources to immediately set up roadblocks and conduct a dragnet, which was how they'd caught the Ripper on the night Dean Shadwell died. For the three months between Vincent's murder and Dean's, there had been an entire police task force in town. Now it was just Mick and Hugh.

'I'm sure I don't have to tell any of you that we don't want the victim's family finding out about this from social media or the news before we're able to formally notify them,' Mick continued, to general nods. 'I'm not going to seize your phones, but will remind you that the call and text records of everyone here could be called into evidence. I'm also going to have to ask you to please not discuss what you've seen here tonight, or you could influence each other's reports.'

With a sinking feeling, Gemma recognised the routine. They weren't supposed to talk, and it was true that they could inadvertently confuse each other into believing they had seen something they hadn't, but it was also a warning to anyone in the room who might be thinking of putting their heads together and getting their stories straight.

Mick pulled a little black tape recorder from his pocket, and placed it on the table. He clicked the record button, announced the date, time and address, and then named everyone in the room. Then he strode out the door, taking any sense of safety with him.

Gemma hurried over to lock the door and push home the bolts, then finally lowered the blinds. A strange quiet descended, and people made their way back to their seats.

Gemma went into the kitchen and double-checked that the back door and kitchen windows were locked. Then, not sure what else to do, she pulled out a clean teapot and scooped in a mix of chamomile, valerian and lemon balm, ingredients that were supposed to calm people down.

If in doubt, make everyone a cup of tea, right?

The stairs outside squeaked, making Gemma jump. The doorknob rattled, and then Aubrey's pale face appeared close to the window, eyes shaded to peer in.

Gemma unlocked the door and ushered her in. 'Is the upstairs door locked?'

'Of course,' Aubrey said. She pressed a hand to her face. The gesture was so like the one Mick used that Gemma found herself charmed. 'Jesus. I can't believe . . .'

'I know,' Gemma said. 'What are we going to do, Aubs?'

Aubrey reached out and pulled her into a fierce hug. 'Everything will be okay. Mick'll sort it out, yeah?'

'Yeah,' Gemma said, dubious. 'Aren't you worried about him, though? Does he . . .'

They'd talked about a lot of aspects of being married to a police officer. They'd bitched about night shifts, and force politics, and promotions or lack thereof. But Gemma had never asked her if Mick had trouble sleeping, if he had nightmares, if he went into strange moods sometimes. She was afraid Aubrey would say no, and then would look at her differently.

'Can Jac stay tonight?' Aubrey asked. 'I don't know how long the witnesses will need to stay here. But when they let us go home, we'll have to file past the scene. I don't want Jac to see that.'

'Of course,' Gemma said. 'You should stay too,' she added, on impulse. 'Sam and Emily are with your parents, right?'

'Yeah, they're staying the night.' Aubrey laughed, a little bitter. 'It was supposed to be the closest thing Mick and I have had to a date night since Sam was born.'

She wavered for a moment, like she was considering it, when Gemma realised her mistake. 'Wait, the guest room is occupied. But that's alright, I can stay on the lounge.'

'I can't put you out of your own bed,' Aubrey said. 'Besides, I'd hate for Mick to come home to an empty house after the sort of night he's going to have.'

'If you're sure,' Gemma said, faintly relieved.

'Who's in your guest room?'

'Marcus Shadwell. He rented it on Airbnb.'

'Dean Shadwell's brother?'

'Yeah,' Gemma confirmed.

'What the hell is he doing staying in your house? What's wrong with the motel? Wait.' Aubrey clicked her fingers. 'The tour people and Tamara Fleischer are at the motel. It's a small place, maybe they had no vacancies.'

'Maybe,' Gemma said.

'I don't know about this, Gemma,' Aubrey said. 'What if he's literally a murderer?'

Gemma shook her head. 'I don't think that's possible. Lochlan wasn't in the fountain when we came into the shop, and he and I were talking for most of the time between then and when Hugh found the body. He was out of my sight for about thirty seconds walking around the building. I don't think that's enough time to murder someone, and even if it was, he'd have been' – her tongue froze around the words – 'covered in blood.'

Gemma wondered if Marcus had seen the fountain on his way around. If he had, then Lochlan's body couldn't have been there, meaning the murder had happened while she and Marcus were talking upstairs. The idea made her shiver.

'I suppose,' Aubrey said. She thought it over for a moment, then shrugged. 'It's still better than letting Jac see the crime scene. Lesser of two evils, right?'

FOUR

LANE HOLLAND SPRAYED bleach solution in a wide arc over the tiles. The cleaning crew wasn't the most sought-after work detail – that would be the kitchens – but it was indoors, and didn't involve much heavy lifting, and by now Lane could go through the motions and let his mind slip elsewhere.

It wasn't right to say that Lane liked life in the Special Purpose Centre. But, in a life that hadn't contained an abundance of truth, he knew one for sure: everything is relative. Lane's life in the SPC, the Tin, was a good deal more pleasant than the time that had preceded it in general population. It wasn't as nice as his life had been in a caravan in Byron Bay with his sister Lynnie. It was a great deal better than living in a caravan with his parents. It was far worse than the one-bedroom flat above a general store, the last place he'd called home, if only for a few weeks. That was a truth he could only understand when looking back – he had been happy there.

The Tin was a standalone facility outside of Bowral, a holding pen for prisoners who created too much hassle for the staff in other correctional centres if they were left to mingle with the general population. The ones who owed unpayable debts. The once infamous, now infirm. The self-destructive.

Informants.

For a few months, Lane had adjusted to life in prison somewhat well. It reminded him of the show circuit – rough accommodations and dreadful food, but the company was decent if you kept one eye open for the shifting politics and posturing.

Lane even got a measure of respect. He'd been arrested and convicted for kidnapping and (as far as the legal system knew) shooting his father, a man responsible for the murders of at least two innocent girls. Some of his fellow detainees admired that, and the rest at least saw him as someone it was better not to mess with. Not to mention that several of them had served time with his father, and envied Lane for being the one to shoot him.

But over time whispers spread about Lane's previous life as a private investigator. About other people he'd put away. About his far-too-generous plea deal. Soon it was considered common knowledge that Lane was a plant, trying to get information out of the other detainees about unsolved crimes. Every friendly overture from him was met with suspicion. Anything that made his life bearable – commissary money from his sister, letters, visits, a decent work detail – were assumed to be special privileges.

After the third time he got the shit kicked out of him, he was moved to the Tin.

'Hey, Holland?' It was his work partner, Ludwig.

'Hmm?' Lane said. Ludwig was a talker. Lane didn't care for it.

'I saw your girlfriend in the paper, eh?'

'You must be thinking of someone else,' Lane said, trying to sound uninterested but not so bored that Ludwig would take offence and pick a fight.

'Aw, go on. You know who I mean,' Ludwig needled. 'It must be cool. Only thing I ever got in the paper was one of those local court write-ups, and they just kept calling me "the defendant".'

'Well, you're still young,' Lane said, moving on to the next wall.

He didn't know why Ludwig was in the Tin instead of a regular prison. There were only two types of detainees here – the ones where it was obvious, and the ones where it was none of Lane's business.

Footsteps echoed in the concrete hallway outside, and a detainee and guard appeared in the bathroom doorway.

'Showers are closed for cleaning,' Lane said. He looked over, and nearly dropped his spray bottle when he saw who it was.

Jan Henning-Klosner.

The guard must have been a new hire, or a recent transfer, because Lane didn't recognise him. He made a tsk noise. 'You're behind schedule.'

Lane frowned. 'We're on this bathroom between nine and ten every day.' He waited a long beat, then added, 'Sir.'

The guard looked at his watch. 'Huh. Must be wrong. Did daylight savings jump forwards or something?'

'I don't think so,' Lane said.

'I told you,' Henning-Klosner said.

'Shut it.' The guard pointed to the shower head at the far right of the room. 'Just use that one – they're done with it.'

Lane spoke up, his skin crawling. 'Sir, there can't be three of us in here at the same time. The rules –'

'You scared of an old man?' the guard sneered. 'He's not gonna bite you. Have you even still got your teeth, Janny?'

'It's Jan,' Henning-Klosner said, sounding tired. 'The J is pronounced like a Y.'

'Then why not just spell it with a Y?' Ludwig asked.

'I really don't think –' Lane tried.

'Aw, shit,' Ludwig said, his face lighting up. 'You're that fucking guy, aren't you? Whatsit. Jack the Ripper.'

'Yes,' Jan deadpanned, unbuttoning his jumpsuit. 'I'm Jack the Ripper.'

'Jack the Ripper's dead, genius,' the guard said. 'Yeh-Jan here is the Rainier Ripper.'

'Just Jan is fine,' the Ripper said, stepping into the spray.

'Get back to work, Ludwig. I don't want to be at this all day,' Lane said.

Ludwig did get back to scrubbing, much to Lane's relief. It wasn't like he was the kid's supervisor, so he couldn't tell him what to do. He hoped that the guard who was meant to be supervising them would come check in soon, and maybe boot the other guard out.

'The Rainier Ripper,' Ludwig muttered to himself. 'That's, like, properly famous.' His eyes were too bright. Like he'd taken something, or forgotten to take something. 'He's even got a Wikipedia page.'

'So what?' Lane asked. 'My father has a Wikipedia page. It's not an achievement.'

Ludwig shot a look at him. 'You've got one too, eh? Because you killed him.'

'That's what the courts say,' Lane said.

Ludwig abandoned the section he was supposed to be scrubbing and drifted closer to Jan. 'Do you get those letters?' he asked. His whole body leaned forwards, and Lane suspected the only thing keeping him out of Jan's personal space was the spray of water. 'You know, from girls. The crazy ones.'

'Ludwig,' Lane sighed, knowing it was futile. He looked over at the guard, who didn't seem to think this warranted any intervention. Lane had heard rumours that the prison was having trouble filling shifts and covering call-outs, which must be true, if this wet-behind-the-ears idiot had been left to manage the Tin's most carefully watched detainee.

Jan acted like Ludwig wasn't there, staring fixedly at the opposite wall and soaping himself up.

The guard's radio crackled with a mush of almost-words.

It all happened very slowly. Lane thought he might have reacted better if it happened quickly. Some instinct or adrenaline might have taken over.

The guard lifted the radio. 'Can you repeat that? Over.'

The sound came again, in the same cadence but with no more clarity. The guard sighed and, ignoring Lane's yelped objection, stepped out of the bathroom, probably assuming he would find a stronger signal away from the cage of pipes. The heavy door swung shut behind him.

Jan's head snapped towards the door, and then his gaze swept over Lane and Ludwig. Lane's blood went cold.

He wouldn't do anything. Would he?

The guard was right outside the door.

Lane knew all too well the hunger inside a person like that, and that opportunities were few and far between. He stepped away, bringing his bottle of bleach solution up between them, like it could do anything.

Ludwig, on the other hand, stepped forwards.

He dropped his shoulder and rammed it into the old man, his jumpsuit going dark with the spray of water across him. Jan was flung backwards, and his head cracked against the tiles. The sound echoed.

He slid to the floor, a hand pressed to his temple.

Bizarrely, Lane's first thought was of the spray of blood across the wall that he'd just got done cleaning.

Ludwig went for Jan's throat.

Lane slammed his open palm on the bathroom door and shouted for help. He could open it and run, of course, but Lane already had as many regrets as he could live with; he didn't know what one more would do to him. He sprinted across the room and, not knowing what else to do, sprayed the back of Ludwig's neck with the bleach mix.

Ludwig dropped his hands from Jan's throat and pressed one to the back of his neck, probably more out of surprise at being spritzed like a misbehaving puppy than any pain.

'Do you want to spend the rest of your life in here?' Lane hissed at him.

Ludwig laughed. 'I already am.'

Oh. Apparently Lane had been wrong about who in the room had a frustrated need to cause pain.

The door crashed open and, thankfully, both the idiot guard and several more experienced officers swarmed in. They dragged Ludwig off Jan.

Lane jumped as Jan grabbed his shoulder with a wet hand. The old man looked not at but past Lane, his pupils mismatched and his breathing ragged.

'I need you to tell Tamara,' he said. 'I tried but they won't let me.'

'If you can't, I can't,' Lane said.

'Not for me, for her. She shouldn't have to live thinking she barely escaped something . . . something bad. I wasn't going to hurt her.'

'Something bad' was such a dramatic downplaying of torture and murder that Lane almost wanted to laugh. He was saved from needing to respond by the rough hands of a guard hauling him away.

* * *

The guards took Lane's wet jumpsuit, shoes and the rubber gloves he'd been wearing and put them into evidence bags. There was a terrible sense of deja vu to the procedure that reminded him of when the police finally arrived to the scene of his father's death. The buzz of workers as they secured the scene, the flash of cameras, the static of radios.

That was the last time he'd ever seen Mina McCreery in person, as she was led gently away to a separate squad car.

Jan Henning-Klosner must have survived Ludwig's attack, because the medics had loaded him onto a backboard and wheeled him away on a gurney.

Lane was practically asleep on his feet. He'd been at the end of his shift, and it felt like he'd been held in the bathroom for hours. An unfamiliar female guard brought him a clean jumpsuit that was a few sizes too big, so he had to roll up the cuffs to avoid them dragging on the ground.

Finally, finally the guard gestured for him to follow her down the hallway. He didn't usually think fondly of his bunk, but tonight it was a luxury he couldn't wait to sink into.

But instead of turning towards the cell block, the guard steered him towards the staff offices. Lane sighed, realising that he wasn't going to get to sleep until after he'd given his statement.

The prison governor, Patton Carver, was seated behind his desk. He had on one of the grey knitted jumpers the staff often wore in the winter, but the edge of a tartan collar peeked out underneath, suggesting he might have pulled it on over his pyjamas when he was called in.

'Mr Holland,' Carver said, gesturing to the seat opposite him. He looked over at the guard, who stood in the doorway with her arms crossed. 'Ana, you can go help at the scene. We'll be fine here.'

For a moment Ana looked like she wanted to argue, then she nodded and left, shutting the door firmly behind her.

'Mr Carver,' Lane said. He pressed his hands to his knees, worried he would droop forwards if he relaxed at all.

'You've had a rough night, then?'

'You could say that,' Lane said. He explained what he had seen, trying to stay factual and dispassionate. It was tricky, explaining what the guard had chosen to do without sounding like he was trying to cast blame.

Carver listened, but didn't take any notes. Lane didn't see any sign of a recording device, but he supposed there could be one hidden. Carver hadn't properly announced the commencement of an interview for a recording, though. He'd just let Lane launch into his story.

When Lane was done, Carver leaned back in his chair and said, 'Huh.'

Lane gave him a moment to gather his thoughts, but Carver didn't ask any follow-up questions. Instead he said, 'You wouldn't be aware of this, Holland, but there has been a murder.'

'Here in the SPC?' Lane asked, confused. Carver couldn't mean that Jan had died, given the way he'd put it.

'No.' Carver turned the monitor of his computer towards Lane. There was a news article splashed across it, a picture at the top with crime scene tape and a white coroner's van. 'In Rainier.'

Lane knew the town of Rainier. Everyone knew the town of Rainier, for a tiny flyspeck just off the highway. And everyone who heard the name thought of one thing immediately. A trio of awful murders committed there in a three-month reign of terror. A trio of murders committed by Jan Henning-Klosner.

'Well, I can confirm Henning-Klosner's alibi,' Lane said, then wanted to punch himself in the jaw. No backchat, no dark jokes. If he was going to have any chance at getting out on good behaviour, he needed to keep his head down and his mouth shut. But he was tired, and it had slipped out.

'That you can,' Carver said, smirking. 'You were quite the detective once, weren't you, Holland?'

'I did alright,' Lane said.

'In the course of your investigations, did you ever come across rumours that Jan Henning-Klosner had an accomplice? A second Rainier Ripper who remains at large?'

'No,' Lane said, trying not to let his sinking feeling show on his face. Carver clearly wanted more from him than a statement about the incident. 'The case was closed before I even graduated high school. If there was a second Ripper, there was no reward offered for their capture, so it was of no interest to me.'

'Hmm,' Carver said. He flipped open a file on his desk. Lane's mugshot stared up at them both. 'You're three years into an eight-year sentence, correct?'

'Eligible for parole in six,' Lane said.

'From what I can see here, you've never signed up for one of the vocational courses offered here. How do you think the parole board will view that?'

Lane was too tired to follow this conversation. How had they got from the incident in the bathroom to a lecture on Lane's educational choices? 'I don't see the point until I get closer to being eligible for release.'

Carver sighed. 'You know that you won't be able to work as a private investigator when you're released, don't you? You'll never get a licence, never pass a background check, never be able to carry a gun.'

'Carrying a gun is where I went wrong the first time.'

'Holland, it is a common belief among prisoners that a sentence is just a pause, and afterwards they can pick their lives up where they left off. It is a mistaken belief, and one that the parole board does not react well to. When the time comes, I would like to report that you are ready to re-enter society.' Carver stared at him, and Lane didn't think they were talking about introductory barista training.

'I will take that under advisement,' Lane said.

'Good. Now, it seems the unfortunate Mr Henning-Klosner is going to be in the medical unit for some time.'

'I'm sorry to hear that,' Lane said.

'I'd like to have you admitted as well.'

'Thank you, but I wasn't hurt.' Lane did not consider himself above playing dumb.

'Henning-Klosner almost died today. If that had happened, he would have taken everything he knows with him. Accomplices. Unknown victims. The identity of Eva Nováková and the fate of her baby. He has been in here for close to two decades, and has never shown the slightest inclination to talk about any of it.' Carver leaned in. 'But when he thought he was dying, he spoke to you.'

'I was nearby,' Lane said. 'He's not going to feel the same urge when he's on the mend. And the police will send a trained interviewer, if they think he knows anything about this murder.'

Which he wouldn't. Jan had been on ice too long to have any meaningful connections on the outside. Lane was all too aware of how interest, letters and visits dropped away year by year. And the prison would be going over every request and letter Jan received, looking for anything incriminating.

'You're a trained interviewer,' Carver said. 'One he won't realise is interviewing him. Henning-Klosner knows how to play games with the cops. But you're good at games too, aren't you?'

Lane gestured to his jumpsuit. 'No, I'm not.'

Carver's friendly demeanour slipped a notch. 'Any prisoner would jump at this opportunity. No more cleaning detail. No watching your back in case someone like Ludwig decides to lash out at you next. I've had prisoners literally swallow spoons to get a vacation in the medical unit.'

Lane didn't like this. It was all lining up too neatly, and nothing was ever neat in a place like this. 'Why do you want this so badly?'

'Like I said, he knows things. Maybe he doesn't know anything about this murder, but he sure as hell knows about his own victims.'

'So this is really about Eva Nováková?'

Lane had read about the discovery of her body as a case study in university. From what he could remember, Eva was the victim who sent the Rainier Ripper case stratospheric. The discovery of a young man's body in the town fountain, killed by a slash to the throat, had made some headlines. There had been some tasteless comparisons to the Black Dahlia, an old cold case in Los Angeles. The news cycle would probably have moved on had a crime scene investigator on a cigarette break not noticed an unusual pattern of undergrowth in the park across the street. The spot was exhumed, and a woman's body was found, wrapped in a yellow knit blanket. Her cause of death was catastrophic blood loss, although the post-mortem wasn't able to determine which had been the fatal wound – when the Ripper cut off her hand, or the vicious slash to her stomach. The post-mortem concluded that she had been heavily pregnant, but no fetal remains were found. It was inhumane, it was sadistic, and it kicked off a national frenzy.

The woman remained unidentified. For reasons Lane couldn't recall, it was considered very likely that she was of Czech descent, and so she was eventually buried under the name Eva Nováková, the Czech equivalent of Jane Doe.

Carver turned a framed photo towards Lane. The girl in the picture's straight parted hair, strappy top and wide-legged trousers looked similar to the outfits Lynnie had worn on her recent visits, but given the cyclical nature of fashion and the aged appearance of the photo, Lane suspected it was from the spaghetti strap's first moment in the spotlight. 'This is my Matilda,' Carver said, showing the exhaustion not just of a long night but of many sleepless years. 'She was twenty-one the last time we saw her. She was backpacking around Australia, working on farms, getting practice in to go do the same thing in Europe for a year. Finding herself. At first, she called and wrote to us all the time, but the calls and letters got rarer and rarer, as they do. Then they stopped completely, and no-one who'd worked or travelled with her seemed to know which way she went.'

'I'm sorry,' Lane said. 'But I don't –'

'Then they found Eva Nováková,' Carver said, ignoring him. 'The time frames when she might have gone missing and when Eva might have died are both wide, but the overlap is significant.'

'Surely you could get a DNA test, if you explained this to the police,' Lane said.

'We adopted Matilda,' Carver said. 'From the Czech Republic – Czechia. She has no living relatives who could provide DNA to compare with Eva's, and she was gone for so long that nothing she left behind had a viable sample. The police say her particulars aren't a match for Eva, but I don't see how they can be so sure.'

Lane wondered if anyone in Corrective Services knew that Carver had been put in charge of a prisoner he genuinely believed could have murdered his daughter.

'In my heart, I know that Eva is my daughter,' Carver said. 'And I think you can get Henning-Klosner to tell you what he knows about her – or where the baby is. Matilda had a boyfriend; if he's a match as the baby's father, it would be strong evidence that the body is hers. Even if you find out she isn't Matilda, Eva is someone's daughter. I know what they're going through.'

'I'm sorry,' Lane said. 'But just being suspected of spying on other prisoners made my life hell for months.'

He couldn't look at Carver. He was sorry the man was hurting – and it must have been bad, for him to be willing to show that kind of vulnerability in front of a prisoner like Lane. He just wanted to stay safe and get through the days until he was eligible for parole. Even here, where he was supposed to be safe, he'd come within an inch of getting attacked again. Putting himself in the same room as a sadistic serial killer was the last thing he should do.

FIVE

BY THE TIME Gemma had served a third round of tea, the energy in the shop had waned into an anxious silence.

Mick knocked on the door about an hour after he had left, and Gemma let him in wordlessly.

'Did you find them?' Christian asked, like the answer wasn't obvious from Mick's drawn expression.

'No,' Mick said. Aubrey came and pressed herself against his side, and he wrapped one arm around her. 'No sign of them, and I couldn't identify which way they went, either. The crime scene techs are going to have to process the entire area.'

More deja vu. The same thing had happened when Vincent's body was discovered, with the police declaring every public area within a one-hundred-metre radius of the fountain part of the crime scene. The rule of thumb was to go big in the beginning and then shrink the boundaries as their understanding of what happened made it clear which areas were of most significance. It was much better than drawing a small boundary to begin with, then discovering something important was contaminated.

However, there were a lot of businesses inside that hundred-metre radius that would have to stay closed – including the teashop.

* * *

It was close to 2 am by the time Mick was done taking preliminary statements and sent everyone home with a warning they would be called in for a formal interview in the coming days. Gemma staggered up the stairs, only to be immediately ambushed by three worked-up teenagers.

'Has there really been another murder?' Violet asked.

Gemma bit her lip. It had always been difficult figuring out how much to tell Violet, and when. Gemma wanted to keep her innocent, but the effects of the Ripper murders were just part of life in Rainier, and could crop up unexpectedly. From customers coming into the teashop to ask invasive questions to the posters of Eva Nováková's identity sketch and Jaylene's occasional outbursts of public grief, it couldn't be hidden entirely. At the same time, it was just distant enough to be more intriguing than frightening for the younger generation, the ones who hadn't experienced it directly.

But this was not distant and abstract. This was a body outside their house right now. A real life snuffed out, and a real killer out there somewhere.

'Yes,' Gemma said. She glanced at Jac. The impact on them would be on another level, since it was their father's murder that was being mimicked. Irritation shot through her at Aubrey's decision to go home instead of staying with Jac. At her choosing Mick over her child.

Jac frowned, but they didn't say anything.

'I don't really know much,' Gemma said. 'It will probably be in the papers tomorrow.'

'Who was it?' Fawn asked.

'Lochlan Lewis,' Gemma answered. 'The tour guide. We don't know who killed him just yet.'

'So they haven't been arrested?' Violet asked, an edge of fear in her voice.

'They will be,' Gemma said, with more confidence than she felt. 'Your dad is right outside. He's on tape duty tonight.'

Violet and Jac, both raised by cops, nodded, but Fawn looked confused.

'That means he's guarding the crime scene,' Violet explained.

'He'll keep watch until another officer can take over in the morning,' Gemma said. 'This house is the safest place in the world right now, okay?'

* * *

Gemma lay awake, hyper-alert to every sound in the house. It was early morning, according to her bedside clock, although at this time of year the light wouldn't start to creep in for hours yet.

The night after Vincent's body was found had not been the worst night of her life, but it had felt like it at the time. She envied her younger self for believing that things could not get

66

worse. That was the one thing she now knew for sure: no matter what she did, however carefully she made her decisions, it could always get worse.

She closed her eyes and slowly counted to ten like Dr Nicholls had taught her. Acknowledge the unproductive thought and let it drift away. It didn't go anywhere, no matter how hard she visualised trying to blow it out like the flame on a candle, but at least she had tried.

A thought occurred to her, and she rolled over to check in the little box of bedside essentials Hugh had brought in when they staged the other room for a guest. He had a little seven-day pillbox, and that day's pill was still rattling in its chamber.

She sighed and got up, grabbing her overcoat from the hook on the back of her door. If Hugh had skipped a dose he was probably already feeling nausea or dizziness, and if he forgot tomorrow's too he would quickly become irritable and anxious. The situation was bad enough without white-knuckling it through withdrawals.

She peeked into Violet's room as she passed. Violet had a bunk with a single on top and a double below, plus a daybed by the window, but all three teens were in the double, curled around each other like hardenbergia vines. Gemma missed that, when friendships were simple. Sure, the kids could have their dramas and stresses, but they had so much time ahead to grow past them and remake themselves, let it fade to something they can look back on and laugh at.

The little kitchen upstairs was a bare scrap of a thing, but stocked enough that she could fill a thermos with tea and put together a jam sandwich. She hated the upstairs kitchen and rarely used it, but was glad they had it now.

Outside the cold air bit, even through her coat. She hesitated in the mouth of the alley, bracing herself to see the crime scene again.

The park was transformed, circled by hurricane fencing and police tape. Thankfully, the fountain itself had disappeared inside a crime scene tent, so she didn't need to see it again.

Hugh stood on the corner, hunched over in his jacket. He had his back to her, talking to someone small enough to be completely hidden from view by his body. Gemma couldn't hear what they were saying, their voices low, but Hugh's tone was short and sharp.

After a few moments Hugh shifted to the side, as the person took their leave of him, and Gemma realised with a jolt that he had been talking to Aubrey.

Aubrey didn't see Gemma standing in the shadow of the building, but Hugh did. His eyes cut from her to Aubrey's retreating back, then he waved to her with a smile that Gemma could tell was forced.

He took the proffered food, drink and pill with good grace, but there was an undercurrent of tension in him.

'What was that about?' Gemma asked. 'I thought Aubrey went home with Mick?'

Hugh shook his head. 'Mick hasn't gone home. He's down at the station, riding the phone. Aubrey went to see him, and checked in with me on her way back – same as you're doing,' he said, a little irritation sneaking into his voice.

It hadn't seemed like a friendly check-in, but then it made sense for Hugh to be snappish.

'How are you doing?' she asked.

'Dead on my feet,' he confessed. 'The crime scene unit arrived and started work a few hours ago, but Wagga isn't able to spare any bodies to help secure the scene until the day shift starts.'

'What about the Homicide Squad?' she pressed. 'Are they going to send someone to run the investigation?'

'Why? Last time they sent Mick, and he's here now. It's not like we don't have the experience to run a murder investigation.'

His experience was what she was worried about. 'Just because you *can* do it doesn't mean you should have to,' she said.

'Leave off it,' he snapped. Then he screwed up his face in regret. 'I'm sorry, I'm just . . .'

'I know,' she said.

'Are you okay?' he asked. 'Is Violet?'

'Violet's fine,' she said. 'She's sleeping.' The exchange reminded her painfully of when Violet was a baby and Hugh would phone home to check on her. Yes, she's fine, she's sleeping, she's eating. Are you?

Was Gemma okay? It didn't matter; she didn't have room to be anything else Not when she had so many other people to worry about.

'Will she need to be fingerprinted?' Gemma asked. She had been herself when the scene was being processed after Vincent's murder. Because she lived and worked across the road from the scene, and had visited the fountain at lunchtime that day, the police needed her prints to rule out any she had left on the metal railings. To isolate unidentified prints that might lead somewhere.

She'd found the experience terrifying. That was the first time she met Mick Seabrooke, and his questioning had turned aggressive once he found out she was Vincent's ex-girlfriend. It was clear he'd thought she knew something she was refusing to share.

'It would be different for Violet,' Hugh said, demonstrating that despite everything he could still read her too easily. 'You were nineteen, she's sixteen. Huge difference. You would be able to go in with her.' He hesitated, before adding with regret, 'You might need to give yours again. Your fingerprints aren't stored unless you're convicted of a crime. But it might not be necessary – it's an awful site to pull prints from. All we got last time was rubbish.'

That wasn't reassuring. If it was a difficult site, how would they identify the killer? When would this be over?

SIX

THERE WAS NO point trying to go back to sleep. The kids would be up soon, and if Gemma didn't get ahead of them with a decent breakfast they would eat their way through the pantry before she staggered out again.

But, then, maybe she should just let them. She didn't know how long the shop would need to stay closed, but she was probably going to end up throwing out a ton of fresh fruit, salad fixings, meat and dairy. She didn't keep a huge stock of inventory, but it was still more than her family could eat. She made a note on the pad on the fridge to call the Dillons and cancel this week's dairy run.

After a quick review of what was likely to expire first, she mixed a ham, cheese and egg casserole in the cast-iron Dutch oven, then found herself alone in the too-quiet of the kitchen while it baked.

She had come to a decision. Hugh had decided to put his pride over his wellbeing. She couldn't imagine a worse decision than insisting on being on the front lines of this investigation. Not when the original Ripper murders had dealt such a blow to his mental health that it had nearly cost them their family and him his career.

But while she couldn't force him to make a different choice, what she could do was help. There were things people in this town were willing to talk about with her that they would never tell the police. If someone knew something that could bring this new investigation to a swift end, she would get it out of them.

* * *

She decided to put on a batch of buttermilk scones to take over to Jaylene and Antoine. While they were baking, she looked in on Violet's room. Violet and Jac were still asleep, splayed out under the covers like a two-headed octopus, but Fawn was curled up in the window seat with her sketchbook open on her lap.

'Morning,' Gemma whispered. 'You can bring that into the kitchen if you want – the light is better there.'

'Thanks,' Fawn said. She tucked the sketchbook under her arm, folded open, and Gemma was startled to see the wide, dark eyes of Eva Nováková staring out at her.

'What are you working on?' she asked.

Fawn flashed her a nervous look. 'Some concept sketches for my visual art major project. I'm just batting some ideas around at this point.'

She put the book down on the kitchen table, and Gemma got a good look at the sketch. Fawn had clearly used the police reconstruction image as a reference, but had taken artistic licence, giving Eva a melancholy but relaxed expression and waves of soft hair falling around her face.

'Did you do this today?'

'Yeah.' Fawn ran her thumb down the edge of the page. 'I'm sorry.'

'We all have our own ways of processing what happened. It's beautiful.'

'Did you ever see her?'

'When she was alive?'

'No, when they were trying to identify her.'

Gemma shook her head. 'They brought me in to have a look at the blanket she was wrapped in, to see if I remembered selling someone that shade of yarn, but it was acrylic – not one of ours. I never saw her body.'

'She feels very familiar,' Fawn said.

'I'm not surprised. That poster with her picture has been up in the community hall since before you could walk,' Gemma said.

She pulled on her oven mitts and brought the casserole out of the oven. She opened the top, letting a cloud of cheesy steam escape, then closed it again and left the pot on the stovetop to cool a bit.

'That smells amazing,' Fawn said. She started to carefully letter something at the top of the sketch.

Gemma smiled. 'Tell me more about your project.'

'Have you ever read the short story "The Nine Billion Names of God"?'

'That's the one with the space monks, right? I think we read it in high school.'

'Ha, us too. They use a computer to list out every possible combination of letters up to nine characters, because they believe among them will be the true name of God. So I thought, if I write out the top hundred girls' names from Czechia, then Australia, the US, New Zealand, Canada and the rest of Europe, there's a good chance I will have labelled her portrait with her real name, even if we don't know which one it is.'

Something cold ran through Gemma at the idea. 'Wow.'

'I don't know how practical it is, though. The canvas would need to be huge to fit them all.'

'What about a mural? A wall would be big enough.'

Fawn laughed. 'Not at our house. Mum won't even let me put up a poster that's off the colour scheme. Plus' – she turned the book so she could continue lettering down the side of the page – 'she gets a bit weird when I bring this stuff up.'

Gemma sympathised. She always tried to discourage any interest from Violet, so she understood where Lotte was coming from.

Gemma could now read Fawn's lettering – *I toto jed* – meaning that she was writing out the text of the tattoo on Eva's ankle: *I toto jednou pomine*, the Czech for 'this too shall pass'. It was the reason the police speculated that Eva was from Czechia, or had spent some time there.

'You could use the back wall of our courtyard,' Gemma suggested. 'If it's for a school project.'

It was a knee-jerk impulse. She knew Violet didn't need her in the background, pandering to her friends like they needed to be bribed. Jac and Fawn genuinely loved Violet, because she was kind and funny and interesting. But part of Gemma would always be that mother sending her daughter off to high school way too young, terrified that the next six years were going to be miserable.

'That would be amazing,' Fawn said.

'You know, if you're interested in Eva Nováková, Tamara Fleischer brought up something during the tour,' Gemma said. 'Apparently scientists can figure out a lot more from DNA these days. Not her identity, unless there's something in the database to match it against, but other information, like her ancestry and ethnicity. That would cut down your list of names.'

'I think I've read about that. We're doing a unit on DNA in biology.' Fawn grabbed her phone and within seconds was scrolling through articles. 'Oh, creepy. Look – they can even do identikit pictures based on the genetic information.'

She held up the phone, displaying rows of pictures that were almost but not quite human.

Three sharp knocks cut through the air. They were too distinct to be something being bumped over or dropped, but coming from the wrong direction to be a knock at the door. It had come from down the hall – the locked door of the room where Marcus Shadwell was staying.

'Sorry to disturb you,' he said when she opened the door. He wore black trackpants and a white t-shirt. She assumed those were his pyjamas, but he'd combed his hair and looked freshly shaved. 'I woke up this morning and just couldn't seem to . . .'

She understood immediately. If he had left his room through the external door, he would have to pass above the murder scene again, and in the full light of morning.

'Of course.' She stepped back to let him come through the hallway. 'Would you like some coffee? I was just about to put on a pot.'

'I would be eternally grateful.' He followed her into the kitchen. 'Something smells amazing,' he said, reaching for the lid of the pot.

'Don't touch that!' Gemma shouted, but it was too late. He closed his hand around the cast-iron handle, still searing hot from the oven.

He gasped in pain, a hiss of breath through his teeth, and grabbed his wrist. 'Oh god!'

'Why would you touch that?' Gemma raced over and turned the kitchen tap on full blast, then grabbed his forearm and pushed his hand into the flow of cool water.

'It's a handle! Why would the handle be hot?'

'There's no heatproofing, it's an antique,' she said.

He tried to pull his hand back out of the water, but she squeezed his arm harder.

'It feels fine now,' he said. 'I barely touched it.'

'It feels fine because the water is numbing it,' she said. 'You need to keep it there for at least ten minutes, otherwise the skin will keep burning.'

'Do you want me to call my father?' Fawn asked.

Gemma nodded. 'That would be great.'

Marcus shifted next to her. They were pressed hip to hip in the narrow space in front of the sink, but she didn't trust him to keep his hand in the water if she stepped away. She had enough men in her life who would rather have their pride than their health.

She pulled out her phone to count off the minutes, and it rang in her hand. It was Jennifer, Hugh's father's wife, wanting to FaceTime. Gemma considered declining and calling back once she'd had a chance to put some concealer on the dark circles under her eyes, but she didn't want to leave Hugh's family worrying.

She regretted it immediately when Jennifer appeared on screen. Jennifer was completely lovely, a stunning Wiradjuri woman, and she looked immaculate despite the early hour.

'Gemma, my hen, I just heard on the news,' she said, before Gemma could even say hello. 'Are you alright?'

'Everyone here is just fine,' Gemma said, and Marcus chuckled beside her, his hand still in the water.

'Is that Hugh? Can I say hi?'

'No, Hugh's still at work. He'll be home any minute, though. I can get him to give you a call once he's had a kip.'

'Oh, don't have the poor thing go to any trouble. Eric's tied up too, getting ready for morning services. But please let Hugh know he's thinking of him, yeah?'

Gemma rolled her eyes. She hated the way Hugh and Eric seemed perfectly happy to conduct their relationship through their wives as proxies. 'Will do. Thanks, Jenn.'

She hung up, and let go of Marcus's wrist. 'That should be right now, but put it back under if it starts to sting.'

'Was that your sister?' Marcus asked.

'Mother-in-law,' Gemma said, then, at his look of surprise, she corrected it to, 'Stepmother-in-law.'

Jennifer was only ten years older than Gemma, making her only five years older than Hugh, which could be awkward at times.

But they'd been in their thirties, and Jennifer in her forties, when Eric moved to Moree and the two of them met, so it wasn't like he'd married a twenty-something while he still had a teenager at home, like she'd seen some men do. Jennifer had taken twenty years off Eric's age, dragging him to music festivals and art galleries and on hikes and campouts. It more than made up for any lingering weirdness.

Her phone buzzed with a voicemail left while she was talking to Jennifer, and then immediately rang again. It really had hit the news, then.

She stepped out of the room when she saw it was her mother, and headed into the lounge.

'Oh darling, I'm so relieved to hear your voice,' her mother said. 'Tell me Violet is okay.'

'She's fine, Mum,' Gemma said. 'What's the news saying?'

'Oh, dreadful, dreadful things. Just awful. I'm glad I didn't see it until this morning – I wouldn't have slept at all if I'd known.'

'Yeah, I didn't sleep particularly well.'

'Of course not, darling, you must be terrified. And poor, poor Violet. You can't stay there, of course, not with some lunatic on the loose. You must drive up and stay with us.'

78

Gemma smiled. 'The three of us aren't going to fit on your sofa bed.'

Her parents had retired to a one-bedroom unit on the Gold Coast. It was absolutely tiny, but if you wedged yourself into the far-left corner of the balcony and stood on a folding chair, you could see a glimmer of ocean, so they loved it.

In the background her father's voice muttered, 'They'd fit if they left the Foreskin behind.'

Gemma's good humour fled immediately.

'She can hear you, you ridiculous man,' her mother snapped. 'It's on speaker.'

'How was I to know that?'

'How did you think you were hearing her half of the conversation?'

There was something comforting about her parents bickering. They squabbled with a sense of complete security in their relationship, and never escalated to outright fighting.

'I've got to go, Mum,' Gemma said. 'Thanks for calling.'

A shadow fell over her, startling her so badly she stumbled forwards. When she saw it was Marcus in the doorway, she forced a fake smile to cover up her embarrassment. It was absurd how on edge she was.

'I apologise if you heard any of that,' she said.

'I didn't. But even if I had, I can't judge. My parents made some mortifying calls in their time.'

Well done, Gemma. Whinge about your parents to a man who has no family left at all.

'How's your hand feeling?' she asked.

'It feels like I've been caned,' he said. He held it out for her to see. The line across his palm was a painful-looking shade of pink.

'Pain is good,' she said. 'A burn with no pain means it's gone deep enough to damage the nerves.'

'That's funny,' he said, staring down at his palm. 'My therapist said the same thing once.'

* * *

'It's good you acted so quickly,' Dr Nicholls said, examining Marcus's hand in the sunlight from the kitchen window.

It embarrassed Gemma how much that pleased her. It was hard not to think of Dr Nicholls as an authority figure. He'd been her doctor growing up. When she found out she was pregnant with Violet he'd been the only person to ask what she wanted instead of immediately pushing for one option or the other.

It felt odd to have him in her house. Their girls were old enough to come and go on their own, so even though Fawn half-lived in their house, her father had never come by. Lotte had stopped by a few times, looking elegantly out of place in their cramped little rooms, but never Dr Nicholls.

When Violet had been younger, playdates had always been at the other child's house or down at the oval. No-one had ever said they didn't want to bring their children to the murder house, but there was always a swift offer to host when the suggestion of a get-together came up. Most of those families had moved away now, in the gradual exodus from town. That was odd, she reflected.

It seemed like those who had stuck it out and remained in Rainier were also those most closely tied to the murders. The Tjibaous, the Holsts, the Dillons, the Seabrookes.

'You shouldn't see any loss of function long term, although you might have a scar,' Dr Nicholls was saying to Marcus. 'I'll put on some cream and bandage it, and you'll need to be careful to keep it clean. I'll take a look in a few days.' He unzipped his bag and started laying out supplies. 'Call me earlier if the pain gets worse, or you suspect it's infected, or if you start to feel unwell.'

Once the doctor was done, Marcus excused himself to have a lie-down until the painkillers kicked in, leaving Gemma and Dr Nicholls alone in the kitchen.

'Fawn is in the lounge,' Gemma told him.

'Thanks,' the doctor replied. 'If it's not too much trouble, do you think she could stay a little longer?'

'Always,' Gemma said immediately. 'But the police have set up a crime scene tent, so she won't see anything if she heads out today.'

'I saw. But,' he lowered his voice, 'Lotte was pretty shaken by what happened last night. I don't want her to worry about Fawn seeing her freak out.'

In other circumstances Gemma would have been charmed by that. Lotte had to be made of stern stuff to survive in the career she'd chosen, but Dr Nicholls was still protective of her.

But Gemma had also seen the body in the fountain. Didn't he think she deserved a bit of privacy and space too?

Her mixed feelings must have been obvious, because his face creased into his familiar look of concern.

'I'm sorry if that was thoughtless of me,' he said. 'To be honest, you've always struck me as someone who manages best when you have something to focus on. Someone to take care of.'

She smiled at that. He knew her well. 'I'm alright, really. And my parents offered to have me visit, if I need extra support.'

'That's good, I'm glad.' He put a hand on her shoulder and squeezed. 'Do you want something for your anxiety? Something to help you sleep?'

She was utterly shattered from lack of sleep, but the idea terrified her. What if she knocked herself out with pills and then someone tried to get in? Or what if Violet needed her? She couldn't risk it.

'I'm fine. Did you see Hugh on the way in?'

'Yes, but I didn't stop to chat. He was in the park, talking to another officer.'

'Did he look okay to you?'

'He wasn't the patient I was on my way to see. Do you want me to come back when he gets home?'

Gemma considered it, but pushing so soon after their conversation that morning might do more harm than good. 'No, I should let you get on with your day.'

* * *

Aubrey picked up on the third ring, sounding groggy. Ordinarily Gemma would feel guilty about that, but not today.

'I wanted to let you know that Fawn is staying again tonight. Jac's welcome to stay too. I think it would be good for the three of them to hang out together today, focus on other things,' she said in a rush. 'But if you would prefer for Jac to be home with you, I'll send them over. The crime scene is covered up.'

But Aubrey knew that already.

'Yeah, sure.' Aubrey yawned loudly. 'Whatever Jac wants to do.'

'It's on the news,' Gemma said. 'Mum called, so it's already national. I'm not even going to try to keep the kids from reading about it – they've probably seen all the details on their phones by now anyway. I'm sure this is going to be especially hard for Jac, is there anything you want me to do for them?'

'I'm sure they'll be fine,' Aubrey said. 'I mean, it was fucking heart-stopping to see it . . . but Jac wasn't around the first time. It's not going to affect them the way it does me or Vincent's parents. It was before they were born, and they've got a great father.'

'If you're sure,' Gemma said, dubious. She waited for a deliberate beat, then added, 'Hugh mentioned you checked in on him last night. Thanks for that.'

Aubrey was silent for long enough to confirm that she definitely had not expected Hugh to tell Gemma that he saw her. 'Of course,' she said.

'Just like you'd look out for Mick, right?'

'Right,' Gemma said. It made perfect sense. So why was there any need for secrecy? What had they really been talking about?

SEVEN

LANE COULD BARELY keep his eyes open, but he hadn't missed a visiting hour in three years and he wasn't going to start today. Lynnie's visits were getting further and further apart, something he bit his tongue about. He knew she was having a rough time out there on her own. But the sight of her waiting for him at the table made his whole body lurch with a desperation he couldn't let himself feel in the times in between. Nothing could communicate how unspeakably lonely prison was.

Her smile fell away as he approached. 'Are you okay?'

'Right as rain,' he said. He knew there was nothing he could do to hide his foggy reactions or the deep shadows under his eyes. 'I didn't sleep particularly well last night, but it's nothing serious.'

'Right,' she said, giving that as much credence as it deserved.

'How's uni going?' he jumped in to ask.

'Great!' she said, brightening. 'Things are super busy at work, given that it's the end of financial year, but it's not too much to juggle.'

Lynnie had transferred out of her English degree in her second year into an accounting cadetship. It was a good deal – she worked part time, went to university part time, and the firm paid for her studies and enough of a salary for her to survive on alone. It wasn't what she had wanted, but she insisted she liked it. That her work was like solving puzzles for a living. He wanted to believe her, but he had to wonder if she told him that in the same way he assured her that prison was exactly the sort of free resort lifestyle the radio shock jocks insisted it was.

'Good, good. That's really good.'

'Yeah, it's good.'

'Good.'

They smiled awkwardly at each other, and Lane clawed for something to say to put some puff back into the conversation.

'Are you seeing anyone?'

Lynnie laughed. 'Oh my god, Lane. Not you too.'

'Sorry.' Lane joined her in laughing, and that was something at least.

'Mina was in the paper yesterday,' Lynnie said. She took a folded page from her purse and laid it out on the table.

Mina McCreery's twin sister, Evelyn, had disappeared from their family farm in 1999, when the girls were nine years old. Mina had only been in Lane's life for a few months, but their stories had been entwined for decades. He'd approached her, wanting to prove the theory that had tormented him for years: that Evelyn had been murdered by his father, Lane Holland Senior.

He'd been right, but in his desperation he'd made the rash, stupid decision to abduct his father and try to force a confession out of him. It had ended with his father dead and him in prison.

The picture was newspaper quality, but it showed Mina McCreery seated with the family of a missing woman at an inquest into the lack of police action in the critical early hours of her disappearance. She looked good. Sombre, as the occasion called for, but there was an air of calm around her that was nice to see.

'I'm happy for her,' he said. He pushed it back across the table. 'You don't need to keep tabs on her for me, Lynnie. She's free to live her own life now.'

'You should keep it,' she said. 'I think it would help.'

'The prison's not going to let me keep that,' he said.

He did want it, and that want sat uncomfortably in his chest. It was easy to lose himself in here, sink into bitterness at his own choices. His connection to Lynnie was one anchor, and another was telling himself that he had made life better for Mina. He couldn't contact her – that could only happen if she chose it, unless he wanted say goodbye to his hopes of parole. So far, she hadn't showed any inclination to reach out to him.

Which was fine. That was her decision. She didn't owe him anything. What he'd done *for* her was dwarfed by what he'd done *to* her.

'Lane,' Lynnie said. 'You've completely zoned out.'

'Sorry.' He shook his head. This time was precious, and he was wasting it. 'I've just got stuff on my mind.'

'What? Do you need to be moved again?'

'No!' he reassured her. His move to the SPC had added an hour to her commute to see him, on top of an already significant trip from Canberra. 'Well, hopefully not.'

It hadn't occurred to him, in his sleep-deprived state, but it should have. If the governor got pissed at Lane for turning down his request, could he find himself dumped back in the general population? Was he only in the Tin in the first place because the governor wanted him here?

'You know hiding shit from me isn't going to stop me worrying, Lane,' Lynnie said. 'Spit it out.'

He glanced around the visiting room to see how close they were to any other prisoners, then leaned in. 'The governor wants me to do something for him.'

He explained the situation as briefly and quietly as he could, leaving out the part where he'd been in danger in the bathroom. To his surprise, Lynnie's face screwed up in a frown.

'And you said no?'

'Of course I said no,' he hissed. 'All I want to do is keep my file clean and tick my days off.'

'Don't be ridiculous,' she said, waving a hand at him.

'You want me to get up close and personal with a serial killer?'

'Lane, you've been more alive in the past three minutes than I've seen you in the past three years,' she said.

87

He couldn't deny that. But was that feeling a real sense of purpose, or the desperation of an addict trying to suck the last dregs out of a bottle?

'I think not doing it would be dangerous,' Lynnie said. 'You need this. Of course you're going to do it.'

She pushed the newspaper page back across the table to him. 'Don't ask them to let you keep this article,' she said. She flipped it over. On the other side was a piece titled: MURDER TOWN PONDERS DARK TOURISM, with a picture of a quaint little teashop, the shadow of a fountain lurking in the corner of the photo. 'Apply to keep this one.'

EIGHT

THE TJIBAOU FAMILY home was behind the church, barely a hundred
metres from the teashop, but only if you went through the Fountain
Park, which wasn't possible with the police activity. Today, she
had to go the long way around.

Rainier had a simple layout. If the old highway was the town's
spine, the residential streets ran off it like ribs. Instead of going
out the gate and down the alley to the main road, she went the
other direction, which opened on Clarence Street. From there,
a footpath ran behind the buildings that lined Sydney Road.
She followed the path until she reached the little car park of the
IGA, and then cut through. She crossed the roads, which were
still eerily quiet, and didn't let herself look back down the street
towards the park.

She held the batch of scones against her chest, enjoying the residual heat soaking through the tea towel she had wrapped them in.

The house had once been a weatherboard church hall, but the Tjibaous had bought it and converted it into a ramshackle cottage. When Gemma and Vincent were children the backyard was filled with project cars, swings, a trampoline, bikes and sporting equipment. But over the past decades it had become Jaylene's space, filled with pallet-wood raised garden beds, windchimes made of Salvation Army teaspoons, broken mirror mosaics and succulents growing in mismatched coffee mugs.

Gemma knocked on the door, but got no answer. She sat on a little concrete bench in the garden, in a nook shielded by a stand of casuarinas. Looking at the ground, she saw there were tiny privet seedlings coming up amid the mulch and leaned forwards to yank them out. All it took was one tree in town, and the birds would eat the berries and spread the seeds for miles.

Nice spaces like this only stayed nice if someone was fighting to keep them that way all the time. The seedlings were all small, shorter than her thumb with a few leaves on each side. She bet there were no bigger ones because Antoine had been pulling them out. Vincent's father loved people by doing things for them. Once she'd spent the night here and tried to sneak out the next morning, only to catch Antoine in the driveway changing the oil in her car.

It really worried her that he wasn't among the people in the teashop last night: the ones who could be ruled out as Lochlan Lewis's murderer.

Antoine had been Rainier's claim to fame before the murders. He won a bronze medal in weightlifting at the 1984 Olympics and then, after moving from Nouméa to Rainier to marry Jaylene, won the silver twice for Australia at the Commonwealth Games. He had come to Rainier Primary School the day before every athletics carnival to let the kids try on his medals, right up until the year the school closed.

'Gemma!' Jaylene said, opening the front gate. She had the cotton tote she used for grocery shopping slung over her shoulder. 'What a lovely surprise.'

'I've brought you some scones,' Gemma said. 'I can't open the shop today, so the ingredients would have gone to waste.'

'Will you be okay?' Jaylene asked. 'How long do you think you'll need to stay closed?'

Gemma shrugged. The shop closure – especially during the school holidays, one of their busiest periods – was a point of pressure that she hadn't let herself think much about. Accept the things you cannot change, as the prayer went.

Jaylene clucked sympathetically. 'Come inside, love. I've got a kvass brewing that will go beautifully with those, and there's no sense hanging about in the cold.'

'Is Antoine around?'

'He's out camping by the river.'

'By himself?' Gemma probed, hoping that she was conveying concern and not nosiness.

Jaylene sighed. 'He needs to be alone sometimes. This tour idea has him hurting like you wouldn't believe. He doesn't want people to see him get emotional. You know how men are.'

Gemma had wanted to hear that Antoine had an airtight alibi. Ideally that he'd been hundreds of kilometres away and captured by six different security cameras at the time of the murder, two of which were airing live on TV.

Inside, she sank onto Jaylene's lounge. Every scrap of available space held a photograph, and if there was an order to how they were arranged she had never figured it out. Antoine's competition pictures, their wedding, Vincent and Jac's baby pictures and school photos, family snaps and formal portraits were all mixed together. Gemma appeared in a few – she was beside Vincent for his Year Ten and Twelve formals, and his graduation. There were even a couple of pictures of Aubrey, at Jac's birthday parties. There were none with Mick.

Jaylene brought in two glasses of kvass and handed one to Gemma. She had never really warmed to the yeasty, fizzy drink, but if she turned it down she would get a lecture about how good it was for the digestion.

'Does Antoine know yet, what happened?'

Jaylene shook her head. 'I left a message asking him to call me, but he hasn't yet. The place he likes to camp is in a black spot.' She settled in an armchair opposite Gemma. 'To be honest I'm a little relieved. It's going to be a tough conversation.'

'How are you holding up?' Gemma asked. Vincent had been an only child, so with Antoine away, there was no-one to support Jaylene.

'I know it makes no sense,' Jaylene said, 'but after the numbness wore off, my first reaction was anger. I just lay awake all night, completely enraged.'

'That seems really reasonable to me.'

'I wasn't angry at the murderer,' Jaylene confessed. 'I'm angry at Lochlan Lewis.'

'For being murdered?'

'I did say it makes no sense.' Jaylene sighed, and Gemma could hear now how tired she was. Her voice had the roughness that lingered after a long bout of crying. 'He didn't care that he was desecrating Vincent's memory. And now their names are going to be linked forever: the bodies in the fountain.'

'I'm sorry, Jaylene,' Gemma said, reaching over and grabbing the other woman's hand. She squeezed and then dropped it.

'It just doesn't seem right. Like we're in one of those sci-fi shows where the timeline got messed up and everything is in the wrong place.'

'I know,' Gemma said. She took a sip of the kvass so she didn't need to say anything more.

Jaylene patted her knee. 'I'll always think of you as my daughter-in-law. You and Vincent were on different paths, but they would have joined up again in the end. He needed to grow up a bit, but he would have.'

'You know he'd have married Aubrey the second he found out about Jac,' Gemma said.

Mentioning Aubrey made Gemma consider asking Jaylene if she had any idea why Aubrey might have been talking to Hugh that morning. But she dismissed the idea quickly. Jaylene wouldn't keep any secrets for Aubrey, and who knew what she would do if Gemma told her what she'd seen.

'Of course he would have. But the two of them were never made to last. Not like you and him were. You would have been as much Jac's mama as Aubrey, and I wouldn't have had to go through the courts to see my own grandbaby.'

Gemma was holding on to the glass so tightly she was worried it would shatter in her hand. She never knew what to say when Jaylene got like this. It was so damn disrespectful to Aubrey, and to Hugh, but Jaylene was a grieving mother. Gemma couldn't imagine living with the pain Jaylene and Antoine felt every day.

And part of her agreed.

Gemma had been eleven when she decided that she was going to marry Vincent Tjibaou one day. It took until she was fifteen for Vincent to agree, and they dated all through high school. He graduated a year ahead of her and got a job as a truck driver. Local routes at first, then a run to Melbourne once he had some experience. The pay was immense for a man of his age. He would be gone for weeks then come back flush with cash and back-to-back days off. He would whisk her off to Melbourne or Sydney, and once to the Central Coast. They'd spend days on the beach and nights in bars, in warehouse dance clubs, at the parties of people he'd met on the road.

It started to get too much. She had exams and assignments, and her grandmother was starting to lean on her more and more to help run the tearoom as she aged. Work then partying then back to work left her exhausted, not to mention the Tuesday blues. She had her suspicions about how Vincent was managing it.

Their split was gentle and wistful, and she had thought of it more as a pause than a stop. She'd always thought the time would be right for them eventually.

The next time he came back to town it was Aubrey he whisked away. Then one day he was gone.

'I'm frightened,' Jaylene said now.

'Do you want to come stay with us until Antoine gets home?' Gemma asked, relieved to be presented with a problem she could solve. There wasn't really room, but they could shuffle around for a night or two.

'I'm not scared to be alone. When you've had a loss like mine, you don't fear death anymore.' Jaylene closed her eyes. 'I'm frightened that Mick is going to pin this on Antoine.'

Gemma's heart clenched. 'He wouldn't,' she said. But she understood Jaylene's fear. Antoine had a motive. He had no real alibi. He wasn't capable of murder, but that was difficult to prove. Mick loved Aubrey fiercely, and the hurt between Aubrey and the Tjibaous ran long and deep. How sure could she be that he wouldn't let that cloud his judgement?

NINE

THE PRISON GOVERNOR didn't seem surprised to see Lane waiting outside his office. He simply smiled and waved him inside.

'I'm going to need some resources,' Lane said. 'I barely know anything about this case; I can't go in with nothing and just hope for the best. I've put in a request to keep an article given to me by a visitor – can you approve that?'

'Done,' said Carver. 'And I'll see what else I can get for you. There are a couple of books on Henning-Klosner, but for obvious reasons the library here doesn't have them. Anyway, you won't be able to sit beside him flipping through his biography.' He looked thoughtful, then turned to his computer. 'You'll have to be quick with these. Henning-Klosner is in the hospital being patched up, but they'll bring him back here to convalesce. You need to be in the medical unit when he arrives or this all falls apart.'

'I've jumped into cases with less prep time,' Lane said.

Carver's laser printer hummed awake and began to spit out pages. Lane peered over and saw an article illustrated with a photograph of a slender foot.

'I'm basically just dumping out the first page of Google results for you,' Carver admitted. 'I'll keep looking, and if I find anything I think you need I'll try to find a way to get it to you discreetly.'

'What about Matilda? I need to know more about her.'

'I can give you her Missing Persons profile. It's pretty scant, though. Blonde hair, green eyes, one hundred and sixty-five centimetres. Twenty-one when she went missing. She'd be thirty-eight now.'

Carver's words were matter of fact, but his tone was all too familiar to Lane. He'd heard it before, from families who had spent years describing someone they loved as a handful of traits and numbers. The flat recitation was a coping method, not real detachment.

'Was she last seen in the Rainier area?'

'No,' Carver said. 'When we fell out of contact she was working at an organic farm in the Kiewa Valley. When that wrapped up she was going to travel home to Sydney. But she might have changed her mind, for the right opportunity. Rainier isn't known for agriculture, but there were farms hiring in the area at the time.'

'Have you spoken to any of those farmers?'

'Not with any success. Those that would talk to me hadn't seen her. But she might not have intended to go to Rainier.

Henning-Klosner was a truck driver at the time, running from Melbourne to Sydney. They could have crossed paths anywhere on that route.'

'Was she in the habit of hitchhiking?'

Carver's face twisted with sadness. 'I don't know. We warned her not to. If she was desperate she could have called us – we would have done anything to stop her putting herself in danger.'

'Of course.' It was easy to say that in hindsight, Lane thought. Living in the worst-case scenario, it was easy to tell yourself you'd have come to the rescue if given a chance. But it was completely plausible that Matilda, finding herself broke or stuck, might have preferred not to turn to her parents, even if just to avoid judgement or criticism.

Carver pulled the sheets from the printer and passed them over. Up close, Lane saw that the photograph had been included to show the detail of a distinctive script tattoo curving below the woman's ankle bone. '*I toto jednou pomine*,' he read, probably butchering the pronunciation.

'It's Czech,' Carver said. 'It means "this too shall pass".'

That explained the assumption that the woman had some connection to Czechia. 'Did Matilda have this tattoo?' Lane asked. He already knew the answer – a tattoo that distinctive would have made the identification open and shut.

'No,' Carver said. 'But at her age, getting a tattoo while travelling and not telling your parents about it is practically compulsory.'

'Surely her friends would have known about it, though?' Lane ran his thumb over the words. He was uncomfortably aware that the picture must have been taken at the crime scene, or in the morgue. That he was looking at a picture of a human's body.

'She could have had it done after she left Kiewa.'

Lane said nothing. The tattoo didn't look fresh. On the other hand, it might not have been quality work to begin with, and foot tattoos were notorious for fading quickly. Not to mention that it might have looked very different pre-mortem.

'Do you know if tattoo artists were canvassed at the time? It would have stuck in the artist's memory better than a random kanji symbol or a flash butterfly.'

'I couldn't tell you,' Carver said, with obvious regret.

Lane flipped to the next page, which showed the forensic sketch of Eva's face. It was of decent quality, but not the best he'd seen. The artist had drawn Eva with overly large eyes. He'd seen a lot of these sketches, and found that the artists almost always went with exaggeratedly large eyes, perhaps in the hope of catching the viewer's attention. Her nose was long, narrow and straight. Her jawline was small and round.

Lane looked at Carver's photograph of his daughter. He supposed that the noses were close enough, but Matilda's jaw was distinctly square.

He tapped the sketch. 'Do you think this looks like Matilda?'

'Some days I do,' Carver said. 'But – and I'm not trying to be funny here – you know those are more art than science. Sometimes when an identification is made, you see the sketch and the photograph side by side and its eerie. Other times, the sketch is off the map entirely.'

'Is there any information on how this was created?' Lane asked. There were a couple of different ways a Jane Doe sketch might be completed, depending on what evidence was available. Sometimes they were sketched using the remains as a reference, because circulating a picture would be too distressing, or to remove bruising or other facial injuries that might get in the way of identification. Sometimes they were made using the skull, based on bone markers, tissue density and educated guesses. Sometimes they were sketched from witness descriptions, by people who had seen the victim alive.

Or by the killer.

'Not much,' Carver said. 'The medical examiner estimated Eva Nováková had been buried for about three months before she was discovered. Her torso and legs were wrapped in an acrylic blanket, but her face was in direct contact with the soil. I think the sketch is based partially on the remains and partially on the bone structure.'

Lane nodded. She was found in the winter, meaning that the soil would have been cold during the time she was buried, but other than that the conditions of her burial were perfect for a fast decomposition. He resisted the urge to press for more detail. While he was eager for every crumb he could get, he was conscious that Carver really thought this was his daughter they were talking about.

'Did you view the remains?' Lane asked.

'No,' Carver said. 'I reached out as soon as the news broke that they'd found an unidentified body and asked to come down and look. The officer I spoke to said he'd get back to me, and then I got a call a week later saying that they had ruled Matilda out as a possible match and not to make the trip.'

'You didn't fight that?'

Carver sighed. 'You need to understand that at the time Matilda had only been out of contact for four months. When the police told us the body wasn't her, our first reaction was relief. We genuinely wanted to believe that she was just angry with us for some reason, or wanted space to find herself.'

'Had there been tension?'

A tattoo that read 'this too shall pass' did not suggest someone who was in a great place emotionally.

'A little.' Carver spoke quickly, looking down at the picture instead of at Lane. 'It's a tough age. Legally she was an adult, but she still had a lot of maturing to do. Add her being adopted to the mix, and things got messy at times. Intellectually, I knew her wanting to explore her origins was natural, but there's always that tiny voice that wants to take it as a rejection. Her mother could get emotional.' His expression turned grim. 'Eventually it was obvious that she wasn't going to just ring the doorbell one day and beg for forgiveness. So I went back over the public particulars of the case and our communication with the police, and doubts started to creep in. By then the Rainier Ripper case was closed. The hearings were over, and Eva Nováková had been interred. We reached out again, and got stonewalled.'

'Did they explain how they ruled her out? Was it based on the tattoo?'

Carver shook his head. 'They said "it is clear from the particulars", but when we asked for more we got a stock line about the public interest.'

That was intriguing. Perhaps there was some detail about Eva that had been withheld from the public. But why? Her killer had been caught, tried and sentenced.

Maybe there was some substance to the idea that there was a second Ripper still at large . . .

'When we didn't get anywhere with the police, we applied to access the coronial documents relating to Eva. We argued that we had an appropriate interest as possible relatives.' He opened his bottom drawer and withdrew an envelope. Lane wondered if he had brought it in anticipation of this conversation, or if he had always kept it in his work desk.

The letter inside was on the official stationery of the New South Wales State Coroner's Court. It was brief.

'*Due to the particulars of the case, I am not satisfied that the applicant meets the necessary criteria to be considered appropriately interested,*' Lane read aloud. It was signed by Lotte Nicholls, an assistant state coroner. 'Cold,' he remarked.

'She called us,' Carver said. 'She was kind, but she couldn't help us with answers. So we're at an impasse. We think Eva is Matilda, the police say she's not. But even if we got them to concede it's possible, that's still a long way from proving it's her. Without something more to go on, we're just going around in circles.'

He looked expectantly at Lane, who apparently had missed his cue to declare grandly that he couldn't wait to get Henning-Klosner to crack and reveal all. But the conversation had left him with the sinking feeling that Carver was grasping at straws.

'Has Henning-Klosner ever spoken about Eva?'

'No,' Carver said. 'When he was questioned about her, he stuck to the Ronald Reagan special: "I don't know" and "I can't recall".'

'Maybe he really doesn't know. If it was a random attack, he might never have known her name, or might have forgotten it.'

'Maybe. But he was connected to the other two victims before their deaths. Vincent Tjibaou was a fellow trucker, and Dean Shadwell was often seen at the service centre.'

'The service centre?'

'Outside of Rainier. Henning-Klosner usually stopped there for a meal on his Sydney-to-Melbourne route. It's where he was arrested.'

'Ah. Well, it's not uncommon for serial killers to start with strangers and then move on to people in their circle.'

'True. But he won't answer any other questions, even ones he must know the answer to. Like where the murder took place. Why he concealed her body, but displayed Vincent Tjibaou's. What happened to the baby. He knows exactly who she is, and refusing to give that up is the only powerplay he has left.'

* * *

Armed with his folder of printed treasure, Lane hurried to the SPC's recreation yard. The yard was a square space created by the office wing and the three accommodation units, which were all tall enough to prevent the yard from getting sun anytime except noon. There was a narrow strip of struggling grass on one side, and a concrete patch on the other that was ostensibly for ball games. In the centre, a tower was topped by a halo of security cameras covering every inch of the yard.

Excitement was humming underneath Lane's skin. Before entering prison he hadn't understood that the worst part was the numbness of it all. Day after day without any purpose or connection. Lynnie was right. He did need this.

The first few printouts were newspaper articles, surface-level stuff that he skimmed and then flicked past. Then he hit gold – a slightly skew-whiff scanned document, fuzzy but readable. It was a leaked copy of Jan Henning-Klosner's signed confession.

It was brief, only two pages long. Of those, a page and a half was devoted to the murder of Vincent Tjibaou, to a level of detail that left even Lane sick to the stomach. Eva Nováková warranted one sentence: *I killed the woman and buried her in the shadow of the church, where I prayed for her soul.*

The woman. No name, no date, nothing to go on. Lane read the confession again, trying to make sense of it. The third and final victim, Dean Shadwell, got a similarly glancing acknowledgement.

I stabbed Dean Shadwell in the park. I did not mean to frighten the girl in the shop. I fled to the service centre on the highway, where I got into an altercation with Tamara Fleischer, and would have killed her had the police not arrived.

The statement was bizarre. Confessions always were, a natural result of flattening out horrendous acts and pinning them to a page. But this was strange in a way Lane couldn't quite put his finger on.

He wondered if Henning-Klosner focused on Vincent more than the others because he was his favourite. Three victims – four if he counted Fleischer: a white woman, a Melanesian man, a white man then another white woman. That was unusual for a serial killer. In most cases, a serial killer's victims were all of a single race – usually the killer's own – and a single gender.

They were all around the same age, though, and Tjibaou and Shadwell were of roughly the same economic background, a truck driver and an itinerant worker. If the speculation that Nováková was a sex worker at the service centre was correct, that would link the four. If she was Matilda Carver, she didn't fit at all. Perhaps all of them were victims of opportunity, and Tjibaou fit Henning-Klosner's preferences better than the others.

He read the statement again, like he could squeeze out something more about Nováková with enough effort.

I killed the woman and buried her in the shadow of the church, where I prayed for her soul.

TEN

GEMMA WAS SO used to cutting through the cemetery to get home from the Tjibaou house that she was through the gate before she even noticed which way she was going.

Eva Nováková's grave was close to the front, and as Gemma passed she noticed someone had laid a single white rose on it.

The grave had no real headstone. Instead it was marked with a low brick wall, which curved around the head of the plot like a hug. The rose was lying on top, with a small white card tied to the stem with a pink ribbon.

Gemma delicately flipped the card over. There was no message, but it had been signed with big, swoopy handwriting. *LL*.

Lochlan Lewis.

She wasn't sure how she felt about that. It was a nice gesture, but at the same time his motives seemed suspect. He'd wanted it to be clear who had left it.

She wasn't surprised to find an identical flower on Dean Shadwell's grave. She had no idea why Dean was buried in Rainier, rather than closer to his family. She'd always assumed it was a cost issue, that perhaps his family lived far away and couldn't afford to have his body returned home, but now she knew that Marcus lived in Sydney, only a few hundred kilometres away, it seemed odd. She doubted it was something she could ask him about, though.

She leaned over and yanked out a knee-high fleabane that was growing on the grave. She would hate for Marcus to come over here and see it looking neglected. She tossed the weed in the bin on her way through the cemetery.

Vincent was buried with Jaylene's parents, and there was a vacant double plot beside him. Gemma wondered what it was like for Jaylene and Antoine, knowing exactly where they would be buried. Every time they visited Vincent, they also visited their own future graves.

She almost snatched the third rose off the top of Vincent's headstone to throw out with the fleabane. She was sure Jaylene would be hurt and angry if she saw it. But she stopped herself – she needed to mention the roses to Mick, as it could be significant that Lochlan was there in the hours before his death. She might get in trouble for interfering with them.

Her phone buzzed. The screen showed the call was from an unknown number, which was always the case when Hugh called from the station phone.

But when she answered, it wasn't Hugh.

'Gemma, it's Mick Seabrooke.'

107

Speak of the devil.

'Is Hugh okay?' She could count on one hand the number of times Mick had called her, and it was usually because Hugh was injured or unwell.

'I was going to ask you that. He seemed fine when he headed home. Look, I need you to come down to the station for a spell. Do you want me to send someone to pick you up?'

It must be time for her interview. She hadn't given it much thought, but of course Mick would have to be the one to conduct it. Hugh wouldn't be able to interview his own wife.

'No, I can be there in a few minutes.' She could see the blue sign of the station from the cemetery's back wall.

* * *

She hadn't seen this many people in the station for years. Christian and Ruth stood in front of the empty reception desk, talking to Mick.

'How long is Fountain Park going to be closed?' Ruth asked.

'As long as it needs to be,' Mick replied.

Ruth frowned. 'But we're supposed to get married at St Michael's next Saturday,' she said. 'What happens if it's still a crime scene?'

Shit. Gemma was supposed to cater the punch and cake reception after the ceremony. It should have been the least of her worries, but she'd been banking on the extra money from it.

'That's what the event insurance is for,' Christian interjected. 'We'll sort it out – Mick has enough to worry about.'

'We're getting the scenes processed as quickly as we can,' Mick said. He gestured for Gemma to follow him.

The interview room hadn't changed at all. The linoleum had faded more and started to crack in one corner of the room, but the walls had been freshly painted in the same shade of gunmetal grey she remembered. Gemma took a seat on the far side of the table, while Mick got the audio recording set up.

'Marcus Shadwell is staying with you, is that correct?' Mick asked.

Gemma wasn't sure what she'd expected his opening question to be, but it wasn't that. 'Yes. I talked to Aubrey about it before she left Jac with us last night. Did she mention it to you when she came to the station?'

Mick didn't answer that, but also didn't seem confused by the mention of Aubrey visiting him, so it seemed like she really had stopped to talk to Hugh on her way back from the station. Maybe Gemma was making something out of nothing.

Mick cleared his throat. 'Do you recall what time he arrived at the teashop?'

'You would probably know better than me, you were at the back of the group coming in, weren't you?'

Mick gave her a stern look. 'I was there, but I need to hear your version. I don't want to influence your answers.'

Gemma looked down at her hands. She knew this from what Hugh had shared over the years when he refreshed his training on how to conduct interviews. But sitting here, she was suddenly nineteen again. Her first interview with Mick, after Vincent's murder, had felt like being mugged. He'd seemed less interested in what she might have seen, living and working so close to the murder scene, and more interested in the details of their break-up. He kept circling back to it, asking the same questions again and again, and accused her of lying to him about their split being amicable. She'd left the station shaking, and feeling weirdly guilty, like maybe she really had been lying to him.

This Mick couldn't be more different, and she tried to remember that.

'Marcus was with our group at the fountain, and would have come in within a couple of minutes. Oh!' She pulled out her phone, and opened the Service NSW app. She showed him the time she had checked in: 6.08 pm. 'It would have been five to ten minutes after that. I'm afraid I didn't stand at the door making sure people were checking in properly, but Dr Nicholls reminded them. If he did, he might be able to give you a more exact time.'

'Did he leave at any point?'

Nerves were starting to build in Gemma's stomach about the very specific direction of his questions. Did she need to be worried about Marcus? She took a deep breath. She knew he wasn't the killer. 'Not until he went upstairs.'

'How sure are you?'

'I looked up every time the bell above the door rang. It was always people coming in, never Marcus going out.'

When had Marcus come in, though? She hadn't really noticed him until she saw him reading the plaque. He must have been

part of the first flurry; she'd definitely have noticed if he was one
of the stragglers that arrived separately.

'Did he have a bag with him?'

She tried to picture him as he'd stood alone. Still rugged up
against the cold even inside the heated teashop, she remembered
that much. A heavy black coat and scarf. But he'd had his hands
free and the lines of his outfit were sleek, no satchel.

'I don't think so. I think maybe he went to get it from the
coat rack?'

'So you separated at that point? Do you know what time
that was?'

She shook her head. 'I'm sorry.' She looked at her phone again,
opened the call log, and noticed that she had a missed call from
a number she didn't recognise. She scrolled back to the previous
night. 'Hugh's call came at six thirty-two pm. So between six oh
eight and six thirty-two, but I can't be more specific than that.'

'How long was he gone for, when he went to get his bag?'

'Less than a minute. I went through the kitchen to let him in,
and by the time I got to the kitchen window I could see him
standing outside the gate.'

'Is the fountain visible from that spot in the alley?' Mick
asked, looking thoughtful.

'No, the front corner of the shop blocks it. But he would
have had a clear view when he walked around.'

Mick nodded, scribbling something down on a notepad.

'What's this about?' Gemma asked. 'Marcus is at my home
right now. Do I need to be worried about him?'

'From the sounds of things,' Mick said, 'Marcus Shadwell is one of the only people in town who can be ruled out.' He grinned. 'Unless the two of you are in on it together.'

'Not funny,' Gemma said. She wanted to put her head down on the table and scream.

'Sorry, mate,' Mick said. 'I'm just whistling past the graveyard. We do what we need to do to handle it, but I shouldn't bring you into it.'

Gemma couldn't let that opening go. 'Have you asked for extra help?'

'Yes, there's some extra uniforms in town, and the specialists are processing the scene.'

'What about extra detectives?'

Mick looked genuinely offended at the suggestion. 'We can handle it. If there's one thing Hugh and I know how to do, it's run a murder case.'

'Of course,' she said. 'I wanted to let you know, I was in the cemetery this morning and I found something. Lochlan Lewis must have visited before the tour presentation. He left flowers on the victims' graves, with a card attached.'

'Hmm,' Mick said. 'That's interesting, although I'm not sure it's significant. I don't think I've ever seen a victim whose movements in the hours before a murder were more thoroughly documented. It's the gap between when we left him and when Hugh found the body that's key.' He made a note in his notebook anyway. 'It might have stirred someone up, though.'

'Because it feels a little fake?' Gemma suggested, relieved she wasn't the only person whose mind went there.

'Was that your read on Lochlan? That he seemed fake?'

For a moment Gemma had forgotten that she was being interviewed by police, not chatting with her husband's colleague. 'Maybe that's unfair. He knew he was under a spotlight, so of course he was a little performative. But some of the things he said, well, it wouldn't surprise me if he had a dossier with dot points of helpful facts on all of us.'

A smile flashed across Mick's face, gone in an instant, and Gemma wondered if they actually had found something like that in his personal effects.

Mick switched off the recorder, signalling the interview was done. 'I wanted to discuss something else while you're here. The Lewis family is located in the UK. One of our counterparts at Scotland Yard broke the news to them this morning. They want Lochlan's body returned to the UK when we're ready to release it, and they'll hold a funeral there. Which is understandable, but funerals are useful for us to identify the victim's friends and associates, and other people of interest.'

'Are you struggling with that?' she asked.

Mick gave her an unimpressed look, and ignored the question. 'We've had some funds approved to hold a memorial service at St Michael's on Thursday. We'd like you to cater it.'

'Does that mean we'll have access to the shop's kitchen by then?'

Mick grimaced. 'I can't give you a timeline on that. Christian has agreed to let you use the pub's kitchen, if necessary.'

Gemma almost asked why they didn't cut out the middleman and have Christian cater, then realised they were throwing her a bone, because they felt bad about forcing her to close the shop.

'I think that's all I need from you for now, Gem, but I'm sure you'll hear from me again. While I've got you here, would you be willing to provide your fingerprints? It would help us separate fingerprints that might have been left on the fountain during the tour from ones that might have been left by our killer.'

'I don't think I touched the fountain or the railings,' Gemma said. 'It was cold, I kept my hands in my pockets mostly. But sure.'

She was stunned by how the procedure had changed. The first time she'd had to clean her hands carefully with alcohol before pressing her fingers in ink and rolling them onto the paper one at a time. She'd then had to wash the ink off afterwards. Now the station had a digital fingerprint scanner, and the longest part of the process was signing the consent form.

Even so, she found herself walking to the little sink in the hallway outside the station toilets, the same way she had the first time she was fingerprinted. There was no ink on her hands, but she was still desperate to wash it off.

Her hands shook as she rinsed away the soap, and she turned off the cold tap, hoping that a blast of hot water would make it stop. But the station's hot-water heater had been on its last legs for years, and what she got was barely lukewarm.

The men's room door swung open, and Christian stepped out. Gemma stepped back to let him use the sink, and wiped her hands with one of the coarse paper towels.

'You alright, Gem?'

'Getting there,' she said, balling up the towel and tossing it in the bin.

'I know Ruth was being a bit . . . Ruth . . . out there. But this wedding means a lot to her.'

'Of course,' Gemma said. As Ruth's caterer, she had seen firsthand how important the wedding was to her. 'Postponing a wedding is a massive thing, I understand.'

'Thanks. Plus, it's extra emotional for Ruth. She's had it rough, bringing up Nico by herself. Dragging him up, really. She never got to do the things she always planned. She never got to be princess for a day.'

Not like Gemma had, was the unsaid part. It seemed ridiculous to her that someone might look at the choices she'd made and consider them something to envy. But Gemma couldn't put so much energy into pretending everything was fine and then get mad that other people thought she really was fine.

She felt a little prickle of guilt, too. Because her parents had pointed to poor Ruth Tanner, who ruined her life so young, when Gemma told them she'd decided to keep her baby. Apparently that gaze had gone both ways.

'How are you holding up?' she asked, desperate to change the subject. 'I guess last night must have been especially rough for you.'

'What do you mean?' he asked sharply.

'I just thought it might have brought some things up for you,' she explained. 'About finding Vincent's body.'

'Oh,' he said. He kept his eyes fixed on his hands, following the whole sequence laid out on the poster above the sink – palms, backs, between the fingers, up the wrists. 'I'm fine. To be honest, in all the madness I haven't really thought about it.'

'Then I'm sorry to have brought it up,' she said.

'Thank you for thinking of me,' he said. He glanced around, then added, 'I bet the council are regretting voting no on the proposal to demolish the fountain.'

'Hmm?' Gemma didn't remember that. 'That must have been while I was away.'

'Right, yeah. It was quite soon after everything happened. Somebody, I don't even remember who, suggested that we get rid of the fountain and remodel the park. But the council said no, too much historic interest – it was opened by Lizzie during her visit in the fifties, you know. I think at the time a lot of people still believed life would go back to normal soon enough. Denial.'

'It's powerful,' Gemma said. 'But then, you could argue that the people who wanted to renovate were just bargaining.'

'Bargaining?'

'You know, the stages of grief. People talk about denial and anger, but I think bargaining is the most dangerous stage. Treating grief like it's a problem that can be solved. It means people make some questionable decisions.'

'What do you mean?'

'I don't know.' Gemma sighed. 'I'm very tired, please don't pay any attention to my rambling.'

* * *

Gemma took the long way home again, crossing Melbourne and Sydney roads with her eyes cast firmly away from the crime scene, aside from a quick check to the right for oncoming traffic. Many of the buildings had footpaths between them, so she cut through to the road behind their house, walking past the walled courtyard on her way to the gate.

At the back entrance to the alley she encountered Hugh on his way out. He was dressed in his uniform, and looked like he'd got at least some sleep that morning, although he still had a pinched look around the eyes.

'I'll be home tonight, but don't hold up dinner waiting for me, okay?' he said.

'I'll leave you a plate in the fridge,' she said.

She froze at a flash of movement over his shoulder. Someone had sprinted up the alley and into their courtyard.

Someone who had been waiting at the other end for Hugh to leave?

'Hugh,' she whispered. 'There's someone in our house.'

She'd only caught a glimpse, but they were too big to be any of the kids and too small to be Marcus Shadwell.

He frowned, but any argument was immediately quashed by the familiar sound of someone walking up the back stairs.

'Stay here,' he said. 'It's probably just a reporter or someone, trying to get a good vantage point on the crime scene.'

Gemma nodded, but her insides twisted. Someone was sneaking around her home. Where her child was.

Hugh stalked towards the house, and she backed up until she could see over the garden wall to the verandah. Whoever it was had moved out of sight, headed around either to Marcus's door or the front of the house. She watched Hugh climb the stairs and disappear around the corner, blocking in whoever was there.

A moment later he reappeared, his hand on the shoulder of a figure in a black hoodie and jeans. Gemma relaxed immediately, feeling stupid. It was Nico Tanner, the young man who lived at the pub with his mother, Ruth, and Christian Holst.

'Sorry, Mrs Guillory,' Nico called, probably at Hugh's prompting. It looked like Hugh had scared the wits out of the poor kid.

Gemma went into the courtyard and stood at the foot of the stairs, arms crossed. 'That's not the way to our door, Nico,' she said, but fought a smile. She'd had her fair share of visitors tap on the windows instead of the front door when she was a teenager.

'I know – sorry,' he repeated.

'How old are you again, Nico?' Hugh asked. 'You're not in school anymore, right?'

'I'll be twenty next month, sir,' Nico said.

'Then you'd better not have been looking for Violet,' Hugh said, but he was smiling too. 'Off home with you, alright? It's a bloody stupid time for surprise drop-ins.'

Nico nodded, a little frantic, and scooted out the gate as soon as Hugh dropped the hand from his shoulder.

'My money says he's keen on Fawn,' Hugh said, turning the smile on Gemma.

Gemma had started to feel a little shaky. It might have been a false alarm, but her terror had been real. Now that it was over she couldn't help feeling angry at Nico's thoughtlessness. She also knew how this was going to go. Soon it would be a funny story about how Gemma freaked out over nothing.

He hovered for a second, leaned in a fraction like he was going to kiss her goodbye, then opted to pat her on the shoulder before setting off.

ELEVEN

Transcript of the interrogation of Jan Henning-Klosner

Detective Michael Seabrooke: *Do you know what this is?*
[Transcription note: the suspect was shown a picture of items recovered from the female victim's grave, found at Appendix 2F]
JHK: *A candle?*
Seabrooke: *What kind of candle?*
JHK: *I don't know.*
Seabrooke: *You don't know what kind of candle this is? You think it might be a birthday candle?*
JHK: *I guess it looks kind of like a votive.*
Seabrooke: *A votive. Like they use in churches?*
JHK: *The one I went to as a kid had those candles.*
Seabrooke: *So you're saying this is a church candle.*
JHK: *Could be.*

Seabrooke: *Why did you bury her with a votive, Jan? Did you pray
    for her soul?*

* * *

A nurse strapped Lane's left wrist and then bundled it into a fake
sling to pre-empt any questions from Jan Henning-Klosner about
why he was in the medical unit.

Henning-Klosner lay in the bed to the right of Lane's, eyes
closed and mouth slack. His body was covered with a white waffle-
knit blanket, but there were shackles anchored to the end of the
bed that disappeared underneath around his ankles. His hands
were free, but a chest strap held him down. Lane wasn't sure if
that was a security measure, or to stop him from slipping off the
bed as he drifted in and out of sedation.

Lane held his right hand out, just to test. With his fingers
stretched as far as they would go, he bridged less than half the
distance, so unless Henning-Klosner had a freakishly long arm
span, they wouldn't be able to invade each other's space.

'You,' Henning-Klosner said, then fell silent.

'Sorry?' Lane said. When he looked over, the man had gone
back to sleep.

After a few minutes, Henning-Klosner spoke again. 'He got
you too, huh?'

'You bore the brunt,' Lane said.

'I definitely thought . . .' Henning-Klosner paused and Lane
thought for a moment that he had slipped back under. 'Thought
my bags were packed,' he finished.

Well, now Lane was going to have Peter, Paul and Mary stuck in his head for the rest of the day. 'You were trying to tell me something on your way out.'

'I'm sure I was.'

Lane picked at his blanket. 'Something about a woman. Uh, Tammy, or Tara . . .'

'Tamara.' He coughed. 'Forget it. Trying to get my fucking deathbed confession in. Unconfession.' He laughed, and it turned into another cough. 'We're all innocent here, right?'

Lane didn't have any choice but to laugh as well.

'I get it,' he said. 'If I thought I was on the way out, there are things I would want to get on the record. Information that I wouldn't want to die with me.' He cringed internally. He'd taken blows to the face that were more subtle than that.

'You want one of those specials? *The Lane Holland Tapes*.'

Lane went cold. 'I didn't realise we'd been introduced.'

'You've been in the Tin long enough to know there's fuck all to do except gossip. You know who I am, I know who you are, don't get precious.'

Henning-Klosner shot a look at him sideways, and Lane was painfully reminded that he wasn't just chatting to a frail old man. The shackles, and the man's weakened condition, meant he was perfectly harmless, but the Ripper still lurked just below the surface.

'I served some time with your old man, you know. Up in Goulburn. God, that place makes this seem like Club Med. You ever been?'

'Not as a prisoner. I went as a visitor once.'

For some reason Henning-Klosner found that amusing. 'Looked at the lion, didja?'

'Sorry?'

'The stone lion.' He waved a hand around his head like an imaginary mane. 'Above the gate. There's an old superstition that you have to avert your eyes from it. If you look right at it, you're cursed to one day pass under it as a prisoner.'

Lane had looked at the lion. It was an almost reassuring thought, that he wasn't here due to his own impulses and terrible decisions but because he'd recklessly admired a bit of stonework.

'Were you and my father friends, then?'

It made sense if they felt a camaraderie. Being with Lane Holland Senior was probably the only time in his life Jan Henning-Klosner wasn't the worst person in the room.

But if they were friends – or enemies – Henning-Klosner might have a score to settle with Lane.

'Nah, barely knew him. He spent most of his time in the segregation unit anyway. You know, in Goulburn the inmates have a special welcoming ceremony for –'

'For child molesters.' It wasn't all he'd done, but it was the only crime Lane's father had faced justice for. Unless you counted what Lane did to him.

'That's not what we usually call 'em.' Henning-Klosner chuckled.

That was a point where Lane always stumbled. Even after years inside, he was reluctant to use prison slang. It just didn't feel right in his mouth, and he was sure he would sound like he was trying too hard. The ironic part was that he knew it made it sound like he thought he was better than the other prisoners, that he was trying to hold himself separate from them. He lived to get in his own way.

'But I saw him enough to know he was a right arsehole,' Henning-Klosner added.

'That he was,' Lane agreed.

'They fuck you up,' Henning-Klosner mumbled. 'God, how does that poem go? All his faults, and some extra just for you.'

Lane didn't know. Lynnie would probably know, she loved poetry.

'So you had a shitty dad too?'

'I'm not your therapist, Holland.'

He'd made a mistake – the first rule of interviews was never to answer the other person's questions, never to let them turn the conversation back on you. But this wasn't an interview. He didn't have the power here and couldn't just keep firing questions at the man until he cracked. Which meant walking a tightrope – making it feel enough like an equal exchange to keep Henning-Klosner talking, but not giving so much of himself up that the other man could get his claws in.

'So this Tamara,' he said. 'She must have been something, if you're still thinking of her after all these years.'

'She was alright. Nice.'

'Nice?'

'That service centre was the earth's armpit, but she always had a smile for you.'

Because that was her job, Lane thought.

'I saw her on TV once,' Jan said. 'She was interviewed on one of those morning shows. The shit one, with the guy.'

'You've just described all of them.'

'She looked beautiful on that. She looked happy.'

Lane thought uncomfortably of the photo clipped from the newspaper that he had stashed among the printouts in his cell.

'Television is fake,' Lane said. Everything in here was fake. Everything was filtered. Television, newspapers, highly restricted books, what little their visitors chose to tell them. There was no truth here.

TWELVE

GEMMA SAT ON a low brick wall in the courtyard, giving herself a moment to get her equilibrium back before she went inside.

Upstairs the back door opened and Marcus stepped out. As soon as the door was shut behind him he stopped to light a cigarette, fumbling to do everything with his uninjured hand. He looked abashed when he saw her, and hurried to stub it out.

'I quit when Gabby . . . I quit,' he said, tucking the extinguished butt back into the package. 'But I seem to have backslid recently.'

'That's understandable.'

He walked down the stairs. 'I tried to call you earlier.'

'Oh.' That must have been the unknown number on her phone. 'What's up?'

'Do you have security cameras here? In the house or the shop?'

'No,' she said. She'd considered putting some up, but Rainier had been quiet for years, and she didn't like the idea of being recorded all the time. 'I would have told you if you were on camera.'

He let out a frustrated huff. 'Fair enough. A lot of Airbnb hosts have them, so I hoped you might. Someone's been in my bag.'

Gemma stiffened. 'How do you know?'

'There's something missing. My knife.'

'Your *knife*?' she said. 'Why would you bring a knife into my house? What knife?'

'I'm sorry. I didn't think about how it would look. I've just . . .' He tapped the cigarette package with his thumb. The warning photo showed a man dying of lung cancer in a hospital bed, his thin, exposed throat reminding Gemma uncomfortably of Lochlan. 'I've struggled a lot with anxiety since Dean died. Carrying that knife helped.'

'And it's gone?'

Gemma's chest went cold. She saw what had happened: Marcus had reported his knife missing to the police, and then Gemma was called in to confirm his story that he was upstairs at the time of the murder . . .

The murderer must have used a knife. Had the police found it at the scene? Had the police found *Marcus's* knife at the scene?

'I'm not casual with it. I keep it in a specific pocket of my bag, and I'm sure it's gone.'

'I can ask Violet and her friends,' she said. 'But they're good kids. They wouldn't go through someone's bag and take things. When did you last see it?'

'It was definitely still in my bag when I got out of my car yesterday.'

'What does it look like?'

'It's an Opinel folding knife,' he said. He held his hands a disturbing distance apart. 'About this long when unfolded. It has a wooden handle, with my initials burned in.'

'MS or MH?'

'MS. It was a gift from my grandfather for my eighteenth birthday.' He scrubbed a hand over his face. 'I don't know what I'm going to do if it was used in a murder. I've got so little left from my family.'

* * *

Gemma found the kids in the lounge room, all three of them tucked under a blanket as they watched some technicolour Regency show on Netflix. Violet scrambled for the remote when she saw Gemma, and hit pause. Gemma smiled to herself. If watching something risqué was their idea of getting up to mischief, she was doing alright.

Gemma leaned against the doorframe. 'Were you expecting a visitor, by any chance?'

She got three identical blank expressions in return.

'Why, is someone here?' Violet asked. 'I didn't hear the doorbell, sorry.'

'Nico Tanner?' Gemma asked.

The mystified looks she got in return might have been faked, but she didn't think so. 'Your dad caught him on the verandah before.'

'Gross,' Violet said. 'You think he was trying to get a look at the crime scene?'

'Maybe he was trying to film it for TikTok or something,' Fawn suggested.

'Or sell the pictures,' Jac said.

'Have you noticed that there haven't really been any reporters?' Fawn asked. 'Mum said that they were the worst part last time.'

How nice for Lotte, Gemma thought, for that to have been the worst part.

'Yeah, well, there's been about a billion rounds of newsroom layoffs since then,' Jac said. 'Mick says that most articles you see these days are just pulled from police press reports.'

'Ugh,' Violet muttered.

Gemma knew she should ask them about Marcus's missing knife, but she couldn't bring herself to. She was sure they didn't have anything to do with it, and didn't want to frighten them about a possible burglar. If her theory was right, the knife was gone before Marcus brought the bag upstairs. Instead, she went into the kitchen to start lunch.

She pulled a day-old loaf out of the bread box and plugged in the electric carving knife to slice it. She had a proper bread slicer downstairs, but it was still part of the crime scene, so this would do. She found it easier to think with the din of the motor drowning everything else out.

Assuming she was right, and Marcus's stolen knife was the murder weapon, why? Why risk stealing a weapon that could be bought almost anywhere? The bag had been on the coat rack in full view of everyone – how had the murderer even got the knife out when she was sure no-one had left?

Unless it was already gone by the time Marcus hung it up. He said he had it when he got out of the car. So it had to have gone missing between when he joined the tour and when he hung the bag up inside the teashop.

Which meant that someone on the tour was involved, but couldn't have committed the actual murder. Anyone sufficiently light-fingered could have lifted the knife while everyone else was focused on Lochlan's talk or getting ready to cross the road, and left it in the park for the murderer.

But again, why?

She wished she could put up one of those boards like in the movies, with photos and maps and spiderwebs of string. But she couldn't risk Hugh seeing it, or finding any notes she made, so she would have to build one in her mind and hope for the best.

Assuming for a moment that she was right about this, the murderer had to be connected to one of the people who attended the tour.

There was Jaylene and Antoine, of course. Jaylene had quick hands – she loved to make things, and she was a decent juggler. Gemma wouldn't be surprised if she could pick a pocket undetected. Not that Gemma could take the idea of the Tjibaous committing murder seriously.

Aubrey's parents weren't there, but they were at home with the two younger Seabrooke children.

Aside from Lotte's friendship with Aubrey, she and Dr Nicholls tended to hold themselves separate, and Gemma couldn't think of anyone they were close enough to that they might have plausibly plotted murder together. Not to mention that they didn't have any personal connection to the Ripper murders.

Tamara Fleischer was a complete wildcard. She could have brought any number of accomplices to town with her.

The front door opened and shut, and Marcus passed by in the hall, his posture all agitation.

'Would you like some lunch?' she called. She wasn't running a bed and breakfast, but nowhere would be open for lunch under the circumstances, and she doubted he'd packed his own food.

'Oh, I couldn't impose,' he said.

'It's fine,' she said. 'I'm going to have to throw out a heart-breaking amount of food; I'd rather see it end up in people's stomachs.'

'At least let me pay you for it,' he said.

Gemma shrugged, and started laying out sliced cheese, ham and shredded lettuce.

'Um, I thought I'd better speak to you before booking it through the website, but I was hoping I could extend my stay by a few days.'

Gemma paused. 'You want to stay in Rainier?'

'Yes. Detective Seabrooke says I can go home when my inter-view is done, and I can visit the station in Sydney if they need to ask any follow-up questions. But honestly, I'd . . .' He traced the outside edge of his bandage with the thumb of his other hand.

'I know this probably sounds ridiculous, but in Sydney this all feels like it happened to someone else. It's Marcus Shadwell's problem, not Mark Herald's. I don't want this to touch my life there.'

'I don't think it's ridiculous,' Gemma said. She envied him the fact that changing his name and starting a new chapter had actually worked. She supposed that living far away was the key. 'Book as long as you need.'

'Thank you. Also, do you know if there's anyone in town who has an electric vehicle charger?'

'I don't think so.' The Nicholls were the only family she could think of that could afford an electric car, but she was pretty sure they drove a hybrid.

'The nearest public charger is in Gundagai. Then there isn't another one until Goulburn, unless you go into Canberra.' He held up his phone, showing a map with a couple of very spaced-out icons. 'I charged up in Goulburn on the way here and was just going to stop again on the way home, but that might be tricky if I'm staying longer.'

'You could ask Christian,' she said. 'A while back he pitched the idea of installing a charger to get more people to stop here. If there are others around, he might know about it.'

'I'll figure something out.'

'Can I ask you a probably inappropriate question?'

'Please do, I'm intrigued.'

'Yesterday, when you walked around the building to meet me in the courtyard, did you notice anything off in the fountain? Was anyone there?'

He laughed without any real humour. 'You think I saw the murder go down and forgot to mention it?'

She flushed. 'No, of course not. So the fountain was empty at that time?'

'I don't know. I was fishing in my bag for my cigarettes and lighter. I think I'd have noticed Lochlan's body if it was already there, but I can't swear it on my life.'

'I wouldn't ask you to. I guess it's just been bothering me.'

'The unanswered questions can get to you, if you let them.'

'If you know some trick for stopping that, please tell me,' she said.

* * *

Lunch was an awkward affair. Their table normally sat four, so Gemma needed to bring in Hugh's desk chair to sit on, and she, Marcus, Violet, Jac and Fawn ended up crammed elbow to elbow.

'Do you think this means that the tour idea is done?' Jac asked, as Gemma was about to bite into her sandwich.

Gemma paused. If one of the other two kids had asked, she would have hushed them for Jac's sake. But if Jac wanted to talk about it, she would.

'I'd say so. Even if Lochlan Lewis's business partners still want to go ahead, it will need to be delayed until after any trial is finished. And then Lochlan's family would get to have their say.'

'It just feels . . .' Jac sighed. 'Mamy and Pépère don't want the tour to go ahead. Now Lochlan Lewis has died, and it's done? It feels like his death is more important than my dad's.'

Fawn shot them a sympathetic look, and Violet reached out and covered Jac's hand with her own.

Gemma glanced uncomfortably at Marcus, who was listening thoughtfully to Jac but didn't seem upset by the direction of the conversation.

'Have you talked to your mum about this?' Gemma asked.

Jac sighed. 'It's complicated. They don't talk about it with me, but I think Mick was planning to vote yes. He's the star of the show, the lead detective who brought down the Ripper. And where Mick goes, Mum follows.'

'Do you think a lot of people would have voted yes?' Marcus asked.

'Maybe,' Jac said.

'There's different factions,' Violet explained. She had found the whole thing fascinating. 'Mr and Mrs Tjibaou were a no, obvs. Some people think it's distasteful but will be good for the town. Some people think it's not worth fighting about because it will fail on its own.'

'I've wondered about that,' Marcus said. 'How much interest could there really be?'

'Did Lewis and Co. send you the printed proposal?' Fawn asked. 'They had all these flyers for similar businesses. Did you know that the bar where Aileen Wuornos was arrested sells commemorative t-shirts?'

'Would you have sold t-shirts?' Jac asked, looking at Gemma.

'Of course not,' Gemma said.

'You should see the Glenrowan main street, though,' Violet said. 'Bakeries and gift shops everywhere. It works.'

'But Ned Kelly died centuries ago,' Jac said.

'Yeah,' Violet said. 'Sorry.'

The doorbell rang, and a ripple of shock went through the table at the sudden, loud noise. Everyone was so on edge. Gemma excused herself to answer it, resisting an irrational urge to ask the kids to lock the kitchen door behind her just in case.

Through the window she saw a tall dark shape, the familiar silhouette of a Driza-Bone overcoat, and relaxed instantly.

'Antoine,' she said when she threw the door open, and he greeted her by wrapping her in a bear hug that made her feel nine years old again.

Antoine was the gentlest, most patient person she had ever met. She'd never heard him raise his voice or snap at someone. Jaylene had done all of the shouting and scolding when they were kids. Even in the depths of grief he'd kept his composure, rubbing Jaylene's back as she screamed and howled with it, and stepped away when it got too much. Vincent had explained to Gemma once when they were young teens, with an air of second-hand embarrassment, that she didn't get it. With a weightlifter's physique and Kanak heritage, Antoine had to work constantly to appear as unthreatening as possible. His petite white wife could shriek all she wanted, but that wasn't an option for him.

'Gemmy,' he said now, his voice all warmth.

135

'Has someone told you?' she asked, praying she didn't have to be the one to break it to him.

'Ayup, Jaylene and Hugh both gave it a go,' he said softly. 'But it's just beyond belief.'

'I know.'

'Jaylene's on the phones now, trying to get a lawyer to drive down for our interviews. Chaps a bit to shell out that much when all I can tell the police is that it was bloody freezing at the creek last night, but better safe than sorry.'

'That's a good idea,' Gemma said. 'I'm sure you'll be ruled out quickly.' She wished she believed it.

Antoine looked sad. 'I hope so. I see how it looks. But even if I was capable of murder, I would never spit on Vincent's memory by doing it like that. Whoever did it was a goddamn – ' He cut off abruptly, looking past Gemma's shoulder.

She turned and saw the kids hovering in the hallway. She stepped away from Antoine, letting Jac take her place.

'Hi, Pépère,' they said.

Antoine muttered something in French, and Jac nodded against his chest.

'I am sorry to interrupt your time with your friends,' he said. 'But today is our visitation, and I know it would mean a lot to your mamy to see you.'

Gemma's understanding of the situation was through the grapevine, but what she had been told was this: Aubrey had voluntarily let Jaylene and Antoine care for Jac as a baby. Then, sometime after Jac returned to live with her, things fell apart;

Aubrey tried to cut them off, refusing to let Jac visit, and they sued for grandparents rights and won. They were entitled to four hours of visitation a month, which they took as an hour every Sunday.

Aubrey was still immensely bitter about it. Gemma tried to avoid discussing the subject with her.

'Don't let Mum hear you say that,' Jac said. 'You know how she goes off about me not being your emotional support animal.'

'Yes, yes, god forbid we should want our family around us on tough days. But perhaps this isn't a good subject for poor Gemmy's hallway.'

'Thank you for staying with us, Jac,' Gemma said. 'Come back any time,' she added, on reflex, then regretted it. She loved Jac, but was relieved to be down to only two teenagers to keep safe.

THIRTEEN

**Transcript of the interrogation of Jan Henning-Klosner
(continued)**

Seabrooke: *Do you recognise this woman?*
[Transcription note: the suspect was shown the picture of the
female victim, found at Appendix 2A]
JHK: *Jesus. Jesus.*
Seabrooke: *Not as pretty as when you last saw her, huh?*
JHK: *No, I –*
Seabrooke: *No? You think she looks prettier like this? How about
    this one?*
[Transcription note: the suspect was shown the picture of the
female victim, found at Appendix 2B]
JHK: *What the fuck?*

Seabrooke: *Hey. Hey. Look, it's just you and me here right now. I get it, you know. Such a pretty girl, even like this. Was she your girlfriend? Maybe not even your girlfriend. But she was pregnant. Was she trying to trap you? You can tell me.*

JHK: *She was pregnant.*

Seabrooke: *Now entering the room is Constable Hugh Guillory. The time is one forty-five am.*

Guillory: *He's crying.*

Seabrooke: *Yep.*

Guillory: *Are you crying because you're sorry, or because you got caught?*

JHK: *I'm sorry. I'm so sorry.*

* * *

Lane had been ignoring Jan, for the most part. He doubted it would go well if he seemed too eager to keep chatting with him, so instead he pretended to read a book, letting Jan get used to his presence. Jan mostly napped, although Lane wasn't sure how much genuine rest he was getting. He shifted and rolled constantly, mumbled incoherently and groaned in his sleep. While supposedly reading, Lane had actually spent the time making an 'interview' plan in his head. His accreditations had expired, but he'd been formally trained in interrogation techniques. He intended to stick as closely to the PEACE model as he could: Plan, Engage and Explain, Account, Closure and Evaluation. PEACE was the closest thing he had to a religion. Of course, he was going to fall down at the second hurdle. In a properly run interview, it was imperative to lay out to the interviewee exactly how things were going to work, and what to expect. He couldn't do that with Jan. What he was going to do here would sit uncomfortably close to the old ways – calculated games to confuse and manipulate the suspect.

'Tell me,' he said, once Jan was awake and tucking into his dinner; Lane figured a bit of chitchat at meal times wouldn't seem odd. 'Is the food getting worse over time, or is my tolerance for it getting lower? I swear, what they served when I first came in was dire, but this is something else.'

Jan grunted and shrugged.

'You want to know the best meal I ever had?' Lane asked, slicing off a square of corned beef and pushing it around with his fork. 'It was a steak at the Commercial Hotel, a pub in Central New South Wales. The kind of place where they could tell you your steak was mooing that morning, and it wouldn't be an exaggeration.'

'Uh-huh,' Jan said.

'You ever slaughter a cow?' Lane asked, taking a calculated risk.

Jan snorted. 'Have you?'

'Yes, actually. My family went in on a cow with some friends one year. One of those deals where you pay a deposit and they feed up a calf until you're ready to buy it. I mean, I didn't cut its throat myself, but I was there.'

Lane let the words 'cut its throat' linger between them. Jan didn't look interested, didn't even glance his way. He kept eating his dinner.

Lane returned his attention to his own dinner. He was surprised that hadn't sparked any interest in Jan. But at the same time, he was relieved that discussions of gore and death didn't seem to be the key to building a rapport here.

FOURTEEN

GEMMA HEARD THE back door open as she was brushing her teeth, and then the familiar sound of Hugh's footsteps trudging down the hallway.

He paused outside Violet's bedroom, and Gemma rinsed and spat to the low murmur of a brief but affectionate exchange between them.

She locked the ensuite door, and turned the shower on as hot as it would go. Their old hot-water system couldn't get it hot enough to really burn, but it was close enough to be pleasantly distracting. She leaned her forehead against the tiles and let the water drum against her back.

By the time she came out dressed in her pyjamas, Hugh was sprawled across the right side of the bed, his face mashed into the pillow like he had passed out the moment he put his head down.

Her heartbeat picked up as she approached the bed. She folded back her side of the blankets and just stood, staring down at the expanse of pale pink sheets. This was stupid. She was stupid. She should be able to sleep beside her own husband without acting like the bed was full of redback spiders.

Hugh shifted, probably from the cold air she was letting under the blankets, and crab-walked one hand into her side of the bed, looking for her. She imagined him putting his hands on her in the night and dropped the blanket.

She went to the hallway linen cupboard, took out the spare doona and the crocheted granny square blanket that smelled faintly of naphthalene, and set herself up on the lounge.

* * *

The locked shop door rattled, startling Gemma out of her focus. She'd closed up hours ago, but had the light on so she could count skeins of wool for the taxman. That didn't mean she was trying to invite midnight visitors. It was a man, huddled inside a large black jacket. He slapped his hand against the glass, and with every impact painted it with a bright streak of blood, until the window was covered in a mosaic of desperate red handprints.

'Gemma, help me!' the man screamed with Vincent's voice.

This time she raced over and threw back the bolt. She opened the door and Vincent collapsed into her. He pressed his face into her neck and something hot and wet slid over her skin and into her shirt. She was too frightened to check if he was crying, or if it was the blood gushing from his throat.

Something outside growled, low and guttural. She looked around desperately for Hugh, but of course he wasn't there. An enormous, shapeless thing flung itself through the door and slammed her to the ground. Vincent dissolved to nothing and it was just her and the monster, a knife pressed to her neck.

* * *

Gemma hurled herself upright, hands pressed to her mouth to stop herself screaming. Her skin prickled with sweat, and her heart was thundering so hard she was sure she was about to pass out. She forced herself to calm down, dragging in deep breaths of cold night air, as the reality of the nightmare slipped away.

She hadn't had that one for a while.

Someone cleared their throat and she yelped, pulling the blankets up as if they could shield her.

'Sorry,' Marcus whispered. 'I'm so sorry. I could hear you, and I came to check you were okay, just in case . . . you know.'

'Yeah,' she said. Suddenly, being attacked in bed was a very real possibility, not paranoia. 'I'm sorry I was loud,' she said.

'You weren't. I doubt you woke the girls. My room is right next to this one, and I'm sort of attuned to night terrors. Dean had them when he came to live with us, so I got used to the sound.'

'Your brother didn't always live with you?' she asked. Her heartbeat was beginning to return to something like a normal speed.

'Dean and I were half-brothers. Same father, different mothers. My mother was my father's wife, and Dean's mother . . . was not.'

'I see,' she said. 'I'm sorry.'

'Thanks. In a lot of ways I think it was worse for Dean than for me, even if the whole thing was pretty confusing. Even at his age, I think he knew that nobody really wanted him.'

'How old were you?'

'He was five, and I was just about to turn six.'

'Ah.' Gemma felt terrible for Marcus's mother, then. There was something extra cruel about cheating on a woman when she was pregnant or had a newborn. It was such an intensely vulnerable time.

'Our father was paying Dean's mother to keep quiet, but she started asking for more and more, until it was too much for our father to hide from my mother. What he had neglected to tell Dean's mum was that our family's wealth came from my mother's side. Dad made an okay living, but the designer clothes and flashy car that had turned her head were gifts. When he couldn't pay anymore, she dumped Dean on our doorstep and disappeared.'

'That's awful,' Gemma said, although she couldn't help but notice that she must be hearing the version of the story Marcus's family had told him. She wondered what Dean's mother's version would sound like.

'Mum was fucking ropeable, but she was very much a "stay together for the kids" type. So we took Dean in and lived as one big, miserable family until Mum and Dad's accident.' Marcus stared out the window, where the first grey light was starting to creep through. 'The ironic thing is Mum was probably the kindest adult Dean ever had in his life. It wasn't fair. He wasn't the one who did something wrong. It was complete luck of the draw that I was born to my mum and he was born to his, and it meant completely different lives.' He paused for a moment, perhaps noticing how increasingly raw his voice had become. 'After they died, I went to live with Grandad, my mother's father, and Dean went into the foster care system. Grandad wouldn't hear of him coming to live with us.'

It was beginning to make sense why Dean was buried in Rainier. Burying him with the rest of Marcus's family was clearly out of the question, but bringing him back to Sydney only to be buried apart from them would have been painful too.

'I went to university with my rent and bills fully paid, and then Grandad parachuted me into a do-nothing job with the family business.' He took a shuddering breath. 'Dean aged out of foster care at eighteen, and that went exactly as well as you would expect. I don't even know how he ended up here. He texted me saying he needed help, asking me to come here, and I brushed it off. A few days later he was dead, and I can't help but wonder if I'd been quicker to help him . . .'

'I'm sorry,' Gemma said uselessly.

'No, I'm sorry.' Marcus stood up. 'I came in to see if you were okay and somehow ended up vomiting my emotions all over you. Not cool.'

'It's fine,' Gemma said, although she kind of agreed. 'And for what it's worth, I think it sounds like you had it really rough too.'

He shook his head. 'Not even the same league.'

* * *

Once again Gemma found herself awake at that awkward hour when it was too late to go back to bed, but too early to really start the day. So she put the kettle on, and hovered over it so she could snatch it off the stove before it began to whistle.

Marcus came into the kitchen, with his hair wet from the shower and looking a little red around the eyes. Gemma decided that the best solution was pancakes.

Marcus sat at the table with a cup of tea, and they talked with surprising ease about the merits of various pancake toppings, Marcus speaking with surprising passion about the difference between real maple syrup and the synthetic dreck you could get in supermarkets.

This had somehow segued into the topic of organised crime's involvement in the counterfeit olive oil trade when Hugh entered the kitchen, dressed in a fresh uniform.

He looked from Gemma to Marcus, and suspicion clouded his face. She realised it probably looked odd: the early hour, their easy camaraderie, her still in her pyjamas with a near stranger.

He then looked down at the table, where Fawn's sketchbook lay open at a half-finished sketch of Eva Nováková. Fawn must have been working there after dinner.

'What's this?' he asked. 'Is this Violet's?'

'No,' Gemma said. 'It's Fawn's. She's working on a mural for a visual arts project. I said she could use our courtyard wall.'

She realised as she said it that she probably should have run that by Hugh first.

'Are you kidding?' he said. 'How could you possibly think that's appropriate?'

Marcus shot her a deer-in-the-headlights look, and then looked longingly at the kitchen door.

'I wasn't thinking much of anything,' she admitted. 'Fawn needed a space and I had one. I'm sorry, we can talk about it more later if –'

'Oh, you just happened to have one. Great idea, Gemma – let's use a vulnerable teenage girl to turn this place into even more of a freak show attraction.'

'Hey,' she said, holding her hands up. 'The courtyard is part of our private space. I have never said anything about letting customers back there.'

Also, she thought calling Fawn vulnerable was a bit of a reach.

'Sure,' Hugh said, his voice dripping with sarcasm.

'What the hell is your problem?' Gemma asked. 'I've never done anything to make you not able to trust me.'

There was a very long silence. Then Hugh said, very quietly, 'Unlike me, right?'

'I'm just going to . . .' Marcus gestured towards the door.

'You can always trust Gemma, right? Gemma's so kind. Gemma just wants to help everybody.' He reached out and put a hand on Marcus's uninjured arm as their guest tried to slide past him. 'You know she sells fake memorabilia on the internet from your brother's murder, right? Sells tea towels to sick fucks and tells people they're the ones she used to mop up his blood.'

* * *

Gemma found Hugh in the courtyard, sitting on the ground with his back to the brick wall and his hands pressed to his eyes.

'I'm sorry,' he said.

'What was that?' she hissed. 'You just went from zero to terminal velocity over nothing.'

'I know,' he said. 'I'm sorry – I don't know what came over me.'

'You do know,' she said quietly. 'You do. I'm sorry too; I should have thought more about how that picture of Eva would affect you, especially when you know so much more about what really happened to that poor woman.'

He flinched, but nodded.

'I should have thought more about what you needed. But . . .' She took a deep breath. A marriage counsellor they'd seen once had told them that in an apology the word 'but' strikes out everything that came before it. 'That said, you're not thinking about what you need either. You're not okay, Hugh. Please. Why don't you talk to Dr Nicholls?'

'Talk to Dr Nicholls,' he repeated, as if it were the most absurd suggestion he'd ever heard.

Gemma held back a shriek of frustration. If Hugh had his head cut off he would use his last thirty seconds of consciousness to accuse her of being hysterical.

'At least talk to Mick. Tell him you need some leave.'

'What I need is to be able to focus on my job without you piling more stress on me,' he said. 'Anyway, it'll cause a mess if I ask now,' he said. 'I've been asked to go up to the Special Purpose Centre today to interview Jan Henning-Klosner, to see if he knows anything.'

She wanted to throw her hands up and scream at him. Hugh had been the one who managed to get the Ripper to confess, but that didn't mean he had any particular interviewing expertise. There was no reason for him to be the one to go, to put himself back in a room with that man. 'He's in prison. He's been there longer than Violet has been alive. Why would he know something?'

'Maybe, if this is a copycat, they reached out to him.'

'A copycat,' she said, feeling a wave of dread. So the police were seriously considering the possibility that there was another serial killer stalking the town.

'It's just one angle we're pursuing,' Hugh said. 'I think it's far more likely that someone targeted Lochlan specifically.'

Gemma nodded, not reassured. 'Wouldn't it be easier to send someone local to the prison to conduct the interview?'

'I don't tell you how to brew tea,' he snapped, then made a face. 'I'm sorry. I'm just saying, it's complicated. It's all organised, they've booked my hotel, it would be a pain to change it now.'

That sounded ridiculous to her, but she couldn't scrape up the energy to fight anymore. At least she would get her own bed to herself for a night.

* * *

Gemma steeled herself and rapped gently on Marcus's door. Talking to Hugh had been hard, but this was genuinely frightening. She didn't know Marcus, she didn't know how angry he was or how he was likely to express that anger.

Thankfully Violet and Fawn, typical teenagers that they were, had still been fast asleep when she looked in on them, and hadn't heard the fight. Small mercies.

To her surprise, Marcus opened the door with a look of concern, not anger.

'Are you okay?' he asked. 'That was . . . unexpected.'

'Am *I* okay?' she repeated. 'I'm fine. I'm sorry you had to be tangled up in that. Hugh's under a lot of stress.'

'Seriously,' he said. 'If you need help . . .'

'It's not like that,' she said.

'Are you sure?' he asked. 'He put you in an awful position, and now everything is fine again? You're just going to sweep it under the rug?'

'Are you really taking my side, after what I've done?' She rushed to add, 'I'm really sorry. I understand if you want to cancel the rest of your stay, and I'll refund everything.'

'I'm not taking a side. Besides, I already knew about the memorabilia.'

'What?'

'A friend found an auction listing and sent it to me, maybe this time last year?'

'Oh.'

'I know that Rainier is doing it tough,' he explained. 'We wouldn't all be here otherwise. You have to admit, this tour idea has the whiff of desperation about it.'

'Yes,' she said, with something like relief. 'We're holding on by our fingertips here. The teashop, the house . . .' She sighed.

She supposed she should be relieved that Marcus had accepted it so calmly, but it niggled at her. His reaction to the tour proposal seemed to be nothing more than mild curiosity. He wasn't upset about her little side hustle. He hadn't asked her any questions about Dean's death, and she couldn't claim that was all due to her attempts to avoid them. What did he want? Why was he even here?

'Would you like to sit down?' he asked, stepping back. He sat on the edge of the bed, and gestured to the tub chair in the corner.

She sat, feeling weird about being invited into her own space. Hugh's space, really.

'You remind me a bit of my mum,' Marcus said.

'Oof.'

He laughed. 'Not in a bad way. Or maybe a little in a bad way. In a concerned way. Oh god, I'm terrible at this. Gabby would be cracking up if she was here.'

'Go on,' Gemma said, smiling. 'You can't just drop something like that and leave me hanging.'

'My mother was . . . well, she would probably prefer me to call her a peacemaker, but actually she was a peacekeeper. Always running around stamping out little spot fires, forcing us to give each other fake apologies, insisting that nobody go to bed angry – which in practice meant that all arguments got shut down unresolved at nine pm sharp, and she wouldn't let us return to the subject in the morning. That would be bringing up old fights and refusing to let things go.'

'That doesn't sound like me,' Gemma said. If anything she was the queen of refusing to let things go.

'You know yourself best. But I noticed the way you were practically patrolling the room during the post-tour dinner. And the way you shuffled Tamara around, like you were supervising a children's party instead of a group of adults who could handle their own problems.'

'I didn't realise you were watching,' Gemma said. She hoped no-one else had overheard her conversation with Tamara.

'I just pay a lot of attention to what's going on around me,' he said.

'Not enough to avoid getting pickpocketed,' she snapped, then pressed a hand to her mouth. 'Sorry.'

'Don't apologise!' he said. 'More of that, please. I know what it's like to live in a house where the fights were never allowed to really catch fire, but it meant there was this constant, smouldering tension. Maybe if we'd fought it out we could have actually resolved something.'

'You're assuming it could have been resolved. Maybe it just would have gone out of control, beyond the point of repair.'

'That's a resolution of sorts.'

'Then what?' she asked, dropping the pretence that they were talking about hypotheticals. 'My other option is to be pushing forty, single, unemployed and living in my parents' flat.'

'Pushing forty,' he said, laughing. 'You've got plenty of time to start again.'

She said nothing. That was such a rich person thing to say.

'What did you want to do? When you were a kid, I mean.'

'Honestly? This.' She gestured around her, trying to encompass their home, the dark courtyard, the teashop below them. 'Growing up I loved spending time in the teashop with my grandmother, helping to make the blends and do the baking. I wanted to grow up and run the shop and get married and raise my kids here. All my dreams came true.' She sighed. 'Are you familiar with the term "stigmatised property"?'

He shook his head.

'When a house is the site of a murder, its value tanks.' She took in a shuddering breath. 'I know it's selfish to talk about this, when you lost so much more, but this house's history knocked about a hundred grand off its value. Which, given that the house and shop have been in the family for generations, shouldn't make that much difference to us. But before the murders, before the highway bypass, my grandmother took out a mortgage on the building to pay for her nursing home care. Back then, the loan amount was modest compared to the building's value. Not so much anymore. Property in Rainier is hard to sell at the best of times; it's not exactly an active market. And that's not even getting into how much expensive maintenance an old building like this needs.'

'You shouldn't have been responsible for your grandmother's debt, though.'

'No, I shouldn't have been. I know I made a choice.'

'And now you're stuck.'

'Like flies between the screen and the window. With what the teashop brings in and Hugh's salary, we cover the payments, but barely. Sometimes the shop has a run of really bad weeks, or one of our engines blows a seal, or Violet's braces payment comes due the same week our rego expires. And I get desperate enough to email back one of the creeps that reach out to me looking for a souvenir. So we make the ends meet, and we have a beautiful home to live in. We can't complain, really. But if we split up . . . Well, I can't cover the payments just from my revenue and I can't get a job that would make more than the shop does. I've tried. I can't refinance, and I can't sell.'

'Unless you can raise the building's value again. You need to turn the shop's reputation around. Make the dark history an asset.'

'Or make a better go of the business. We almost managed to sell it as a going concern once, to a couple who wanted to rent the space from us and run the shop.'

Something shifted in Marcus. He sat up straight. 'You'd lose a lot of control that way. It seems like you run the shop really respectfully, and try to downplay the connection to Dean's death. Not like that bar the kids were talking about.'

She nodded. 'You and Hugh are on the same page there. He had a million questions for the buyers, and wanted them to agree to a criminal background check. It ended up nuking the deal.'

'I'm sorry,' he said, although it didn't sound sincere. She didn't blame him. 'You never know. Maybe Holst will push forwards with the tour once the dust settles. It'll certainly stir up a lot more interest in the case.'

'Holst? Our Holst?'

'Yeah, the dude who owns the pub.'

'Why do you think he'd take over the tour idea?'

'You don't know?' Marcus looked surprised. 'I got my CFO to request the company details on Lewis and Co. from ASIC. Christian Holst is the "and Co." in "Lewis and Co.".'

FIFTEEN

Transcript of the interrogation of Jan Henning-Klosner (continued)

Guillory: *You frightened the daylights out of* [redacted], *you know.*

JHK: *Who?*

Guillory: *Who, he asks. Doesn't even care.* [redacted]*'s the girl from the teashop.*

JHK: *Across from the fountain?*

Guillory: *That's right. The sweetest girl you'd ever meet. She'd do anything for anyone. Now she's too scared to be left alone. You've probably scarred her for life.*

JHK: *I'm sorry, I didn't mean to frighten her.*

Guillory: *Who gives a shit what you meant to do?*

Seabrooke: *Steady on, mate. Of course it matters. You never intended for things to go this far, did you, Jan? Things got out of hand.*

JHK: *It doesn't make any difference. I'm fucked, right?*

Seabrooke: *Hey, it makes a difference. The more you help us, the more we can help you. There's two sides to every story, right?*

Guillory: *I'm not here to help him.*

Seabrooke: *Guillory, stop getting worked up.*

Seabrooke: *Guillory doesn't have to be here, you know. If you just want to talk to me, I can get him to take a break.*

JHK: *Could I take a break?*

Seabrooke: *Yeah, we're all tired. Guillory, why don't you go home for a bit?*

Seabrooke: *Constable Hugh Guillory has now left the room. The time is eleven thirty-five am.*

* * *

Lane dreamed that he held both of Mina's hands in one of his as he emptied a water bottle over them. The water poured between their fingers and splashed on the ground, the smell of wet dust mingling with the smell of fresh blood.

He woke up with a gasp, and the faint bleach smell of the medical unit was suddenly overwhelming.

Jan chuckled. 'Prison turns us all back into teenagers, doesn't it?'

'It wasn't that kind of dream,' Lane mumbled, earning him a disbelieving snort.

This would be the perfect moment to turn the conversation to the subject of sex and romance, to try to get Jan to open up about the women he once knew out there. He certainly wasn't going to tell Jan anything at all about Mina, but maybe he could make up some grand romance.

'There's going to be some shuffling around today,' Jan said, while Lane was still brainstorming possible backstories for his fictional star-crossed lover. 'The Rainier police want to come have a chat about some new murder down there.'

That took Lane by surprise, and worried him. He doubted that Carver had bothered clearing his little plan with the police. 'Is your lawyer coming?'

Jan laughed. 'Mate, my lawyer died in 2008. Bloody flu, if you can believe it.'

'You should have a lawyer. I could call mine, if you want. He'd love it.'

'What are they going to do? Pin this new one on me? I might need you to give me an alibi, tell them I was busy getting my head smashed in at the time.'

'What about older cases?'

'They can charge me with a thousand murders if they want to,' Jan said with a sigh. He closed his eyes. 'I'm going to die here. Probably before they manage to get a trial date.'

An orderly arrived with their breakfast trays, already cold from the walk from the kitchens. Lane ate his soggy toast mechanically, trying to make sense of Jan. He didn't seem to care about defending himself against false accusations, nor did he seem to have any interest in inflating his reputation with false confessions and bluster like some did.

'Are you actually dying of something, or just being dramatic?' he asked.

'Actually dying,' Jan said, poking at his eggs. 'I've got a bad heart. I mean literally – I'm not trying to be poetic. The quacks over at the hospital want to cut me open, but I don't see the point. Sounds like a lot of pain and time stuck in one of these beds just to buy some extra years to spend in here.'

That made everything more clear, and more unsettling at the same time. It had worried Lane that Governor Carver had put this plan together at lightning speed, amid the chaos of a late-night violent incident. But if he had known for a while that Jan was dying, he could have been quietly plotting in the background, then taken advantage of the opening. The question was, had Carver just waited for an opportunity, or had he created one? And how long had he been moving playing pieces around?

'Have you got a bucket list?' he asked.

'Oh yeah – I'm going skydiving, right after I climb Everest,' Jan joked.

'There are things we can do in here, though,' Lane said. 'Make our peace.'

Jan sighed. 'This again.'

'Well, sorry for trying to make conversation,' Lane said with a forced huff.

'Bloody nosy is what you are.'

'Maybe I'm a bit rusty,' Lane admitted. 'This place really does a number on your social skills.'

And his interview skills, clearly.

'Just you wait,' Jan said, pushing his tray table away and sinking back down into the pillows. 'It only gets worse.'

SIXTEEN

GEMMA MEASURED OUT a scoop of green tea. The act of pouring the tea-leaves into the top of the teapot, a motion she'd gone through thousands of times, suddenly felt like she was trying to hit a bullseye on a moving target. She took a deep breath and focused, tilting the scoop slowly to let the leaves tumble in bit by bit. Her hand trembled.

She'd been going back over her conversation with Marcus, worried that she'd crossed a line. It embarrassed her how much she'd overshared. At the same time, it had felt good to have someone to talk to about it. Someone who wouldn't say 'I told you so', like her parents were inclined to do. Someone who wouldn't spread it all over town or decide they should bring it up with Hugh.

But she didn't feel like she'd been particularly honest with Marcus. She wasn't trapped here. She could decide to go, if she needed to. But panic clawed through her at the idea of doing it.

Every major life decision she'd ever made had turned out to be wrong, even the ones that had seemed perfectly reasonable at the time. What they had here was good enough. She would be an idiot to torpedo it.

What was this? How had she got here? How could this possibly be how she lived?

Okay. She knew this one. 'Hi there, derealisation,' she said, giving the monster its name.

She turned to the kettle and gripped the handle, so the heat of the boiled water warmed her knuckles where they pressed against the body of the kettle. Dr Nicholls had advised her that when anxiety started to creep in she should try touching something hot or cold to ground her and pick an object to focus on.

'This is my kettle,' she whispered. 'It is blue. My great-aunt Sadie gave it to me at my bridal shower, meaning it is seventeen years old.'

'It's nice,' Fawn Nicholls said behind her, making her jump.

'Thank you,' Gemma said. Her voice sounded far away and didn't feel like her own. 'Cup of tea?'

'Got anything stronger?'

'Like . . . whisky?'

'Like coffee.' Fawn frowned. 'Are you okay?'

No.

'I'm fine. Do you girls have plans for the day?'

'We have a biology assignment we were thinking we could knock out today. It's on DNA.'

'I wish I was so sensible when I was your age,' Gemma said. She poured her tea into a travel cup, thinking that a walk might help.

* * *

Gemma went out the back gate and down the alley towards Clarence Street. This time she followed it to its end, and within a few minutes at a slow amble she was at the edge of the town.

Outside of the town was a mix of paddocks and bushland. Walking beneath the trees, Gemma couldn't help wondering why the Ripper had taken the risk of burying Eva Nováková in the park, so close to potential witnesses, when he could have hidden her body here. Why the park? Why Rainier, for that matter? The Ripper maintained that he had no other victims, and the police had never managed to connect him to any other unsolved murders or disappearances along his trucking route. Why had he chosen to terrorise Rainier? He wasn't born here, he never lived here, he only ever passed through. What about her home had inspired him to destroy their lives?

Gemma sighed. So much for a walk helping to calm her thoughts.

She decided to do a full loop around the outskirts of town before going home. When she passed the motel, she saw a flash of pink hair in the smokers garden. That had to be Tamara, sitting at the table at the back, and there was someone else with her. Gemma didn't think much of it, until she drew close enough to recognise Jac's voice.

They didn't notice Gemma, and while she didn't hide, she also didn't make any effort to draw their attention to her approach.

'I didn't know your dad that well,' Tamara was saying. 'When I was in the area I worked out of the service centre, and crashed with a friend further up the highway. Your dad only stopped there if he absolutely needed to; once he was that close to home, he wanted to blow straight through to get back to your mama.'

'But you did meet him?'

'A handful of times. He was absolutely thrilled about becoming a dad.'

That took Gemma by surprise. She'd always been under the impression that Vincent hadn't known about Aubrey's pregnancy when he died. He certainly hadn't told his parents, and the Tjibaous didn't find out until they ran into a visibly pregnant Aubrey during the trial. But if that was news to Jac, they didn't show it.

'He absolutely loved your mother, too,' Tamara said with a fond smile. 'The first conversation I ever had with him, he went on and on about how wonderful she was and how much he loved her beautiful blue eyes.'

Jac, who had been slouching in their chair, sat up abruptly. Aubrey didn't have blue eyes.

Gemma cleared her throat. 'Sorry, couldn't help overhearing,' she said, knowing it would be completely obvious she'd been eavesdropping. She pointed at her own blue eyes. 'That must have been before your mum and dad got together, Jac. He was probably talking about me, and probably waxing rhapsodic because our relationship was limping towards its end. You know, like when people get on social media to gush about how great their partner is it always means they're days away from announcing a break-up.'

Jac didn't look mollified, but shrugged. 'Sounds about right.'

'Or I could be forgetting the colour,' Tamara said. 'It was a long time ago.' Then she sighed. 'Though it feels like yesterday, some days.'

'I know that feeling,' Gemma said.

Jac pushed back their chair. 'Thanks for answering my questions, Tamara, but I've got to go. Mum and Mrs Nicholls are going for lunch in Wagga, so she needs me to babysit.'

That stung a little. Gemma, Aubrey and Lotte were friends, in the sense that Gemma and Aubrey were friends, and Aubrey and Lotte were friends, and their children were friends, so they all spent time together. She knew that Aubrey and Lotte did things without her sometimes, but considering that she'd been feeding and watching over Fawn for days now, it would have been nice to get an invite to a girls' lunch.

As Jac disappeared down the street, Tamara turned to Gemma. 'They came to see me, I didn't invite them here,' she said. 'And we were outdoors the whole time.'

Ah. That explained the choice of the smokers garden when there was no sign of Tamara having cigarettes. 'I wasn't going to accuse you of anything.'

'Just making sure the air is clear,' Tamara said. She leaned back, tipping her face up to catch the weak winter sun. 'When

MURDER TOWN

you're in sex work, or adjacent to it, being seen talking to teenagers can be fraught.'

'Were they just asking about Vincent?' Gemma asked. 'We're always happy to tell them anything about him they want to hear.'

'I'm sure you are, but I think Jac wants to hear a version that isn't filtered through their dad's grieving family and friends. At that age, teenagers are desperate to understand who they are. I bet that goes double when you're being raised by a man like Mick Seabrooke.'

'Have you had issues with Mick?' Gemma asked.

'Not really,' Tamara said with a shrug. 'The guy just always gave me douche chills. I always get a vibe like he resents me for not grovelling with gratitude because he saved me from Jan.'

It sent a chill through Gemma to hear the Ripper referred to so casually.

'Plus, the guy was middle-aged when he married a, what, twenty-one-year-old single mother? Thinking he has a white knight complex is the charitable interpretation of that mess.'

'She was about to turn twenty-three,' Gemma said, which she supposed wasn't exactly a rebuttal. She didn't feel comfortable talking about Aubrey like this, but she didn't want to say something that could come across as chiding and make Tamara clam up. 'I hope she didn't say anything to you in the teashop, before I pulled you away.'

'No, although her face was screaming it.' She shrugged again. 'Not the worst thing that's happened to me in my line of work. Hell, it wasn't even the worst thing that happened that night.'

167

'That's true,' Gemma said. She hesitated. She could take the opening to steer the conversation towards the death of Lochlan Lewis, but that might make her seem ghoulish. 'I heard that you work for a non-profit now?'

'That's right. It's a different role but the same industry. I'm a policy officer for the Australian Sex Workers Alliance. The pay cut was tough, but I couldn't keep up the work I was doing.'

'I'm sorry.'

'Well, I'm the one who agreed to let the press reveal my name.'

Gemma wasn't sure what that meant. She'd assumed Tamara had changed careers due to the trauma of being attacked by Jan, but she didn't see what her name had to do with that. 'You were harassed?'

'In a way. In the months following Jan's arrest, my bookings went way up.'

It took a moment for the implications to sink in. 'That's awful.'

'Yep. Lewis and Co. are hardly the first tourists.'

Gemma grimaced. 'It must be a bit of a relief to have the tour called off, then.'

'Eh. I doubt the tour was going to move the needle much. Nothing like the way Lochlan Lewis's murder is going to stir up attention.'

'I'm sorry,' Gemma said. She couldn't help it, but she was mentally sorting the people in town into two groups – the people who were worse off due to Lochlan's murder, and so had no motive, and the people who weren't. She added Tamara to the first group. 'And I'm sorry that you won't get the funding you were hoping for to have Eva's DNA profiled.'

Tamara sighed. 'Lochlan was never going to stump up the money.'

'Does it cost that much? I've been getting ads for those genealogy tests lately – it's just a couple of hundred dollars.'

Tamara shook her head. 'Those are novelties. Plus, they ask you to provide a huge sample. The police only have a little bit of DNA on file for Eva, unless they exhume her to get more, and the analysis it would go through is much more robust. I can send you an article if you'd like.'

'That'd be great,' Gemma said. 'Are you going to keep trying? If you have a fundraising link I'd be happy to send it around.'

'I don't know. The Alliance never has enough for the living people we support. If I ask someone to donate a dollar for Eva, that's a dollar they can't give for emergency housing or legal help or the education fund. Lochlan had no reason to give to those campaigns, but I could hit him up for Eva. I knew it was a long shot – unless he thought it could lead to more media attention for the tour.'

'Did you have much to do with him? I never spoke to him outside of a few pleasantries before the tour started.'

'We exchanged a few texts. He wanted to interview me, to help him write the tour script. I have to respect that; at least he wasn't planning to just repeat some of the bullshit that's floating around about the case.'

Unless he was just hoping for some juicy new angle to set his tour apart from those existing books and websites, Gemma thought.

'I would have preferred him to say as little about me as possible,' Tamara continued. 'I agreed to participate as a representative of the Alliance, really. I was worried about how they were going to talk about Eva, since there's no family to speak for her.'

'Did you know her?'

Gemma knew Tamara had always said she didn't, but she seemed very concerned about Eva for a stranger.

'No. Which is important. I knew who my competition was. I knew every woman and man working out of that service centre, and I knew who was working out of their homes here in town. You keep tabs on your competition, don't you?'

'I guess.'

'I told Seabrooke that, back when they were first trying to identify her. But he went and made an offhand remark to the press about how she might have been a sex worker at the service centre, and the media ran with it.'

'She wasn't living in town, though,' Gemma said. 'No-one here knew her either, and we never got a lot of new arrivals. Just travellers passing through.'

'But if she was a traveller she should have had friends and family looking for her. There would have been a matching missing person. If no-one cared, she must have been one of us, right?' Tamara said bitterly.

'That's not what I meant,' Gemma said, although she couldn't articulate what she had meant, if not that.

'It's alright,' Tamara said. 'Eva's like an ink blot test. The details are just vague enough for everyone to look and see what they need to see. Because she was unknown, people could see her as innocent. The papers couldn't pull old arrest records like they did with Dean. And Vincent was. . .'

'Vincent was innocent,' Gemma said. 'He was just a kid enjoying his twenties – he never hurt anyone.'

'I know, he was a complete sweetheart,' Tamara said, laying a hand on Gemma's arm. 'But you know the readers of a certain kind of rag wouldn't see him that way. But on Eva they could project the image of a beautiful, white, lost angel. At the same time, though, they assumed she was a sex worker, so it felt safe to objectify her. Have you ever heard the term "the less dead"?'

'No.'

'It refers to murder victims who were homeless or addicted or doing sex work, or some combination of the three. People who aren't living on the edge don't see them as really living, so it makes their deaths that little bit less sad. Do you think this tour idea would even be considered if the victims were all middle-class blonde women?'

Gemma couldn't disagree.

'Did you know' – Gemma caught herself before calling him 'the Ripper' – 'Jan Henning-Klosner before he . . . before he attacked you?'

'A little,' Tamara said. 'Better than I knew Vincent, but not by much. I get the impression I meant more to him than he did to me.' She said it matter-of-factly, without any trace of sympathy.

'Did he seem off?'

'Yes and no. He could be cranky sometimes, but trucking means long hours and unreasonable pressure. If he was erratic, I chalked it up to him being on uppers. I never felt like I was in danger with him, until I was.'

'Did you ever set any store by the rumour that there was a second Ripper?' Gemma cringed. 'I mean, that he had an accomplice?'

'Maybe,' Tamara said. 'But if there was, they didn't kill Lochlan Lewis.'

'What makes you so sure?'

'Because Jan was only ever close to two people. Me, who he was paying, and Dean Shadwell, who he killed.'

SEVENTEEN

Transcript of the interrogation of Jan Henning-Klosner (continued)

Seabrooke: *The crime scene unit found Dean Shadwell's phone, dropped in the park near where he died. We –*

JHK: *Dean's dead?*

Guillory: *Didn't stick around for that part, huh? He was declared dead on site.*

Seabrooke: *As I was saying, we found an interesting text message sent by Dean to your number about half an hour before he was killed. Would you like me to read it to you?*

JHK: *I know what it says.*

Seabrooke: *'Jan. I can't do this anymore. I'm going to the cops.'*

Guillory: *That must have really scared you. What was he going to tell us, Jan?*

* * *

An orderly brought a wheelchair for Lane, so that Jan and the police could have the medical unit for the interview, rather than risk moving Jan.

Instead of taking Lane back to his cell as he expected, the orderly pushed him through the heavy medical unit doors, then immediately hooked left and pushed open a door painted the same colour as the hallway wall, which Lane had assumed was a storage cupboard.

Inside was a room not much larger than a single bed, containing nothing but a plastic chair. On the wall shared with the medical unit was a small window, with the distinct off-colour sheen of a two-way mirror. It was small, and discreetly placed enough that Lane hadn't noticed it before, the way he would have immediately clocked a full-size observation window.

He wondered how many of his conversations with Jan had been watched.

The orderly parked him in the small open space, and used his foot to apply the wheelchair's brake. He left without saying anything to Lane, or even making eye contact.

After a few minutes the door opened again, and Governor Carver walked in and took the other seat. He gave Lane a small nod.

'Was this necessary?' Lane asked, indicating the wheelchair. 'Isn't it supposed to be my arm that's injured?'

'You think he's going to watch you get up and walk out of the medical unit on your own and not start wondering why you need to be in there?' Carver crossed his arms. 'Has he given you anything?'

Lane shrugged. 'Mostly he sleeps. We've had a few chats; I think there are angles I can work.'

'You're being subtle, right?'

'As subtle as I can be. But that limits how effective I am. I could just come out and ask him, but I'm trying to convince him that I'm bored and nosy, so that it doesn't seem odd when I badger him for details.'

'Is that working?'

'Well, he definitely thinks I'm nosy.' Lane shifted on the uncomfortable seat of the wheelchair. 'You must be aware that he's dying.'

'Yes,' Carver admitted. 'He's a heart attack in waiting. Maybe next year, maybe during this interview. It makes it difficult to be patient.'

'I think it's the wedge, though. When he thought his death was imminent, he wanted to set the record straight with Tamara Fleischer.' He paused. 'What if you contacted Tamara? This prison has a restorative justice program, doesn't it?'

Carver grimaced. 'The families and survivors know the option is available to them. Henning-Klosner could put in a request, but the paperwork would take months. If Fleischer came voluntarily, we could get them in a room together, but I can't reach out. Especially not to someone like Fleischer. If I overstep with her she'd raise a ruckus. It would be all over the papers, especially with interest in the case high again.'

The medical unit door opened, and Lane sat up straighter. Watching the interview without Jan's knowledge was deeply unethical – but, then, so was everything about this little game.

Two uniformed officers entered: a man about Lane's age and a young woman. The woman looked like she was having trouble with her poker face, letting her wide-eyed nerves show when she spotted Jan.

'Mr Henning-Klosner,' the man said, tucking his hat under his arm. 'I'm Sergeant Hugh Guillory and this is Probationary Constable Panipak Seesondee.'

'We've met,' Jan said. He looked at Panipak. 'I mean him; I'm pretty sure you weren't even born when Guillory and I became acquainted.'

'I was five,' Panipak said, then flushed.

Hugh Guillory. Lane recognised the name – he was one of the officers on record for Jan's confession. He wasn't sure what angle the Rainier police were playing. They'd sent someone completely tangled up in the Ripper's history, and a probationary constable – someone who had been a cop for less than a year. Probably much less than a year, if Panipak was green enough to volunteer personal information like that. She was basically in this interview as a seat warmer.

'How have you been, Guillory? I heard you went mental.'

Guillory ignored the comment and consulted his notes. He ran through the preliminaries of the interview robotically – date, time, location and names of all present.

'When was the last time you had contact with someone from Rainier?' he asked.

'Well, there's this chat we're having right now. Before that, I guess it would be the time that Vincent's mother stood up in the courtroom and screamed that she couldn't wait for me to burn in hell. Wait.' He clicked his fingers. 'Do the letters your dad used to send me count?'

Guillory didn't school his expression fast enough. That was genuine news to him. 'I doubt that's pertinent. No-one else has written to you, or visited?'

'No.'

'Have you had any other contact that you think we should know about? Maybe someone who seems a little too interested in the details of your crimes, or has told you they'd like to do the same?'

'No.'

'We will be consulting your visitor records and interviewing the nominated officer who checks your mail, so there's no point trying to conceal it if someone has contacted you.'

'They'll tell you the same thing: I don't get visitors or letters. Even the fetish freaks and God-botherers have lost interest.'

Guillory nodded, and wrote something down in his notepad. 'Did you choose the fountain, Jan?'

'What?'

Guillory looked up from his notes, and looked Jan in the eye. 'The fountain. Did you take Vincent there, or was that just where he was when you attacked him?'

Jan stared at him for a long time, then shrugged. 'I chose the fountain.'

'Why?'

'You've given this more thought than I ever did. It was public enough that Vincent didn't think he was being lured into danger, but with the trees, the sound wouldn't carry to the shops. I see you guys cut them down. Looks nice. Bet the greenies pitched a fit.'

Lane wondered how on earth Jan knew that, but Guillory apparently didn't see it as worth following up.

'So the site didn't have any particular significance for you?'

'Not at that time, no.'

Carver shifted in his chair, and Lane empathised. He wanted to bash on the window and shout at Guillory to ask about Eva, but he understood why Vincent was the focus of the interview, given the nature of this new, possibly copycat murder.

'Ask about the church,' Carver muttered. 'The fountain was within sight of where he buried Eva – that has to be significant.'

Clearly Guillory wasn't picking up on Lane and Carver's telepathic messages, because he flipped to a new page of his notebook.

'Where did you get the knife that you used to attack Vincent Tjibaou and Dean Shadwell?'

Lane glanced at Carver, wondering if he had noticed the obvious implication there – either Eva's body had been buried for too long for them to be able to positively match the weapon from the other murders, or she was killed with a different weapon.

'Didn't we go through all this years ago?'

'And yet I'm asking again. It was pretty fancy, wasn't it? French.'

'A French peasant knife isn't fancy. I bought it at some ratfucked camping store in Melbourne. I doubt they remember me.'

'Have you ever told anyone about that knife? Described it to a fellow inmate, or a journalist, or someone who was writing to you?'

'I told you, nobody writes to me. And I don't know what you think this place is like, but we don't sit around bragging about what we did. I don't like to talk about that damn thing. Not like –'

He clammed up, and Lane frowned. Not like who? Who liked to talk about the knife?

He wasn't alluding to Lane, was he? Lane hadn't asked him about the knife.

'Not like who?' For once Guillory asked a question Lane wanted him to.

'Dean,' Jan said, sounding sad. 'He had a chip on his shoulder about it. Told anyone who'd listen that –'

Guillory held a hand up, silencing Jan. 'Don't play games. I'm asking about people who are alive.'

'I'm tired,' Jan said. His voice took on a quaver that Lane had never heard before and doubted was real.

'We just have a few more questions,' Panipak said, giving him a sunny smile. Apparently she was the good cop.

'No. I'm done.'

'This isn't a press conference – you can't walk off when the questions get hard,' Guillory said.

'Oh, I'm well aware of how your interviews work,' Jan said, narrowing his eyes at Guillory. 'I'm not answering any more questions.'

Lane bit back a groan. They hadn't asked a single question about Eva, and now it was clear it wouldn't happen.

'We never released the details of that knife. Can you think of anyone who might know that you used a "French peasant knife"?' Guillory asked, making air quotes with his fingers.

Something seemed to change in Jan. His expression went flat, and he leaned over the edge of the bed, closer to Guillory. The detective didn't flinch, but Lane noticed him shift his weight ever so slightly on his heels. He'd had to stop himself.

Jan let out a high, keening cry. A pitch-perfect imitation of a baby crying. If Lane hadn't been watching, he'd be looking around trying to figure out where the child was.

Panipak looked puzzled, but Guillory went completely white.

Carver jumped to his feet and stormed out of the observation room. A moment later he barrelled into the medical unit. 'That's enough,' he said.

Lane expected Guillory to fight it, but he simply turned on his heel and strode out, looking like he might throw up.

'Tell your dad I said hi,' Jan shouted at his back.

EIGHTEEN

GEMMA WALKED BACK to the teashop, her mind whirling. She had never known much about Dean Shadwell. The time she had known him could be measured in seconds, and she had avoided any articles or news pieces about him. Pictures of him had set her heart racing and brought back that phantom smell of fresh blood.

She had known him only as a victim. She'd had no idea he'd been close friends with his killer.

Could the man who died in her shop have had a hand in Vincent's death? In Eva's?

Gemma was so caught up in her thoughts that she didn't notice the fresh crime scene tape closing off a section of the footpath until she'd almost stormed through it like a first-place sprinter.

'Ma'am, you're going to need to go around,' an unfamiliar police officer said. He looked fresh out of training, barely older than Violet. It was a sign of Gemma's age that more and more authority figures looked like absolute babies to her. Behind him, a crime scene investigator was photographing the grate of a stormwater drain.

'What's happened?' she asked. 'Has there been another murder?'

'No,' he said.

'I found something,' another voice said. On the far side of the taped-off section stood Nico Tanner, Ruth's son. 'I was walking home from the oval and noticed something sticking out. It was flapping around in the breeze.'

'What is it?'

'Move along, please,' the officer said.

But Gemma felt like her feet were melted into the footpath. Satisfied with the pictures, the crime scene investigator reached into the gap and carefully lifted out a rumpled bundle of clear plastic. At least, the parts that weren't striped with dark, dried blood were clear.

Something about the shape of the thing was familiar, but Gemma couldn't place it.

'Well,' Nico said, sounding nauseous. 'At least now we know which way the killer ran.'

Gemma looked to her right, towards the fountain, then back down the street. It made sense for the killer to run this way – away from the windows of the teashop and all the witnesses inside. But if they were trying to avoid that, why dump the body in the fountain? Why take such a risk?

The motel was at that end of the street. Was the killer staying there? Or perhaps looking for something in Lochlan's room?

'The pub has a security camera, doesn't it?' she asked Nico. 'They would have run past.'

Nico shook his head. 'Our security camera only covers the inside, the bar and the gaming room. It would have recorded anyone coming in and out, but we were closed. We already handed over the footage, but it didn't capture anything through the windows. Not even a shadow.'

'Do you want me to walk you home?' Gemma asked. The poor kid looked ready to drop. 'It's no trouble, I need to talk to your dad about using the kitchen for the memorial.'

'He's not my dad,' Nico corrected, falling into step beside her. 'I mean, he's fine and all, but I was seventeen when they started going out. Feels weird to call him my dad, or stepdad.'

'Sorry,' Gemma said. She was too used to navigating the minefield of how to refer to Mick – if Aubrey was around he had to be referred to as Jac's dad.

* * *

The pub was a single-storey red-brick building with tinted windows. Usually they had the weekly schedule written on the glass in bright chalk paint: Cheap Tuesday Pizza, the Thursday Meat Raffle, sometimes a band on Fridays. But someone had scrubbed the windows clean and taped a closed sign over the opening hours.

Christian was inside, vacuuming the dining area. He greeted them with a cheerful smile that dropped when he saw Nico's face.

'What's happened, mate?'

Nico gave him a clipped explanation of what he had found outside and then announced he was going to his room. Christian watched him go, looking pensive.

'Has he been okay?' Gemma asked.

'Yeah, well, that kind of stroppiness is pretty standard, so it's hard to tell.'

'It's hard figuring out how to help them, isn't it? Luckily Violet's been happy to stay home, where she's safe. She seems totally fine with everything – a little too fine sometimes; she's eager for all the details she can get from the news.'

'Kids are resilient,' he said.

'Mmm. I guess I just don't want this to follow her the way it's followed us.'

Especially given the struggles on both Hugh and Gemma's sides, they'd handed their daughter a ticking time bomb of a genetic predisposition.

'You know,' Christian said, 'if you're having trouble with it, there's help available.'

'I'm alright. I talk to Dr Nicholls sometimes.'

'He's not a counsellor, though.'

'If he thought I needed one, I'm sure he'd refer me.'

'Look, I don't want to make you uncomfortable, but' – he lowered his voice – 'if money's an issue, the Victims Support Scheme will pay for counselling.'

'I'm not a victim,' she said.

'You watched Dean Shadwell die,' he said. 'That qualifies.

There's a time limit on applying for compensation, but not for the free counselling. You can still access it.'

'You seem to know a lot about it,' she said. 'Have you done it?'

'Yes. Plus, I pour the drinks in this town. I started keeping pamphlets under the bar years ago to give to the people using me as a counsellor when they clearly need a real one.'

'Don't you think . . .' She was probably going to regret this, but she couldn't help herself. 'If you've seen the way people were hurting, why did you partner with Lochlan Lewis on the tour?'

He stared at her. 'How did you find out about that?'

'Marcus told me.'

'Marcus?' He looked puzzled.

'Marcus Shadwell. He looked up Lewis and Co. in the ASIC register. But that's not really the important part, is it? Why did you keep it a secret? You had to know we'd find out eventually.'

'I'd have come clean if the tour was going ahead. I wanted people to cast their votes based on the plan's merits, not feel like they had to support it because it was my business.'

'It wasn't that you wanted to be able to walk away with your reputation intact if the town hated the idea? You still haven't answered my original question: why would you go along with it in the first place?'

'You're right – I know better than anyone how many people are hurting in this town. But I also see the other hurts. People struggling to keep their businesses open. People watching their kids grow up and move away, because there isn't enough for them here.

So when Lochlan reached out with his proposal I thought it could help. But it turned into a shit show.'

'I'm sorry,' she said. 'And I'm sorry you lost your friend.'

'Thanks,' he said, voice gruff. He cleared his throat. 'Since you're here, how about I show you around the kitchen?'

'Sure.'

'Do you know what you're making?'

She shrugged. 'The budget they gave me isn't huge, and I don't know how many to expect. I'm thinking fruit skewers and goat's cheese tarts, to use up what's about to expire on me, and then frozen spring rolls and quiches to fill in the gaps.'

The kitchen was basic, but roomy. There was a wood-fired pizza oven, which she didn't need to know about, a good-sized stove and a walk-in freezer. Christian had a middle-of-the-range coffee machine – a different brand from the one Gemma used in the shop, but she was sure she could figure it out.

'I heard Marcus is still staying at your place,' Christian said. 'Ruth's a little surprised you're so comfortable with a strange man around your daughter.'

Gemma looked at him, taken aback. She hadn't realised she was on the gossip radar. 'Violet's not a little kid, and she still has Fawn with her. Besides, Marcus isn't really in our house. There's a separate suite.'

She didn't mention that he was coming and going through the inside door a little more than she'd planned. It wasn't Christian's business.

NINETEEN

LANE WAS BUZZING, and if he didn't get his hands on a notebook in the next thirty seconds he was going to start scrawling his thoughts on the wall like a lunatic. That was quite possibly the worst interview he'd ever witnessed – Guillory had been scattered and combative and had skimmed straight over every interesting avenue his aimless questioning opened up. But he had opened them up, and Lane was going to dig into them properly as soon as he and Jan were back together.

Carver strode past him, gesturing for Lane to follow. Lane fumbled with the wheelchair, trying to find the brake release, but Carver shook his head. 'Leave it.'

Once they were out in the hallway, Carver escorted him straight past the medical unit door.

'Are we going to your office?' Lane asked.

'I'm returning you to your cell,' Carver snapped.

'What?' Lane would have stopped walking, but he got the feeling that would have made Carver switch to shoving him along. 'Why?'

'Don't you get it?' Carver asked. 'That baby crying garbage was aimed at me. I don't know how he knew I was there listening, but it's obvious he's twigged why you're in there with him.'

'He hasn't,' Lane argued, with creeping desperation. 'He was nothing but friendly, right up to the moment you took me out of there.'

He replayed every interaction with Jan, trying to think of a single moment when he might have slipped up and revealed himself. A moment when Jan had switched from slowly warming to Lane to distrustful again. There was nothing.

'Sir,' Lane said, 'even if Jan has figured it out, I can still help you. I could interview Matilda's friends. Or if you set me up with phone credit, I can canvass tattoo artists. I can call farms and –'

'Just drop it, Holland,' Carver said.

Lane saw now. Carver wasn't angry. He was afraid. That answered the question about whether the department knew about the possible connection between Matilda Carver and Jan. Carver's scheme was unravelling, and he was scared his whole career was about to unravel with it.

* * *

Lane paced in his cell. He couldn't just go back to nothing. Not without any warning. It was a physical itch under his skin, like every nerve ending had been abruptly cut off from a drug.

He threw himself down on the bed and opened the slim folder of printouts. His sad little 'case file'. There had to be something, some hook he could dig into that would convince Carver – or whoever replaced Carver, if he was about to get fired – to let him keep going.

It wasn't really going to happen. He knew it. This was irrational, compulsive. It was exactly the same lack of control, the same refusal to lose, that had landed him in here in the first place. He acknowledged that truth, then ignored it.

He re-read Jan's confession, and the interview transcripts. It was interesting being able to hear Jan's voice as he read them this time, and Hugh Guillory's too. Small moments took on greater meaning now that he had seen Guillory's interview style in action. But it didn't add up to what he needed.

He went through the articles again, the photographs, the sketches.

When he flipped over the last page, he saw an envelope that he had shoved in the back. Inside was the newspaper clipping Lynnie had given him the day she visited. He looked down at Mina's picture for a long moment, then flipped it over.

There was something here. He just had to decide if he was willing to cross a line to keep this going. In the background of the picture stood a teashop. The one that had hosted a gathering the night of the fresh murder. Painted in the window was the word *Reservations*, and a blurry but legible phone number.

TWENTY

ORDINARILY WHEN GEMMA wanted to think she sat on the front verandah with a cup of tea, but she doubted that a view of the crime scene tents would help her right now. Instead she took a kitchen chair out the back. That part of the verandah was little more than a landing at the top of the rear staircase, but it had a peaceful view of their neighbours' roofs and gardens.

She pulled out her phone, and typed *Dean Shadwell* into the search bar. She took a deep breath. If she was serious about this, about trying to ferret out the leads the police weren't considering, she needed to be able to follow them herself. If she couldn't handle the idea of searching for the man's name, she was wasting her time. But the thought of seeing his picture, of seeing those eyes looking at her again, made her head swim.

The search engine offered her some helpful options.

Dean Shadwell murder

Dean Shadwell brother

Dean Shadwell Rainier Ripper

Dean Shadwell second Ripper?

Dean Shadwell memorabilia for sale

She pressed the X button to make the words disappear.

The first time she sold one of the tea towels, the idea hadn't been hers. Some freak in Russia had found her email address and asked if she had anything for sale from the murder scene. It had been a hellacious week, trying to run the shop with a teething Violet in a playpen in the yarn section. When Gemma read that email she'd had a panic attack, and found herself curled up on the lounge room carpet with her head between her knees.

In response to her silence, he'd doubled the offer.

She emailed back that she had nothing. What the police didn't take away had been cleaned, thoroughly.

He replied that he didn't mind if they'd been cleaned.

From there she'd hatched the idea. The shop had a back stock of old-fashioned crochet-edged tea towels that no-one wanted. She tossed one in a box and shipped it off, postmarked Rainier.

The day the cheque cleared she vomited, then pulled herself together and paid off half her outstanding supplier debts.

The back door rattled, and she bit back a sigh when Marcus came out. She couldn't think of a single person she was less ready to talk to right now.

'Hi,' he said. 'Are you okay out here?'

'Just fine,' she said. 'Do you need something?'

'I've been thinking,' he said. 'Can I talk to you?'

'It's bring-your-own chair, I'm afraid.'

'That's alright.' He leaned against the wall. 'I've been doing some research. Looking at real estate listings for buildings of this size in towns like Rainier.' He laughed, sounding uncomfortable. 'Not like Rainier. Nowhere is like Rainier. I mean the same size as Rainier.'

'Are you thinking of moving?'

'No. I like the city. But I'd like to make you an offer.' He reached into his pocket and took out a folded piece of paper. 'For this building. The shop, and the house. Or if you'd like to keep the house, we could negotiate.'

She unfolded the paper and read the number, then read it again. It was well above the last valuation they'd received. Closer to what the property might have been worth if Dean's murder had never happened. More than enough to clear their debts and put down a deposit somewhere new. Somewhere else.

'You can pay this for a building you're not even going to live in?' she asked. Marcus had dropped some hints that he had serious money, but this was on another level.

'I can pay it to make sure you don't have to sell to someone who will turn it into a tacky tourist trap.'

Gemma flinched, and refolded the paper. 'You don't have to do this. I would never –'

'Look, I see how this place weighs on you. I can see it because I feel the same way about the money I inherited. Maybe we can trade.'

Gemma's eyes prickled. 'How can you do this for me after what I've done?'

'With the tea towels?'

'No.' She sniffled. 'With the door, Marcus. I wouldn't open the door. If I'd let him in, if I'd called the ambulance right away, he might –'

'Oh, Gemma,' Marcus said, and for some reason he was smiling. 'Just take the damn money.'

'I'll need to talk to Hugh about it,' she said. Hugh should be pleased. This kind of money could slice away some of the knots that held them together. It would let them really think about what they wanted, without what they needed getting in the way. But he could be unpredictable.

'If it helps any, you don't have to think of this as something I'm doing for you. Think of it as something I'm doing for Dean. I wish I'd come here a long time ago. If I'd understood, I'd have made this offer years ago. I want him to rest in peace, without ghouls obsessing over every detail of how he died. I should have done more for him when he was alive, but I can do this for him now.'

She pushed herself to her feet and wrapped Marcus in a hug. He startled in her arms, then huffed awkwardly and hugged her back.

'I'd suggest picking up a bottle of champagne, but I noticed you don't keep any alcohol in the house,' he said, just above her left ear.

'You've been looking, have you?' she joked, pulling back from him. She was embarrassed about her impulsive move, but he didn't seem bothered by it.

'It sticks out a bit, because this place clearly used to be a pub. You've got a built-in wine rack in the kitchen with nothing in it.'

'It hasn't been a pub for a long time. Longer than I've been alive, or my father has.'

She didn't have any sobriety chips. But when she was staging the house for a guest, one of the things she'd moved out of public view was a glass jar displaying a lifetime's worth.

'Sorry, I shouldn't have assumed.'

'No, it's fine. You're very observant.'

His smile was sad. 'A survival skill, I'm afraid.'

'My grandmother converted this place to a teashop when she inherited it in the 1950s. She told people she didn't want to run the pub in such a busy town, but really it was because she wanted to marry my grandfather, who was in recovery.'

'Is he the Earl Grey from the shop name?'

'No.' She smiled, relaxing a little. 'Earl was her cat.'

'Ah. Even so, a pub owner's daughter in love with an alcoholic. That's romantic.'

'Yes, well.' She folded her arms. 'It's a lovely story, but the reality of being married to an alcoholic didn't always live up to it. My father grew up with an absolute terror of alcohol, so we've never kept it in the house. There's a genetic component to alcoholism, after all.'

She'd never told anyone this before, other than Hugh, but it was comforting. Marcus was easy to talk to, and it was a little easier opening up to someone who would leave soon and take her secrets with her.

* * *

She texted Hugh about the offer before heading into the ensuite to brush her teeth, and was surprised when he called within minutes.

She spat the toothpaste out and answered.

'I don't want to sell,' he said instead of a proper hello.

'What do you mean?' she asked. 'We've spent years trying to get an offer half this good.'

'*You've* spent years.' His voice had a fuzzy edge to it.

'Have you been drinking?'

'Bit.'

She sighed. 'Let's talk about this when you come home tomorrow. Sober.'

'I don't want to sell,' he repeated. 'And you can't do it without me. My name's on it.'

'I can, actually,' she said quietly. If they divorced, she could force a sale.

He was silent for an achingly long time. She might as well have shouted it.

'What's keeping us here, Hugh? Your family is gone. My family is gone. Violet will be gone before we blink.'

'Rainier is home,' he said. 'I can't abandon my job. I owe Mick for holding it for me.'

'That wasn't him doing you a favour, that was New South Wales Police trying to avoid a compensation claim.' She pinched the bridge of her nose. 'Forget it – we'll talk tomorrow.'

She was going to sleep tonight, properly and deeply, and she didn't want to have a pointless argument while he was drunk and maudlin.

* * *

Gemma hummed as she stirred the porridge the next morning.

'You're cheerful,' Violet said. She dropped heavily into a chair at the kitchen table.

Gemma cut off her humming and leaned against the counter to look at her daughter. She didn't know how Violet was likely to react to the possibility of moving out of here. Maybe out of town altogether. But she also knew that the days of them living together as a family were numbered. Violet was bright and ambitious. She belonged at a big university. Gemma's parents had floated the idea of Violet coming to live with them and attending school on the Gold Coast. Gemma hated the idea, but also knew it was the best option.

That morning she'd woken up early and lay in bed scrolling through Gold Coast real estate listings on her phone. Flats she and Hugh could afford together.

Flats she could afford on her own.

'How did your assignment go?' she asked.

'We got most of the way there,' Violet said. 'It got me wondering, though.'

'That's good,' Gemma said, spooning porridge into a bowl for her.

'Red hair is recessive, right?' Violet asked, twisting a lock of her own red hair around her index finger. 'Which means I need a copy of the gene from both sides.'

'You'd know,' Gemma said. 'Biology was twenty years ago for me.'

Fawn stumbled into the kitchen, yawning, and took the seat beside Violet.

'Well, I know that Granddad has red hair, but where did it come from on Dad's side?'

'Your dad's mother was a redhead,' Gemma said, setting the full bowl in front of Violet. 'She was pleased as punch when you came out with it too.' She ran a hand through Violet's hair.

'She has brown hair in your wedding portrait, though,' Fawn said.

Gemma shot her a sideways look. She had no idea why Fawn would be paying such close attention to their family pictures. 'That was a wig, I'm afraid. She was sick by then and going through chemo. She said all of the red wigs in the store made her look like a clown.'

'Right,' Violet said, sounding sad. 'I'm glad I don't have to worry about that, since she was on Dad's side of the family. Breast cancer risk comes from your mother's side, right?'

'No,' Fawn said. She had gone oddly still. 'The gene can come from either side.'

Gemma paused, wondering if there was something going on in the Nicholls family that she didn't know about yet.

'That's why I want to do one of those DNA tests,' Violet said. 'They can tell you everything you should be looking out for.'

'No way,' Gemma said.

'Why not?'

'Because the fine print on those kits is a mess. You don't want some company having rights to your genetic information.'

'Are you worried one of our relatives will get outed as a serial killer?' Violet asked. 'You know that's how they caught the Golden State Killer: they matched DNA found at the crime scenes to one of his cousins.'

'Violet,' Gemma snapped. 'Don't joke about that – especially with Marcus in the house. How do you think he'd feel if he heard you?'

'Sorry,' Violet mumbled.

Gemma's phone buzzed with a call from Hugh. She shot Violet a 'this conversation is not over' look, and answered.

'Is this Gemma Guillory?' a woman's voice asked.

'Yes,' Gemma said, going cold. Why did a woman have Hugh's phone?

'I'm calling because you're tagged as the emergency contact in this phone.'

'Is Hugh alright?' Gemma asked.

Violet looked up in alarm.

'There's been an accident,' the woman said. 'I was on my way south from Cootamundra when I came across his cruiser.

I've called an ambulance – they're on their way. They're going to take him to the hospital.'

'Can I talk to him?' Gemma asked, putting a reassuring hand on Violet's shoulder.

'I'm sorry, but he's unconscious,' the woman said.

In the background, the wail of sirens drew closer.

* * *

Gemma could only remember snatches of what happened next. She explained what had happened to Violet and pulled her into a panicked hug, smoothing her hands over her daughter's back. She remembered the flannel fabric of Violet's pyjama top underneath her palms, but then moments later they were both dressed and standing in the hallway.

Fawn must have called her father to collect her, because suddenly Dr Nicholls was there, taking charge of the situation.

'Let me drive you to the hospital,' he said.

'Oh, I can't let you do that,' Gemma said. 'It's too far out of your way.'

'We don't need two accidents in one day,' he said gently. 'It's no trouble. I go out there a couple of times a week anyway, to visit my patients.'

And then they were at the door of the hospital. 'Maybe I should go in first,' she suggested. She didn't know what they were going to find, what kind of condition Hugh was in.

Violet looked uncertain. 'I want to see Dad,' she said, sounding terribly young.

Gemma's heart ached, but she couldn't let Violet walk in unprepared. 'I'll call you if he's awake, okay?'

'Why don't I take you two girls to the cafe for a bit,' Dr Nicholls cut in. 'We can get a slice of cake while we're waiting.'

* * *

Hugh was in the acute trauma ward, which ramped up Gemma's anxiety. The hospital was frequently overloaded, and she'd heard horror stories of patients left waiting in ambulances outside, so it worried her that he'd been admitted so quickly. How critical did he need to be to fly through in the forty-five minutes it took them to drive from Rainier?

A woman about her age in scrubs, a mask and a face shield met her in the hallway and introduced herself as Dr Ahmad. With only her eyes visible Gemma couldn't read anything in her expression, but her stance was relaxed.

'He received a serious blow to the head, and we're going to take him for an MRI as soon as possible, but his early signs seem good. He's also fractured his left arm, and we're waiting for an orthopaedic consult, but I don't think it's going to require surgery.'

'He's not going to die?' Gemma sagged at the knees with relief, and Dr Ahmad reached out a hand to support her.

'We don't know everything yet, but he's stable.'

'What happened?'

'My understanding is that he ran off the road and hit a tree. There's no sign of any other vehicles involved, and no-one else was hurt.'

Gemma closed her eyes. He'd been drinking the night before. Had it still been in his system when he started to drive home to Rainier? Or perhaps he'd been fatigued, too upset by their conversation or what happened in his interview with the Ripper to sleep.

'How has Hugh's general health been recently? Have you had any concerns about his mental health or mood?'

Gemma wondered if her thoughts had been written all over her face. 'Why do you ask?'

'It's something we have to consider, with a single-car accident – particularly given your husband's admission history.'

'Right.' Was it possible? 'He was stressed and on edge when I saw him yesterday morning, but he hasn't made any threats to hurt himself or showed any suicidal ideation.' She couldn't help noticing how easily the terms rolled off her tongue.

Dr Ahmad nodded. 'I'll schedule a psych consult before he's discharged, just to be safe. I can take you to see him, but he's been given pain relief so he might be asleep.'

* * *

She'd been braced for Hugh to look horrific, but was most struck by how vulnerable he looked in the bed. He'd always been a big man, tall and broad, but he looked small between the metal rails. His head was bandaged, and Gemma had to look away from the streaks of iodine creeping out from underneath. It was too unsettling.

His eyes were closed, but he must have only been dozing lightly because within a few moments of her arrival they blinked open.

'Gemma Grey?' he asked, his voice hoarse.

'I haven't heard that name in a long time,' she said. She remembered an old video that had gone viral of a man waking up from sedation and 'meeting' his own wife, overjoyed at how wonderful she was. She and Hugh were well past that sort of moment.

'You've been in an accident, Hugh,' she said. 'But you're going to be okay.'

'Please don't call my father,' he said.

She wondered where he was in time. 'You're not in any trouble.'

He laughed. 'I definitely am.'

'You don't need to worry about anything. I'm going to call Mick and make sure your leave is sorted.'

'No!' he said.

Anger flared so intensely within her that she couldn't look at him. She pressed her face into her hands, reminding herself that he was doped to the gills and couldn't be held responsible for anything he said. But she was so sick of this. She was so sick of trying to hold the edges of their life together while he stubbornly refused to help at all.

'I'm sorry,' he said, and tried to reach out with his good arm. She batted his hand away, and his face crumpled. 'I'm sorry,' he said again. 'I thought I could fix everything but I just keep making it worse.'

'Fix what?' she snapped.

'The baby,' he said.

'The baby? She's practically an adult,' she said, mystified.

'I know,' he said. 'I'm sorry. I love you. I'm sorry I've fucked everything up.'

She opened her mouth to tell him that she loved him too, but she couldn't make the words come. 'Get some sleep,' she said instead.

* * *

There was a sign on the door of the hospital chapel advising that it was closed, but Gemma went inside anyway. Let security throw her out if they must.

She sat on the floor, her back to the wall. She wasn't sure if she wanted to cry, or scream, or sleep.

What she wanted, desperately, was to understand. There was some piece of the puzzle of her life that had got lost. She understood the forces that had brought them here – the Ripper murders, the debt, their daughter, Hugh's job, their faltering connection. But every step of the way Hugh seemed to be fighting against her, not with her. He wouldn't take the space away from his career that he needed. He didn't want to sell their home and clear their debts.

He loved her? Quite frankly, that was news to her.

'Mum?' Violet sounded scared.

Gemma looked up, surprised. 'Hey. How'd you know I was here?'

Violet held up her phone. 'You've got your location shared, remember?'

'Oh.' They'd put that on so they could track down Violet if needed. She hadn't realised it worked both ways.

She stood up, glad that she hadn't actually melted into a crying heap like she'd thought she might. But judging by Violet's face, she still looked pretty dire.

'Dad's going to be fine,' she said. 'A couple of bad knocks, and he'll need some help for a while as he recovers, that's all.'

Violet sighed with relief. 'When your dot showed up in here, I thought . . .'

'I'm sorry, honey. I didn't mean to scare you.'

Gemma shifted to one of the plastic chairs that served as pews, and Violet sat beside her.

'Where are Dr Nicholls and Fawn?'

'I told them I was okay to find you on my own, so Dr Nicholls has gone to see his patients. He wanted Fawn to go with him. He's trying to convince her to go into medicine.' She took a deep breath. 'Are you sure Dad is going to be okay?'

'Yes,' Gemma said. She was sure, at least, that he wasn't in immediate danger. Whether he would be okay was a much more complicated question. 'Do you want to see him now?'

'Can we maybe sit for a few more minutes?' Violet clasped her hands together in her lap. 'You know this is the first time it's just been the two of us since before the murder?'

'Oh, sweetheart, I'm sorry,' Gemma said. 'I thought having your friends around would help.'

'No, I've liked that part,' Violet said. 'But these past couple of days, it's like you've been afraid to be in the house.'

Tears burned in Gemma's eyes. She bit back the urge to

apologise again. 'I know. It's brought up a lot of stuff for me. And for Dad. We've been trying our best, but it's hard.'

'Can I ask you a question?' Violet asked.

'You can try. I don't feel like I have many answers lately.' She regretted it as soon as the words were out. She was the mother; it was her job to keep her shit together.

'Was I conceived the night Dean Shadwell died?'

Gemma stared at her. 'Why on earth would you ask that?'

Violet grasped the hem of her shirt, and twisted it. 'Just something Marcus said. We were chatting about astrology and when I mentioned my star sign he asked for my birthday, then did the maths.'

Rage washed over Gemma. 'He did what? When? I'll ask him to leave.'

'Yesterday. He wasn't being a creep,' Violet said. 'He cracked a joke, something about "one in, one out". Seriously, it rivalled some of Dad's worst attempts at humour.'

'Even so, that's not appropriate.'

Violet shrugged. 'I mean, I know it's not that precise. But it must have been around that time, right?'

'Do you really want to know about this?' Gemma asked. 'When I was your age this was the last topic I wanted to hear about from my parents.'

'I don't know,' Violet admitted. 'I guess it got me thinking. You guys don't talk much about how you met, or the early days of your relationship.'

'We don't remember meeting,' Gemma said. 'You know what Rainier's like, I was probably in a pram at the time.'

'But you weren't close growing up,' Violet pressed. 'Not like you and Aubrey and Jac's dad.'

'Yeah, your dad was older, so we ran in different circles.' Gemma sighed. 'It wasn't that night.'

'Okay.' Violet looked down at her hands. Gemma was struck by how much her profile looked like Gemma's own. They had the same nose, the same mouth, the same chin. She couldn't believe how quickly Violet had grown, how close she was now to the age Gemma had been when she was thrust abruptly into full adulthood.

'It was the next day,' she said softly. 'I spent all night at the police station, and then your dad took me home in the morning.'

They were quiet for a long time. Violet reached over and took Gemma's hand. 'Was it consensual?'

'Jesus Christ,' Gemma yelped, before she could stop herself. 'Of course. How could you think it wasn't?'

She wondered how long Violet had been silently carrying that question around. What had she done to make her daughter think that?

'Sometimes . . .' Violet said, her voice catching. 'Sometimes it feels like you see Dad and me as just another thing the Ripper did to you.'

'Oh, Violet, no.' Now the tears came. She used one hand to wipe her eyes, keeping a tight hold of Violet with the other. Violet put her head against her shoulder, and Gemma kissed her hair. 'I had a choice, I promise you. I chose you. I'm so sorry I let you think otherwise.'

Violet exhaled, her shoulders shaking. Gemma had thought that Violet was the only one of them who was doing okay, but she could see it now. They had given her an edited version, years of talking around painful facts, and she had filled in the gaps with her own, much worse version.

'It's not a particularly romantic story, I'm sorry. When your father drove me home, there was no-one else around. Your grandparents were with my grandmother in the hospital, and they hadn't been notified yet. I didn't want to be alone in the house, so I asked him to come in with me. I came on to him.'

'He shouldn't have, though. You must have been so vulnerable.'

'So was he,' Gemma said. 'It was a bad idea between two people who weren't in a place to think straight. He was –' She broke off.

'Tell me.'

'He was always a really sweet guy, you know? Then he went into the police, and almost straight away he was on the front line of a horrific serial murder case. He wasn't some seasoned cop with iron skin; he was just a kid who wanted to help people. He had to escort Jaylene and Antoine to identify Vincent's body. He tried to keep Dean Shadwell alive with his bare hands. He made a mistake, and then six weeks later I was on his doorstep with a home pregnancy test in my hands. *But*' – Gemma rushed the word out before Violet could get the wrong idea – 'he was all in. Immediately.'

'Were you?'

Gemma took a deep breath. Full honesty. 'Dr Nicholls talked through the options with me. He offered to refer me for a termination if that was what I wanted. He also told me they had been working with an adoption agency until Lotte finally fell pregnant with Fawn, and could introduce me to them. But when I pictured it, pictured having a tiny soft baby in my arms and then handing her over, I knew I didn't want that. I wanted that baby. I wanted you.'

'Then why?' Violet wiped at her eyes with a sleeve. 'Why are you so angry at Dad all the time?'

'Am I?' It rocked Gemma that Violet saw it that way.

'Yes!'

Gemma sighed. 'When we tell you that having a newborn is shatteringly hard, we're not just trying to scare you off sex. It really is. We didn't sleep for three months straight. I think I took a total of four showers in the first six weeks. And it was somehow even harder for your dad. He would come to bed, and then ten minutes later would get up again to check the front door was locked. He would do that three, four times. One night I woke up to the sound of you crying, and when I went into your room he was there, standing by the cot, just watching you cry.'

'Grandma died right after I was born, right? That must have been hard.'

'Yeah, but' – Gemma squeezed Violet closer – 'when you were four months old, you went through a rough patch where you stopped sleeping. And one day your dad left for work and just never came back.'

'He left?'

'He left. At first I assumed he'd just been caught up and was doing some overtime. I texted. I called. Finally I packed you into a pram and walked down to the station. Mick was shocked to see us, because your dad had put in for a leave of absence days earlier.'

'Wow.' Violet pulled her feet up onto the seat and hugged her knees.

'I went to see your grandpa, but Eric wouldn't tell me where your dad was. He just begged me to be patient. Your grandparents were furious, though. They'd wanted to move out of Rainier for months. There was something of an exodus in the year following the murders. They convinced me to come with them, and the four of us moved to a two-bedroom unit in Wagga.'

'What happened to the teashop?'

'It had been closed since Dean's death. My grandmother owned it, but she had gone into a nursing home. We just left it locked up.'

'How long was Dad gone for?'

Gemma twisted her wedding ring with her finger and thumb. Once Violet knew this, there was no going back. She thought about asking her to wait until Hugh was well enough to tell her himself, but that would be an answer in itself. 'A year, sweetheart. He was gone for a year.'

Gemma rubbed Violet's arm, giving her as long as she needed to process that.

'A few months after your first birthday, your dad reached out. Obviously I told him to piss off. But he kept coming back, and finally I heard him out. He'd had a breakdown and had been in inpatient care. After he was released from the hospital, he convinced himself that he should just leave us alone. But he missed you so desperately, and wanted to make amends and try again.'

'But why did you take him back, if you weren't actually going to forgive him?'

Gemma sighed. 'It's not that simple. And I have forgiven him for leaving. He wasn't well; I can't hold that against him. But we didn't just get back together. We came back to Rainier.'

'Why?'

'I've been trying to figure that out for fifteen years,' Gemma said. 'Sorry. Your great-grandma passed away while we were still figuring out our way forward. We found out that she had substantial debts. She borrowed against the teashop and the house to pay for her end-of-life care, because she didn't want to be a burden on us. The idea is that the borrower doesn't have to make payments during their life, but the bank will sell the property to repay the loan with interest after their death. The interest had been compounding for ten years, and the building had been the site of an infamous murder only two years earlier. It was my mother who stood to actually inherit the situation, but she wanted to just walk away, let the bank take the building.'

'But you didn't want that.'

'At the time the only thing I wanted was a good night's sleep. But your father was convinced it was the universe aligning.

He offered to take out a new mortgage to clear the debt and buy the building from my mother.'

'That sounds like the opposite of a fresh start,' Violet said.

'Well, we'd both been away from Rainier for a year and were still hurting. He thought that the only way forward was to go back. Lash ourselves to the mast and face the storm.' Gemma sighed. 'At the time, we thought if it didn't work out we would just sell up. But then the town was bypassed, and the local real estate market crashed. We were trapped.'

'That doesn't sound like Dad's fault,' Violet said.

'You're right,' Gemma said. 'Feelings aren't always fair.'

She didn't really know how to express fifteen years of feeling brushed off and dismissed any time she hinted, or even outright told him, that she would be happier away from Rainier. Or the creeping feeling that there was more to his refusal than she could understand.

TWENTY-ONE

LANE SHIFTED HIS weight from side to side as he waited for the call to connect. Like anything else he did in prison, getting here had taken a long time and a ream of paperwork.

To make an outgoing phone call, it had to be on his list of approved numbers. Lane was entitled to ten personal phone numbers and three legal numbers. He'd only had two personal numbers registered for his first three years inside – Lynnie's mobile and her work number.

He put through the form requesting eight new numbers. He'd spent the night back in his cell, then had gone straight to the library to trawl through the collection of phone books to find seven contact numbers for cafes and bakeries up and down south-eastern New South Wales, and hidden Earl Grey's Yarn and Teashop among them. He claimed on the form that he wanted the numbers to request informational interviews, because he was considering a post-release career in hospitality.

Frankly he'd expected the request to be refused, and had told himself that he would drop the whole idea once it was. But he'd woken up on Wednesday morning to find it approved, not even twenty-four hours later, which was light speed by prison standards.

Lane wondered if Carver had told his employees to quickly wave through any requests Lane made. Maybe he should ask for more things before Carver remembered to cancel that order.

'Gemma Guillory speaking.'

Lane listed to one side as he abruptly stopped his fidgeting. That was the same family name as the police officer he'd watched Jan torment. 'I'm sorry, I was trying to reach Earl Grey's. Are you any relation to Sergeant Hugh Guillory?'

Lane held his breath. If a guard was monitoring the exchange, as they were supposed to, that could be enough to make them cut the call off. Nothing happened.

'I'm his wife. Is this about his accident?' Gemma's voice took on a panicked edge.

Lane's plan for the conversation was rapidly falling apart. He'd gone from a shot-in-the-dark cold call to talking to the wife of a lead investigator. One who had apparently had an accident? 'No, I'm not calling about Hugh. I didn't realise he owned the teashop.'

'I own the teashop,' Gemma said. 'What is this? Who are you?'

'My name is Lane Holland. I'm a private investigator, and my client has asked me to try to find out the real identity of Eva Nováková.'

If it wasn't for a slight crackle on the line, Lane would have assumed that Gemma had hung up

Finally she sighed and asked, 'Are you aware that at the start of this call they played a recording asking me if I was willing to accept a call from the Special Purpose Centre? I know what that is.'

'I'm calling from the prison, yes. But I am a private investigator. I have access to Jan Henning-Klosner, and I think I'm close to getting him to identify Eva. I just need more leverage.'

'Mr Holland, are you a prisoner?'

Lane had to accept he'd lost that one. The word game he'd been playing had been a long shot.

'Yes. But I'm not lying to you. Before I was in here I worked as a private investigator. You might even have heard of me. I have a degree in criminology, and I really am trying to solve this case.'

'Oh shit.'

Either Gemma had looked him up while he spoke, or she had just remembered where she had heard his name before.

'You shot your father,' she said.

Lane hadn't, actually, but that didn't matter. All that mattered was this: Gemma hadn't hung up. 'It seemed like a good idea at the time.'

'Why are you calling me, Mr Holland?'

'Please call me Lane.' He took a deep breath. 'I'll be

completely honest with you, Mrs Guillory. I'm calling because your number is the only one I have. I'm hoping you can connect me to someone. I want to talk to Tamara Fleischer.'

'Why?' She didn't reciprocate with permission to use her first name, he noticed.

'Jan is in the medical unit. I don't know how much time he has left, but it's close enough that I'm willing to take desperate measures. I think Jan genuinely cares about Tamara's opinion of him, and she could get him to talk.'

'I don't have Tamara's phone number,' Gemma said.

She left a silence hanging that screamed there was an unspoken 'but'.

'I've read a couple of Tamara's articles,' he said. 'I know she cares about Eva. I think if she agreed to a restorative justice meeting with Jan, she might be able to persuade him to give up Eva's real name.'

'You keep calling the Ripper by his first name,' Gemma said. 'Are you friends or something?'

'We're not friends,' he said quickly. 'But we've spoken enough for me to get in the habit. I have to call him by name; he's not going to open up to someone holding him at arm's length.'

Lane shuddered to think how much Gemma's long silences were costing him. He might be able to get Carver to clear the charge off his phone account, but not if nothing came of it. Not when Carver had told him to drop it.

'What's that like?' she asked quietly.

'Unsettling,' he admitted. 'But sometimes I get caught up in chatting. Then I realise I've been nattering away with the Rainier Ripper like he's just another guy, and it's even more unsettling.'

'I had a run-in with him,' Gemma said. 'When I was nineteen. I was in the shop when Dean Shadwell came looking for help. I didn't see the Ripper, but he must have been nearby.'

'Ah,' Lane said. 'He mentioned you in his confession.'

'I've never read it.'

'He said he didn't mean to frighten you.'

'How considerate,' she said. 'Look, with Tamara – I don't think it's a good idea. I didn't even see him and the man terrifies me. She was actually attacked by him. He would have killed her.'

'He told me he wasn't planning to kill her.'

'And you believe that?'

'Honestly? Yes. But even if it's a lie, that's what he would tell her if they had a meeting. Do you think that would help her?'

'I don't know. I just think it's inappropriate. I'm sorry, but I can't talk to her for you.'

'I understand.' He held back a sigh. If she felt that way about Tamara, there was no use asking about anyone connected to Vincent Tjibaou. He racked his brains, trying to come up with something else before she ended the call.

'Thank you,' she said, sounding genuinely surprised that he hadn't kept pushing. 'Even if I can't help, I'm glad you're working on this. You pushing on Eva from your side, while Mick and Hugh try to solve this new murder from their side, I think it's best for everyone.'

'I'm sorry I can't help more with that,' Lane said. Mostly he was sorry for himself, at having a case just out of reach. The idea of going back to his cell and his cleaning shifts and the slow day-by-day countdown was crushing.

'What would you do, if you could?'

'What?'

'If you were out here, in your old life, a private investigator trying to solve Lochlan Lewis's murder. Where would you start?'

'I'm not out there. If I was, I would leave the investigation to the police. They have resources I can't even dream of. I would focus on the cold case, Eva Nováková.'

Gemma chuckled. 'That's a very self-interested answer.'

'I suppose it is. Maybe I'm biased. Look, if you really want to know where I would start, it's with the classics. Means, motive and opportunity.'

'What's the means?'

'Basically, who was capable of it, both physically and mentally. If you have the weapon, you want to know who had access to it.'

'Unfortunately that's just about everyone,' Gemma said with a sigh. 'The murder weapon was a stolen knife. I've been trying to figure out who might have taken it, and I'm getting nowhere.'

'Why you, Gemma?'

'Because I want this solved before it destroys everyone I love. More than it already has, I mean.'

'Do you think the killer could be someone you know?'

'I don't know. I don't want to think it's possible. But it is.'

'Then it sounds like you're uniquely placed to work out the motive.'

'I've been trying,' Gemma said, her voice cracking. 'But everyone has a motive. They didn't want that damn tour going ahead. But the people who were angriest about the tour are the kind of people I could never imagine being capable of slashing someone's throat.'

'Ah,' Lane said. 'A throat wound is a particularly vicious attack. We're so vulnerable there. It's really second only to attacking someone's face, and takes an intense hatred.'

'The thing is, Vincent Tjibaou was murdered that way. And his family wouldn't re-enact his murder, no matter how angry they were. It would kill them to disrespect Vincent's memory.'

'Are you sure?' he asked gently. 'Maybe from their perspective, Lochlan was disrespecting Vincent's memory, and it felt like poetic justice.'

Her only reply was a sharp intake of breath, and he worried that he'd gone too far.

'Is anger at Lewis's disrespect for the dead the only possible motive, though?' he added. 'What if someone doesn't want the extra attention on the case the tour would bring? Someone who doesn't want any extra scrutiny on the original case?'

'If they wanted to avoid scrutiny, they made a big mistake.'

'I'm just throwing out ideas. Think on it.'

'Thank you. I'm sorry I couldn't help you more.'

'Maybe you can. Did you ever meet a woman by the name of Matilda Carver around the time of the original murders?

You'd have been around the same age,' he said remembering that Gemma had said she was nineteen at the time.

'There's no Carver family in Rainier,' she said. 'I can't say I remember meeting someone called that. I went to school with a Matilda Nguyen. But she's Matilda Dillon now, not Carver.'

'Nguyen?' he repeated. 'Is she Vietnamese?'

'Yep.'

'Not her, then.' Of course, the fact Matilda Nguyen went to school in Rainier already ruled her out.

'Why are you asking this?'

'I'm trying to trace a possible match for Eva Nováková. The Rainier police ruled out Matilda Carver, but no-one seems to know why.'

'I'm sorry, Hugh never talks to me about the details of his work.'

'Do you think you could ask him?'

There was a long pause, so he added, 'Matilda's family haven't heard from her in nearly eighteen years. They love her, and not knowing what happened to her causes them a lot of pain.'

'I'm sorry,' Gemma said. 'I'll do what I can, but I don't know how much I can help you.'

'Thank you,' Lane said. He could only hope he hadn't thrown away his call on a dead end.

TWENTY-TWO

GEMMA STARED AT her phone. When she'd heard the message asking if she was willing to accept a call from the Special Purpose Centre, she'd gone into her bedroom and closed the door, assuming the call had something to do with Hugh's accident. Maybe an occupational health and safety officer investigating the accident as an incident relating to the prison.

She hadn't expected *that*.

She felt awful for the family of the missing woman this Lane Holland was looking for. It was hard not to picture them like her own parents, or Vincent's.

Maybe she could ask Tamara. She might have met Matilda at the service centre, or even encountered her later through her work with the Sex Workers Alliance. Maybe Gemma could ask Ruth, too, since she had worked as a cashier at the service centre around that time. She'd have seen everyone coming and going. But Gemma didn't think she could bring it up with Hugh, not in his condition.

The man had made a good point, though. Maybe she had been too focused on the idea that the tour was the killer's motive. Maybe everyone had been.

She went into the bedroom, where her phone was on the charger. She opened a web browser, and plugged in *Lochlan Lewis*.

The first results were news articles, most of which were the same couple of paragraphs cut up and rearranged. Maybe Jac was right, and they were just pulling from the police press releases verbatim.

She found the website for the tour company, although the header still identified it as Lochlan Lewis Tours. The site was basic – a few promotional photos of Lochlan leading groups, gesturing up at a sandstone building with bright eyes, and some quotes from travel articles about the tours. There was a booking form, but all future dates had been greyed out.

She scrolled back through the months, and found she could see the tour dates that had previously been available to book. She clicked on one in June. An error message at the top said *CANNOT BOOK – DATE MUST BE IN FUTURE*, but she could still read the details. A three-hour Razor Gangs walking tour in The Rocks, Sydney, led by Lochlan Lewis.

She clicked through the rest from that month, and noticed that while there were a few different tours running, two details remained the same – they were all in Sydney, and they were all led by Lochlan himself.

Hadn't he pitched the company to them as a thriving multi-city enterprise that employed students as tour guides? Where were the Melbourne tours?

She found them eventually, six months back on the calendar. When Melbourne dates started to pop up, the Sydney dates disappeared. Six months back again, and it became a pattern – Melbourne tours disappeared, and all events were located in Adelaide. No tour was ever listed as being led by someone other than Lochlan.

Lochlan wasn't running a business that was operating in two major cities. He'd changed cities every six months.

She went back to the original search results, and found a Facebook page for Lochlan Lewis Tours. Commenters had turned it into a de facto memorial page. She scrolled past condolences, offers of prayers and pictures of roses. She paused when she noticed one post that had attracted a number of angry reactions.

Hi. Does anyone know who to contact about refunds?

The first response looked like it was from a member of the public, not an admin. *The dude just died. I'm sure they'll sort out getting people's $20 back when they're done with little details like the funeral and murder investigation.*

An admin named John Smith had responded: *Lochlan, may he rest in peace, had no tours scheduled at the time of his death. He had taken some time off to work on the Rainier tour proposal. There are no bookings to refund.*

The original poster replied: *This wasn't for a future tour, it was for the seven-day Footsteps of the Kelly Gang hike that was supposed to happen in 2020. Full sympathy for them having to cancel, but we were still emailing back and forth with Lochlan up until his death. I'm sorry for your loss, but we're not talking about a small amount of money here – our group was chasing a couple of grand.*

John Smith hadn't responded, although the comment was less than a day old. Gemma opened the admin's profile but didn't find much. No other group memberships, no public posts, no picture. It was probably the alias of an employee, or maybe even a sock puppet for Lochlan himself, now being run by a relative.

The sound of the doorbell made her jump. She was so sick of lurching like a spooked cat at the slightest noise.

It was a uniformed policewoman, one Gemma didn't know. Gemma's first thought was that Hugh must have died. Her second thought was that she should probably feel more than a numb resignation at the possibility.

'Good morning, I'm Probationary Constable Panipak Seesondee. Are you Gemma Guillory?'

'That's me. Is this about Hugh?'

The officer shook her head. 'No, ma'am. Detective Seabrooke would like you to come down to the station. He just has some follow-up questions.'

'Of course.' Gemma didn't have the energy to ask herself if her relief was because Hugh was alive, or just because she didn't have to deal with her feelings about his death.

* * *

The furniture in the police station had been rearranged, she assumed to accommodate the sudden influx of loaned officers and activity. The reception area now had a row of plastic seats for visitors to wait on, and just past it in the main room Hugh and Mick's desks had been joined by several more, some pushed at odd angles to make them fit. Panipak asked Gemma to take a seat, and disappeared into the back to let Mick know she'd arrived.

Jac was standing at the reception desk, unloading takeaway coffees from a cardboard carrier.

'Is somewhere open for takeaway again?' Gemma asked them.

'Yeah. Mick gave Christian the green light to open up the pub.' Jac held up a cup and showed Gemma Christian's scrawl on the side. 'Do you think this says soy?'

Gemma squinted. 'Christian should have been a doctor with that handwriting.'

Jac laughed. 'Oh well, this is all going to taste like swamp water anyway. It's a pub, not a coffee shop.'

'How did you end up on coffee duty?'

'Mick offered me some extra cash to help out while they're under the pump. Especially with Hugh injured. How's he doing?' Jac looked abashed for having forgotten to ask right away.

'He'll be fine soon. Is Mick allowed to do that?'

Jac shrugged. 'If anyone asks, I'm the work experience kid. I think it's more about managing Mum's anxiety than me being an actual help. She feels safer with me at the station. She drops in with the kids eight times a day to "say hi".'

'Huh. Do you have access to the file room?' Then Gemma's brain caught up with her mouth, and she realised what she was asking, and who. She held up a hand. 'Ignore me.'

'What are you after?'

'I'm looking for information on Matilda Carver, a possible Eva Nováková match. I'm sorry for the inappropriate question – obviously I'd never ask you to do something unethical for me.'

'Is this for Fawn's art project?'

'Yeah,' Gemma lied.

'She's so obsessed,' Jac said, chuckling.

'Gemma,' Mick called, overly loud and cheerful. 'Thanks for coming in. Come on through.' He reached over and took two of the coffees from the desk, and once again gestured for her to follow him to the interview room.

'I ordered you a basic flat white, since I knew you'd be coming in,' Mick said, putting it in front of her on the table. 'I didn't want to hold Jac up waiting for your order. Hope that's okay.'

'Sure,' Gemma said, although it made something tilt oddly inside her that he had planned for her arrival. 'Jac mentioned that the pub is open again. If you've reduced the size of the crime scene, are we able to access our downstairs again?'

'We did agree to reopen that part of the street to foot traffic,' Mick said. 'I suppose I can disclose this to you, since you were present when Mr Tanner found the item we believe was discarded by the killer. That find means we now have a good picture of the killer's movements and can shrink the perimeter.'

'So is that a yes?'

She was surprised by how annoyed Mick looked by a reasonable question. 'You've been married to Hugh for long enough to know a fair bit about how the crime scene rules work, right?'

'Unfortunately I had to learn the rules well before that.'

Mick's face softened a fraction. 'Sorry, of course. You know that the time we can maintain a crime scene without the building owner's permission is counted in hours, not the days you've generously allowed us. We haven't sought a court order because you've chosen to give us permission.'

'Sure, but does my shop need to remain a crime scene or not?' Nerves were beginning to coil in Gemma's stomach. 'The killer didn't come anywhere near it.'

'As I said, you could insist that we get a court order. But you would need to consider how it would look, if you chose to stop cooperating.'

Gemma couldn't believe what she was hearing. 'Am I a suspect?'

'I just need to ask you a few questions about some new information that's come to light. I'm sure we'll get it all cleared up like that.' He snapped his fingers.

He took his time setting up the interview recording equipment, leaving Gemma stewing.

'Marcus Shadwell. Is he still staying in your home?'

'Yes, he extended his stay for a couple of days.'

'When was the first time you had any communication with Mr Shadwell?'

Gemma frowned. 'When I got a message from him booking the room, although I think the website generates the text for you, and he just hit send. I first talked to him in person in the teashop, on Saturday evening.'

'What about Mark Herald? Have you had any contact with someone by that name?'

'Mark Herald is Marcus. He booked the room under that name.'

'Hmmm.' Mick wrote something down. 'What about prior to Dean Shadwell's death? Did you have any contact with him?'

'With Dean? No.'

'No, with Marcus.'

'No.'

'Or perhaps at the trial? Did you ever speak to Marcus then?'

'No. I was barely aware of his existence before the tour. What's this about?'

Mick flipped open a binder on the table. Inside was a printed photograph. It was fuzzy, just run off an ordinary desktop printer, but it was clear enough.

It showed Marcus and Gemma standing on her back landing, arms wrapped around one another.

Terror raced through her. 'Who took this?'

Someone had been watching her. Had they been there every time the hairs prickled on the back of her neck?

'It was dropped off anonymously. An unmarked envelope in the station letterbox.'

She stared down at the picture. 'This is completely out of context,' she said. 'You've known me for years, Mick. You know I wouldn't.'

Mick sighed. 'I've known Hugh for years as well. Long enough to know a few things. Like that his marriage isn't so crash hot. I've heard it from Aubs as well.'

'I don't talk to Aubrey about my marriage,' Gemma said.

Maybe Aubrey had heard it from Hugh. Could that be why the conversation she saw them having had seemed so weird?

'Well, maybe you should,' he said. 'What somebody isn't saying can speak just as loud.'

'I am not seeing Marcus Shadwell,' she said, enunciating each word carefully. 'Yes, I hugged him. He made an offer on our house, and I was excited. If I was shagging him, don't you think I would be more careful about being spotted?'

'He made an offer on your house?' Mick asked. 'Why?'

'He was worried about who else we might sell to,' Gemma said.

Mick looked dubious. 'I'm going to say this once, and I want you to think hard about it, okay? If you and Marcus are in a relationship' – he put up a hand to stop her immediate objection – 'I said *if* you are in a relationship, then evidence of that will come out. Your statement that Marcus was with you at the time of the murder may not hold up. If he was gone for longer than you said he was, even by a few minutes, you need to come clean now. New evidence has come to light suggesting it would

228

have been possible for the murderer to kill Lochlan, clean up and then return looking relatively normal within a short time span. If he was gone for ten, fifteen minutes, then I need to know.'

'It was two minutes. Three tops.'

The plastic thing the police pulled out of the storm drain. Gemma realised now where she recognised it from. It was one of the clear plastic ponchos they sold in the supermarket. They were cheap, easy to grab and stash in your glove box or purse for emergencies. The killer could have pulled one on, murdered Lochlan, then thrown it down the stormwater drain and walked away without a drop of blood on them.

Her hands were shaking. She pressed them flat on the table to make it stop.

Mick nodded, looking serious. 'We've managed to pull a good print. If you tell me now that you lied for him, I won't pursue you for it. But if that print comes back as a match for Marcus, you'll cop an obstruction of justice charge at best. Last chance, Gemma.'

'Marcus has an injured hand,' Gemma said. 'Do you need all ten prints to clear him?' She didn't want to have to wait until Marcus had healed. She didn't want this hanging over her head.

'Shadwell's prints are in the database,' Mick said. 'Old mischief charge from when he was at university.'

Gemma nodded, relieved. 'Am I free to go?'

'You always have been. But my offer is gone as soon as you leave this room.'

* * *

Gemma was relieved to find Violet alone at the kitchen table when she arrived home. After her exchange with Mick, she wasn't up for a conversation with Marcus.

'Did Marcus go out?' she asked.

'I think he's in his room getting some work done,' Violet said.

Gemma needed to start prepping food for the memorial service. She wiped down the counter with sanitiser, then pulled on a pair of gloves.

'Want some help?' Violet asked.

'I can't pay you for the time,' Gemma warned.

'That's fine,' Violet said, stepping up to the sink to wash her hands.

Gemma pulled a carton of kiwifruit from the pantry and started peeling the fuzzy skin away before sliding them over to Violet to be diced. 'I've been thinking,' she said. 'Maybe you should spend the rest of the school holidays up in Queensland. Your grandparents would be thrilled to have you.'

Violet made a face. 'Mum, I've got so much homework to do. I'd feel really bad going up to visit and then ignoring them the whole time.'

'They wouldn't mind,' Gemma argued, although they probably would. 'I'd just feel better knowing you were away from all this.'

Violet stopped chopping. 'Why? I've been fine.'

Gemma's first instinct was to lie to her, but she remembered how trying to hide things from her daughter had only led to her inventing a worse version in her head. 'The police have a picture of me that someone took and sent to them.'

'What kind of picture?'

'A perfectly innocent picture of me and Marcus that they've taken out of context. But it means that someone was watching me. Watching this house. And that scares me.'

Violet stared down at her knife, thinking. 'We should both go, then.'

'I can't just run off,' Gemma said. That would make her look even more guilty. 'Your dad is going to need help when he's discharged.'

'If it's safe enough for you, it's safe enough for me,' Violet said.

They had finished the kiwifruit and were halfway through chopping up a bag of oranges when the doorbell rang. When this was all over Gemma was going to rip that thing out of the wall. The sound was indelibly linked with this awful week.

Jac stood on their back verandah, ashen-faced.

'Is Violet home?' they asked.

'In the kitchen,' Gemma said, stepping aside to let them come through. 'Has something happened, sweetheart?'

'With Hugh in the hospital, the Homicide Squad sent some new detectives to help with the case,' Jac said.

'I've been hoping they would do that,' Gemma said.

Jac shook their head. 'I'm not allowed at the station anymore. Because it's a "conflict of interest".' They made quotation marks in the air with their fingers. 'They've brought Pépère in for questioning again. Apparently they found one of his fingerprints at the fountain. Of course they did – he prays there more often than he does at church.'

They looked on the edge of tears. Violet wrapped her arms around them. 'It'll be okay, Jac.'

'You can't know that,' Jac said into her shoulder. 'He has no alibi. He has what they see as a motive. He's strong enough to hold Lochlan down.'

'What do you mean, strong enough?' Violet asked, frowning.

Jac groaned. 'Ugh, I shouldn't have told you that. I overheard two of the new cops talking about the medical examiner's report. The cause of death wasn't the injury to Lochlan's throat. The killer suffocated him by covering his mouth and nose.' They mimicked pinching their nose closed, like a swimmer about to duck under, and pressed their palm over their mouth.

'Like Burke and Hare?' Violet asked. 'The body-snatchers?'

'Violet,' Gemma scolded. She understood why Jac was upset, but she thought that making them leave the station was the only smart decision any adult had made all week.

'Yes,' Jac said. 'It's called "burking", after them. It's quick and quiet, but you have to be pretty strong to stop the victim fighting you off. Like, say, a weightlifter.'

'He didn't do it, though,' Violet said.

Jac laughed. 'You think they're going to care, if the pieces are a close enough fit? You think someone like my pépère will be treated fairly?'

Gemma wanted to tell them they were wrong, but she knew it wouldn't offer any reassurance. Jac deserved better than a shallow dismissal. 'Why don't you kids sit down. I'll make some tea.'

'Thank you,' Jac said. They'd managed to fight back the tears, and seemed calmer, which made Gemma oddly sad. She hoped they weren't afraid to cry in front of her.

'I've got something for you,' they said, taking a folded piece of paper from their shirt pocket and putting it on the table. 'A little souvenir I picked up on my way out.'

Gemma unfolded it, half-expecting to see another incriminating picture, or maybe a hint about who had dobbed her in. Her earlier request had slipped her mind, until she saw that it was a photocopied file note about Matilda Carver.

TWENTY-THREE

LANE WAS CHEWING through a cheese sandwich, biting and swallowing without tasting, when a guard rapped on the door to his cell and announced the governor wanted to see him.

Carver's own dinner was on his desk, minestrone soup in a plastic tub. It smelled ten times better than any food Lane had encountered in years.

'You got an interesting email this afternoon,' Carver said, without saying hello.

'I didn't realise I could get email in here.' Lane took a seat opposite Carver at the desk.

'Anything you get by email is processed the same way your mail is. If you received anything through our Email a Prisoner portal, it would have looked the same as your mail.'

Lane nodded. He didn't receive his original letters. The prison opened his mail, checked the contents, and delivered him a photocopy of anything that passed inspection. The originals were destroyed. Not that it mattered to him; it wasn't like anyone was sending him tear-stained letters soaked in perfume.

'When we came to our little arrangement, I nominated myself as the officer responsible for checking your incoming mail. Lucky for you, because any other officer would have shitcanned this.' He slid a printout across the table.

Lane

Eva Nováková still had her wisdom teeth at the time of her death. Matilda Carver's had been removed, according to her family dentist.

Thanks for the advice.
Gemma Guillory

Lane read the message, then read it again. He looked at Carver. 'That's a pretty conclusive discrepancy. That's not like the height of the remains being slightly off your estimate for Matilda, or them refusing to consider her because she was in another state when she went missing. If it was the other way around, and Eva was missing her wisdom teeth while Matilda still had them, then it would be possible that Matilda had had them removed after you lost contact. But the other way around? Wisdom teeth don't grow back.'

Carver just stared down at the printed email.

'It's really unfortunate that they didn't just tell you this,' Lane said. 'Why do you think they were so secretive? It could have saved you years of frustration.'

Carver leaned forwards and said, 'My daughter never had her wisdom teeth removed.'

'What?'

'Matilda still had her wisdom teeth. If she had them removed, it definitely wasn't with our family dentist. In fact, she and my wife had a little tiff about it. Her mother wanted her to get them out before she left for Europe, so there wasn't any risk that she would need to have them removed urgently while she was overseas. But Matilda didn't want to use up her savings on such an expensive procedure if it wasn't necessary.'

'So the file is wrong,' Lane said. His stomach buzzed, like when a roller-coaster is about to crest the peak. This was huge. He'd done it.

At the same time, the excitement was coloured by sadness. It was suddenly very likely that Eva Nováková was Matilda. Which meant that the daughter Carver loved so much was dead.

'More than that,' Carver said. 'Before I had you brought in here, I called our family dentist. Luckily he's still sharp as a tack, and has all of his files still. He checked Matilda's, and confirmed that he never referred her for wisdom tooth removal. He told me he would definitely remember if he'd been contacted by police looking for Matilda's medical records. He hadn't been. Whatever the Rainier police have on file about Matilda isn't just a mistake – it's a lie.'

'Put me back in, coach,' Lane said. He might as well take the shot. 'Get me back in a room with Henning-Klosner. I can press him more about the baby. Even if he knows what my game is, I might be able to get him to talk.'

TWENTY-FOUR

GEMMA STARED UP at her bedroom ceiling, begging herself to fall asleep. She'd only had one decent night of sleep since the murder, and that hadn't been enough to repay the sleep debt from the other nights. She had to be up at the crack of dawn to head over to the pub kitchen to make the hot food for the memorial service.

But the moment she closed her eyes she became convinced that if she opened them again, there would be someone in the doorway watching her.

Sighing, she got up and went into the hallway, walking as slowly as she could so that she wouldn't wake the whole house up by making the floorboards creak. She checked that the back door, which led onto the verandah, was locked, and did the same with the front door. She wanted to go check that the door leading to Marcus's suite was locked too, but didn't want to risk rattling the doorknob.

She put her head in the door of Violet's room, and saw that she was sleeping soundly.

With that small bit of reassurance, Gemma went back to her room and crawled under the doona.

The police weren't putting all their eggs in one basket, it seemed. Mick was pursuing Marcus as a suspect, while the new detectives were focused on Antoine. But that still meant they were fixated on two people whom Gemma was sure were innocent. Meaning that no-one was looking for the actual killer.

A killer who was now stalking Gemma.

* * *

It was almost impossible to drag herself out of bed for the memorial service, after getting barely any rest. She'd gone through the motions of getting the coffee and tea urns ready in a bleary haze, and by the time the guests started drifting in she felt almost human.

She was pleasantly surprised by the turnout. She didn't attend the service itself, not when there was so much setting up to do, but she did pick up an order of service booklet on her way through the church vestibule. She had flipped through it while she waited for the guests to make their way out, trying to ignore the instrumental version of 'My Heart Will Go On' on the sound system.

It was a nice mix of what looked like promotional pictures from the Lewis and Co. website and more personal pictures that must have been sent by the family. The main picture was a group shot on a pebbled beach. In the centre of the group was an older couple who looked like they could be his parents. To their left were two couples with children arrayed in front of them – Lochlan's siblings, their spouses and his nieces and nephews, Gemma guessed. Lochlan stood to the far right of the group, alone but beaming. Next to it was a picture of him in a cap and gown, holding up the diploma of a history degree. Then a candid of Lochlan alone in a backyard, lifting a beer to salute whoever was behind the camera. The rest of the pictures showed him lecturing tour groups, on streets that looked like Sydney, Melbourne and London.

'Do you need any help here, hon?' Ruth Tanner asked.

Gemma jumped a little, and winced in embarrassment. She hadn't heard Ruth walk up to her, thanks to the thick carpets and music next door. God, if she didn't get a grip on herself she was going to end up having a heart attack the next time someone slammed a door or dropped a plate.

'Thanks, but it's about done.'

'Gosh, this looks nice. You've done a great job!' Ruth said, overly cheerful in a way that meant she didn't think so at all. 'Under the circumstances. I'm so sorry to hear about Hugh; you know we would have been happy to take over if you needed.'

'Oh.' It hadn't even occurred to Gemma that she could have pulled out of catering the service after Hugh's accident. It had felt easier just to keep pushing forwards, move on to the next thing to be done. 'It helps to stay busy.'

'How is he doing?'

'He's fine, thanks. He's still in the hospital, but he'll be alright.'

'Oh, I'm so glad.' Ruth took an orange slice and examined it. 'This isn't what you were going to serve at our reception, was it?'

'No, I was going to serve the menu we discussed. I'm sorry you had to postpone.'

'Ah well. It just wouldn't have been respectful. And I wanted a spring wedding anyway; the park is miserable at this time of year.'

'It sure is,' Gemma murmured, turning away from her to line up the water glasses on the serving table.

Mick was the next to arrive, wearing an unassuming grey suit and black tie. He nodded to Gemma, and made himself a cup of coffee without speaking to her. She felt his eyes on her back as she laid out rows of cups, saucers and teaspoons. As the room started to fill properly, she picked up a tray of food and started her rounds.

'Did you hear they're close to making an arrest?' a man asked.

Gemma looked over, thinking he was addressing her, but saw that he was actually speaking to a woman with him.

Gemma was invisible with a serving tray in her hands. People looked at the food, not at her, and didn't even pause their conversations as they made their selections. That phenomenon had annoyed her when she was younger, but now she just found it amusing.

'That's quick,' the woman said, taking a goat's cheese tart from the tray.

'It's pretty open and shut, I hear,' the man said. 'The father of one of the original victims. You have to have some sympathy for that, but what he did to Lochlan was savage.'

A third man approached the pair. 'Were you friends of Lochlan?'

'Why?' the woman asked. 'Are you a reporter?'

'No. I'm trying to find out who the executor of Lochlan's estate is.'

'No idea,' the woman said. 'He was so young – would he even have had a will?'

Gemma moved away, taking the tray to a different group.

After her first loop of the room she noticed Aubrey come in, wearing the black dress with pearl buttons she wore to every funeral. Jac was right behind her, in a navy blue jumpsuit. Instead of going to join Mick, the two of them crossed the room to stand with Lotte and Fawn. Lotte wore one of her normal dark work suits, while Fawn wore a knee-length black dress under a pinstriped blazer Gemma was pretty sure belonged to Lotte.

With a twinge, she remembered the day of Vincent's funeral. Half the girls in attendance had on club dresses, since the only black dresses they owned were the ones they wore to parties. Her grandmother had muttered under her breath about it the whole time, but now Gemma thought it was sad. So many of them had been too young to have ever needed an outfit for sombre occasions.

Jac saw her and smiled, but Gemma wasn't in the mood to talk to Aubrey. Not Aubrey who'd talked behind Gemma's back about her marriage, spilling things she probably only knew because she was having secret late-night chats with Gemma's husband. Gemma gave Jac a little nod, then scanned the room.

Tamara hovered in a corner with a cup of coffee. Gemma made her way over, and held out the tray.

'Goat's cheese tart?' she asked. 'They're handmade.'

'Impressive,' Tamara said, taking one.

'Well, don't ask me about the spring rolls.'

'I heard that your husband had an accident,' Tamara said. 'I'm sorry.'

'I appreciate it.' She didn't want to stand here talking about Hugh. She didn't want Tamara's sympathy. 'How was the service?'

'Surprisingly affecting,' Tamara said. 'I didn't know him well, but there's an energy to funerals that makes me cry every time. When I'm in a pew, I'm right back at every other service I've ever attended.'

She stared past Gemma, who turned to see what had caught her eye. The man looking for Lochlan's executor had moved on to a different group.

'Do you know him?' she asked.

'No. He's been chatting to everyone, though. Just seems like a red flag.'

'I heard him asking about Lochlan Lewis's will earlier,' Gemma said. 'He might be a relative?'

'A relative would know who to talk to, surely? My money says he's a debt collector.'

Gemma clutched her tray tighter. 'At a memorial service?'

She wasn't a complete stranger to debt collection services, but surely that was beyond the pale.

Tamara shrugged. 'If I'm right, it must be enough that they're really sweating about getting that money back.'

'You should point him out to Mick,' Gemma said, tipping her head to the side to indicate where he was still standing, watching the crowd with no expression. He didn't seem to be paying any attention to the strange man.

'I try not to go out of my way to talk to cops,' Tamara said.

That was fair, but Gemma wasn't keen to draw Mick's attention either. Maybe he had already noticed the man, and just didn't want to show it.

'While I've got you, can I ask you a question? Have you ever met a woman named Matilda Carver?'

'Doesn't ring a bell,' Tamara said. 'Sorry.'

'She was looked at as a possible identity for Eva. Dental records ruled her out, but it's a sad story.'

'There's a lot of those around,' Tamara said.

'She was my age,' Gemma said. 'And it got me thinking about Eva. She'd be around my age now too, if she'd lived. She would be a mother. And nobody even knows her name.'

'Except Jan Henning-Klosner,' Tamara said, taking another spring roll. 'Which is worse, in a way. Imagine having that fucker as your only memory keeper.'

'Would you ever consider approaching him about it?' Gemma asked. 'He might be willing to talk to you.'

'That would be a mistake,' Lotte Nicholls interjected. 'Sorry to eavesdrop, but this isn't a movie. A sadist isn't going to help you; he'd just use the opportunity to play mind games.'

Gemma hadn't noticed the ebb and flow of groups in the small room bringing Lotte, Aubrey and the kids over to where she and Tamara were chatting. She smiled uneasily, replaying the conversation to check if they might have overheard anything questionable.

'Ms Fleischer is right, though,' Jac said. 'There are some things that only that man knows. If he dies, it's lost forever.'

'He's had plenty of time to share what he knows about Eva, and he's refused,' Lotte said.

'Maybe no-one's asking the right questions,' Gemma argued. 'Or maybe it's not the right person asking.'

'I agree with Lotte,' Tamara said. 'It's a bad idea. Besides, he's not the only path to getting Eva identified. There's still the DNA analysis option.'

'I'd love to hear more about that,' Fawn piped up. 'Mrs Guillory mentioned it the other day – it sounds really interesting.'

'Why were you talking to my daughter about that?' Lotte asked, a sharpness in her tone that surprised Gemma.

'Lotte,' Aubrey said, a warning in her voice that Gemma found similarly mystifying.

'If you don't even trust me to make small talk with her, why did you trust me to supervise her for days on end?' Gemma snapped back.

'From what I hear there wasn't much supervision going on,' Lotte said.

'Mum!' Fawn said. 'We're not children.'

'Okay,' Tamara interjected. 'It's normal for emotions to run a bit high at a funeral . . .'

'I'm not emotional,' Lotte said. 'I'm sorry. It's just that, in my professional opinion' – she leaned hard on the word 'professional' – 'we, as a society, are rushing in to things we don't understand. We have all these shiny new toys – DNA analysis and databases and whatnot – and everybody is too excited to think things through. Yes, we've had success. Like when the Golden State Killer's DNA was matched to a relative through a genealogy company. But that relative was never able to give informed consent to that. She or he had no idea it was even possible when handing their sample over.'

'Yes, won't someone think of the serial killers,' Tamara muttered.

'Easy to say, but where's the line? US police later used the same technique to nail someone on a burglary charge. Thank god that was struck down.'

Lotte's cheeks were flushed, which was probably the most out of sorts Gemma had ever seen her. She was usually so put together and controlled, it was unnerving. Gemma glanced at Fawn, who was staring at her mother with her brow furrowed.

'I'm not saying it's bad, just that it's too new. We need to get the ethics and the legislation fully ironed out before we take off running with these things.'

'Is that why Eva hasn't been tested through the state program yet?' Tamara asked. 'Have you been advocating against it?'

'No,' Lotte said firmly. 'But I haven't been advocating for it, either.'

* * *

Ordinarily Gemma wouldn't have heard the soft footsteps behind her, given the clatter she was making piling used cups and plates onto her trolley, but she was on high alert.

She turned to see Jac, who started stacking up cups alongside her.

'Where's your mum?'

'She's gone to pick up the kids from the farm. I figured if I went with her I'd end up watching the kids all afternoon while she has a lie down, so I told her you asked me to help clean up.'

She should probably scold Jac for lying to Aubrey, but that would be hypocritical. Why not tell little lies all the time, to make the wheels turn smoother? It saved time, it saved people's feelings. No harm done, right?

'Is she doing that a lot, lately? Lying down, I mean?'

'Mmm.' Jac scraped a plate into the food and organics bin hanging on the trolley. 'I don't think she's sleeping at night.' They looked at Gemma. 'I don't think you are either.'

'I'm fine.' Gemma reached out and grabbed a teaspoon before it tumbled into the bin.

'There's something weird going on.'

'There was a murder,' Gemma said.

'Was it like this the first time?'

'After your father died?'

Jac nodded. 'Was it this – I don't even know how to describe it – this weird?'

'A little,' Gemma said. 'But this isn't just a repeat of that. This is the fourth time, not the first. It's bringing up things that everybody had buried.'

'Please,' Jac said, voice earnest and soft. 'Fawn and I were talking about it, after her mum's little TED Talk. There's more going on here than people being scared, and I know you're involved.'

'What the hell does that mean?'

'When I talked to Fawn,' Jac said slowly, 'she was pretty surprised to hear that you were looking for information about Matilda Carver on her behalf.'

Shit. When Gemma told that lie, she hadn't stopped to think how likely it was Jac would mention it to Fawn, but then the whole point was that she'd done it without thinking. She'd been tired and distracted and just trying to end the conversation with as little friction as possible.

'I'm sorry, Jac. I shouldn't have lied to you. I was just trying to help the Carver family.'

'Why?'

'I got a phone call from someone looking into Matilda Carver. He's a private investigator.' Gemma took a deep breath. No. No more lies. 'He *was* a private investigator. He's a prisoner now. He's in with' – she fumbled for a gentle way to refer to the man – 'with Jan Henning-Klosner. He's trying to get a deathbed confession about who Eva really is.'

Jac paused, a cup in each hand. 'He's dying.'

'Maybe. He's definitely sick.'

'Why did you lie?'

'Expedience, I guess. Or because the truth is pretty strange, and if you knew, you would tell Mick, and it would become a bigger thing than I was ready to deal with.'

'I never tell Mick anything.'

Gemma laughed, then felt bad about it.

'Do you really think you and my dad would have got back together, if he hadn't . . .'

Gemma nearly dropped the mugs she was gathering. 'Did you hear that from Jaylene?'

'Yeah. You tend to come up whenever she's pissed off at Mum. Which is most days.'

'No,' Gemma said. 'No, I don't think we would have. And you know, if we never broke up you and Violet wouldn't exist. I can't think of anything worse than that.' She sighed. 'But some days, when the real world is hard, it's a nice fantasy to retreat to. I get why Jaylene does it, even if I worry about her sometimes.'

'I used to get in a lot of trouble for doing that,' Jac said, their voice barely above a whisper.

'Oh, hon.' Gemma put the mugs down so she could squeeze their shoulder.

'I tried it on a few times, when I was fighting with Mick. *Dad would have let me. Dad wouldn't do this.*'

'You should try talking to your mum,' Gemma said. 'She doesn't know it's affecting you at all. She told me you don't remember anything, that Mick's always been your dad.'

'I worry that if I bring it up, she'll get mad at Mamy and Pépère,' Jac whispered. 'I mean, I don't really remember it, but I looked up the court transcripts. She thought they were hurting me by bringing up Dad all the time, and that it was stopping me from bonding with Mick. So she tried to cut them off for a while, and they took it to court, and it's been a bin fire ever since.'

'Can I hug you?' Gemma asked.

Jac nodded, eyes scrunched shut, and Gemma wrapped them in her arms.

'I want to talk to him,' Jac mumbled into Gemma's shoulder.

'The private investigator?'

'No. The Rainier Ripper.'

TWENTY-FIVE

'DID YOU GET shit kicked again?' Jan asked, once the nurse had fussed around setting Lane up in his hospital bed once more.

Lane watched his face carefully for any hint that Carver was right and Jan knew what they'd been up to. Jan gave him nothing.

'Nah,' Lane said. 'I got transferred to the real hospital to see a specialist. They reckon this might need surgery.' He gestured at his fake sling with the other hand. 'How'd your interrogation go?'

'Waste of time,' Jan said. 'Theirs, anyway. I had fun.'

'I saw the cops in the hallway while I was waiting for my transfer,' Lane said. 'The dude looked like he'd seen a ghost. What the hell did you do to him?' He tried to sound impressed.

'Their fault for sending Guillory,' Jan said. 'Dude had a breakdown way back when. The tiniest bit of needling about it and he collapsed. It was like punching a paper bag.'

'How do you know that?' Lane asked.

'Nosy,' Jan said.

'Go on,' Lane pushed. 'That was the most interesting thing that's happened since I got here – you can't blame me for wanting the details.'

'His dad works for the church. A bishop or something. High up enough to be full of himself. He used to send me letters, trying to save my soul. Laid a bunch of guilt trips about how Hugh was suffering, how everyone in Rainier was suffering. Like bringing me to Jesus could fix that.' Jan sighed. 'I reckon it was his own soul he was worried about.'

'What makes you say that?'

'He just wouldn't let up. Years and years of trying to build some kind of weird-arse relationship with me. The whole family's cracked.'

Lane thought guiltily of Gemma Guillory; he'd only encountered her briefly but she'd seemed unusually kind.

'When they were here, I swear I could hear something like a baby crying. What was that about?'

He'd expected Jan to laugh, or brag, but instead the amused look slid off his face, and he looked tired and a little sad.

'That was in the letters,' he said. 'He couldn't deal with the sound of his own baby crying.'

So Carver had been wrong. The fake crying hadn't been aimed at him at all. Lane decided it was time to take a risk. 'One of your victims was pregnant, wasn't she?' He couldn't stop himself from looking over at the little mirror he now knew was an observation window. He wondered if Carver was on the other side watching them.

'What happened to the baby, Jan?' he asked, dropping his voice as low as he could.

'I got real confused when they asked me about the baby,' Jan said, his own voice barely a whisper. 'I was already all tangled up, and I thought at first they meant Vincent's baby.'

'When you were questioned?' Lane asked. He was feeling pretty damn confused himself. 'Wasn't it obvious which baby they meant?'

'Nothing was obvious,' Jan said. 'That room was a fucking nightmare.'

'The interrogation room?'

'Guillory's an arsehole. I'm glad he's miserable. Just wish they'd sent the other one too.'

'You wanted to talk to them?'

That was one thing he hadn't been able to get his head around. Jan hadn't been obliged to talk to Guillory, but he'd done it. And he'd been quite forthcoming with answers, right up until he decided he was done.

He wasn't nearly as chatty with Lane.

But, then, Guillory hadn't asked a single question about Eva, had he?

'You know the rules. We can't reach out to them, even if we want to talk. They have to come to me. And I've had years to plan what I would do to Guillory if I got a shot at him.'

TWENTY-SIX

'NO.'

It was a word Gemma usually found impossible to say, but it slipped out easily now.

'I just want to know why,' Jac pleaded. 'Why he did it. Why he destroyed my family. And I want him to go to his grave knowing how much hurt he caused.'

'He would enjoy knowing that, Jac. Remember what Lotte said? A sadist isn't going to help you.'

'Remember what *you* said? It's about asking the right questions. Or the right person asking.'

'You are not the right person.' She squeezed Jac tighter. 'There are some things that can't be unlearned. He's not going to be able to give you any answers that will bring your dad back, or make you miss him any less.'

'I just . . .' Jac sagged. 'I just want to know why.'

'Your mother would murder me,' Gemma said. 'Jaylene and Antoine would help her hide the body. It would finally unite the three of them.'

Jac didn't laugh.

'If you want to do something like this, it should be your mother who takes you,' Gemma said.

'She couldn't,' Jac said. 'Even if she supported the idea, she would be terrified that Mamy and Pépère would take her to court for custody again.'

'You're nearly eighteen – the court isn't going to take custody away from your mother.'

'I know. She'd still freak out.'

Gemma understood. You can't talk yourself out of a trauma reaction with facts and logic. 'You'll be able to go yourself when you're eighteen. I'd be happy to accompany you then.'

'He's dying,' Jac said. 'Even if it's hard, even if it's cruel, at least I'll know it. If he dies before I get any answers, it'll torment me my whole life.'

Gemma closed her eyes. She should say no. But what if Jac was right? What if he died, and Jac never forgave her?

'There might be something I can do,' she said. 'Take another day to think about it. If you still want this, come to ours in the morning and we'll talk.'

* * *

Gemma dialled the number of the Special Purpose Centre switchboard. She enunciated her name carefully, and the name of the prisoner she was trying to reach. She didn't know Lane Holland's unique identification number, but hoped for the best.

The phone beeped, and then switched over to a tinny Archie Roach song while the great machinery of justice decided whether or not to connect her. She hummed along, wondering if it would have been better to use the Email a Prisoner portal she'd found while trying to forward Lane the information about Matilda Carver. But something told her that she didn't want to put down in writing what she was about to suggest – and besides, Holland had never responded to that email.

The song cut out.

'Special Purpose Centre, this is Governor Patton Carver speaking,' a male voice said. 'I understand you're trying to reach Lane Holland, Mrs Guillory.'

'Yes, sir,' she said, something uncomfortable prickling in her stomach. 'Did you say your name is Carver?'

'Mmm. I recognise your name, too. You're Holland's little birdie on the outside, correct?'

'You're related to Matilda Carver, then?'

'I'm her father.'

Oh. There was clearly something much more complicated going on here than she'd imagined. 'Are you the client that asked Lane Holland to look into Jan Henning-Klosner?'

There was no real humour in Carver's laugh. 'Is that how he put it? I suppose that's true.'

'I need Mr Holland's help with something. It's a little out there, but I think it could help you too.'

'I'm listening.'

Gemma took a deep breath. She could be about to open herself up to a whole world of trouble, if Carver wasn't as willing to bend the rules as she suspected he was.

TWENTY-SEVEN

LANE PONDERED HIS next steps as he stacked his empty yoghurt container and spoon back on his breakfast tray. The problem was that simply coming out and asking Jan if he had ever met Matilda Carver was the nuclear option. If he had not brought Jan to a place where he was ready to talk by the time Lane dropped that question, it would all be over. So instead he played one of the cheap tricks he'd been holding in reserve.

He hummed 'Waltzing Matilda'.

'I went out with a Matilda for a while,' Lane lied.

'Bet she hated that song,' Jan replied.

'Hmm? Why, did you know a Matilda who hated it?'

The medical unit door opened, and Lane wanted to scream.

It was Governor Carver. At first Lane assumed he had popped out of the observation room to interrupt on purpose, but then he saw that Carver was holding up a mobile phone, its light washing his face with a faint blue tinge.

'Henning-Klosner, there's a call for you, if you're willing to accept,' Carver said.

'That doesn't look like one of the Tin's phones,' Jan said.

Carver hesitated. 'This would be off the record. The caller is Jac Tjibaou. Vincent Tjibaou was their father.'

'Their?' Jan asked.

'Jac is non-binary,' Carver said. 'I've got some pamphlets in my office you can read after, if it matters that much.'

Jan stared at the phone, then looked at Lane. Lane gave him a little nod of encouragement, glad that it fit his persona of drama-hungry bystander.

'We could reschedule for another time, if you'd like to think about it,' Carver said.

'Fuck it,' Jan said. 'I'll talk to 'em.'

TWENTY-EIGHT

THIS WAS A bad idea. This was a bad, bad, bad idea, but she'd set it in motion and she couldn't seem to get the words out to stop it.

Gemma prayed silently that the Ripper would refuse to take the call.

'Here are the ground rules,' she said to Jac while they waited. 'I'll hold the phone. If he tries anything, I'll hang up. If I think you're getting too upset, I'll hang up. If I decide to hang up, I'll hang up. There will be no discussion and no arguments. Yes?'

They were downstairs in the courtyard. It wasn't the most comfortable place, but she couldn't risk doing this upstairs where Violet or Marcus might walk in on them. She was confident they wouldn't be able to hear her from upstairs, as long as no-one started yelling, and she would put an immediate stop to the conversation if it got heated.

'He's not going to be able to do anything to me through the phone,' Jac said.

'He destroyed me without us ever being in the same room,' Gemma said. 'Now, if you need me to end the call at any point, do this.' She balled a fist and held it up.

Governor Carver came back on the line. 'Henning-Klosner has agreed to take your call. This call is not being recorded, and you should be aware that recording from your end without my permission is illegal in New South Wales. You're on speaker. Also present is Lane Holland, another prisoner. We can remove him from the room, but it would cause a significant delay.'

Gemma muted the call. 'That okay with you? Lane Holland is the private investigator I told you about.'

Jac considered this for a moment, then nodded. 'That's probably better, to have him and the governor monitoring Henning-Klosner from their end.'

Gemma unmuted, and gestured for Jac to speak.

'I understand. You're on speaker too, and I have Gemma Guillory with me.'

'Hello,' Gemma said.

'Hello, Gemma, Jac. Can I call you Jac? Mr Tjibaou? Miss Tjibaou?'

Ice filled Gemma's stomach. She'd never heard the Ripper's voice before. She'd avoided attending the trial at any time she wasn't needed to testify, and she'd always changed the channel before the news could show footage of him.

This was a mistake. What was wrong with her?

'Mx Tjibaou, please,' Jac said. They pronounced 'Mx' like 'mix'. 'I'm going to call you Mr Henning-Klosner.'

'You can call me fuckface if you want,' Jan volunteered, with a gentleness that surprised Gemma. 'I wouldn't blame you.'

'Thank you for talking to me,' Jac said.

Gemma rubbed her chest. She couldn't imagine how Jac felt, speaking so politely to their father's killer. She wanted to scream.

'I never knew my father,' Jac continued. 'You – he died before I was born. My mother, my grandparents, they try to tell me his story, but they can't . . .' Jac took a shaky breath. 'I want to know what his final moments were really like.'

Jan paused before answering. 'I know there's a lot of stories out there. Like I got off on watching people bleed out, so I made it as slow as possible. That's bullshit. He . . . I wish I could tell you that he wasn't frightened, but it was quick, at least. He knew he was hurt bad. He knew he was going to die. He called out for his mother.'

Gemma looked at Jac, whose hands were still open by their sides. She muted the call. 'Are you doing alright?'

Jac nodded, drawing in a shaky breath. 'This is what I wanted.'

'You don't have to follow through just because this was your decision,' Gemma said. 'There's no shame in bailing out.'

Jac shook their head, and Gemma unmuted. 'Go on.'

'He lost consciousness fast. It was a horrific end, but not what the media hyped it up to be. There was so much blood.' The Ripper sounded genuinely distressed. A serial killer who couldn't handle the sight of blood? It certainly hadn't stopped him from making a bloody mess of Dean Shadwell.

Jac sniffled, then shot Gemma a fierce look before she could end the call. 'Why did you choose him?'

'I knew your father,' Jan admitted. 'We were sort of nodding acquaintances through our trucking routes; you get to know the faces after a while. He bought from me a couple of times.'

'Bought from you?'

Jan sighed. 'Everybody's got something going on the side, right? Truckers are often looking for a bit of extra energy to help them push through a tight schedule. Or something to cancel out what they took yesterday, so they can get to sleep. A bit of ecstasy to get the most out of their time off, and something to help with the comedown. I was no Tony Mokbel, but I was never short of buyers for a few pills here and there.'

'He was on drugs?' Jac asked. 'I knew about Mum, but . . .'

It took Gemma a moment to realise the question was directed at her, not the Ripper. She nodded. 'Socially, sometimes. It was nothing serious.' She hurried to add, 'Not that it's okay! Stay away from them.'

'A few weeks before . . . before, he started doing a bit of side work for me.'

'Side work?'

'He was keen for some extra cash. Said he had bugger-all savings and a kid on the way. That'd be you, eh?'

'Yeah.'

'He wanted to get him and your mum set up in their own place. So he did a couple of jobs for me. No selling; we'd just occasionally stick a bag of pills under his seat in Sydney and have him make a drop along his route. I think he did it three, maybe four times before I found out I wasn't the only side hustle he had going on.'

'What?'

'He was signing off delivery sheets for fake consignments for a farm in Rainier, to help them launder the money from their marijuana operation,' Jan said.

Gemma drew in a sharp breath. Vincent had been working for the Dillon farm?

'Sometimes he moved people for them, too, bringing in people willing to work on the farm under the table. I was fucking ropeable when I found out Vincent was double dipping. Rule number one is you never commit a crime while you're committing a crime. If he got caught for that other shit, he'd drag my operation down with him. So I paid him a visit on his day off. Suggested we go for a little walk in the park.'

Jac's sniffles had become full-blown sobs now.

'I think we're done here,' Gemma said. She was still trying to process the fact that the Ripper had a motive for killing Vincent. It had always, *always* been spoken of in town as a random attack, one of a spree.

'No,' Jac almost shouted. 'No,' they added more quietly. 'Knowing this is . . . a lot, but I want to keep going.'

'I went there intending to put the fear of God into him. Convince him to drop all of it and walk away, before he ended up in an interrogation room.'

Jan's voice grew husky, and Gemma's stomach twisted as she realised the man was tearing up.

'I kept this folding knife in my truck, for cutting ropes and shit. I took it along with me, trying to scare him with some gangster fucking bullshit. I had the knife to Vincent's throat, and tried to push his head into the fountain.'

'Oh god,' Gemma broke in. 'The water in the fountain.'

'What?' Jac asked.

'It was frozen,' Gemma and Jan both said, almost at the same moment.

'I was just an idiot playing at hard man,' Jan said. 'The unexpected resistance scared me. I panicked and jerked, slashing Vincent's throat.' He broke down. 'I'm sorry, Jac. I'm so fucking sorry.'

'That's still murder,' Jac said. Their voice was eerily calm, their own tears gone.

'I know,' Jan said.

Jac raised a fist, and Gemma ended the call.

Gemma wrapped her arms around Jac, wishing it was possible to hug them tight enough to help at all with their pain.

After what might have been minutes or hours, Jac heaved a wet, shuddering sigh and then said, 'I have to tell Mamy and Pépère.'

'Please don't rush,' Gemma said. 'I'm not sure you understand what the consequences will be.'

'What do you mean?'

'I know what farm Jan was talking about. The one your father was working for. When your grandparents find out it was the reason your dad was killed, it's going to spark World War Three.' Gemma took a deep breath, steeling herself. 'That farm was run by your other grandparents.'

Jac just stared at her. 'Grandma and Grandpa Dillon run a goat farm. They make cheese.'

'Now, yeah. But back when we were growing up, it was an open secret that they grew marijuana. Everyone knew.'

Jac shook their head. 'I know they smoke occasionally, but that's ridiculous.'

'After your dad died, with the massive police presence in town, they thought it was too risky to keep going. They sold what they could and razed the rest.'

She had even heard rumours that they deliberately burned down one of their farm sheds to eliminate evidence, but Gemma had never set much store by that. If it had happened at all, it was more likely an accident while burning off the stubble.

'You should talk to them about this, when you're ready. They weren't living some *Breaking Bad* double life. By the time you were born they were done with it, and they never looked back – especially not once they had a cop for a son-in-law.'

'Oh my god, does Mick know?'

'I have no idea,' Gemma admitted truthfully.

Jac rubbed their face. 'Thank you, Gemma. This has been a deeply fucked-up day, but I'm glad I know.'

'You're welcome. Now, let me drive you home,' Gemma said. Jac looked like they wanted to refuse, but she held up a hand. 'For my sake, let me make sure you make it home safe.'

They drove in silence. Gemma pulled up at the front of the Seabrooke house, and prayed Aubrey wouldn't come out. She wouldn't be able to hold it together if she did.

'Promise me you'll talk to your mum about this, and soon. Before you talk to Jaylene and Antoine. Ask her to take you to a counsellor; you need to process this with a professional.'

'I will.'

Gemma was proud of herself for holding it together until Jac had made it into the house and closed the door. She pulled away, and drove for quite a bit longer than the few minutes it should have taken her to get home.

TWENTY-NINE

LANE AND CARVER were frozen for a moment, a tableau of confusion and shock.

'What about Eva?' Lane asked. 'She died before Vincent. He wasn't your first victim.'

Jan laughed, a cold, desperate sound. 'Did Ludwig hit you in the head?'

Lane hadn't seen it until now. Maybe he'd been refusing to see it. The way Jan had been so open to answering questions for Jac. Eager, even. The way he'd been honest with the police. But when Lane asked questions about Eva, or tried to sidle up to the topic, he'd got nothing more than a brush-off or a blank look.

'You don't know who Eva Nováková is,' Lane said.

'No.'

Carver's face clouded over. 'What do you mean you don't know?'

'He didn't kill her,' Lane said.

'I didn't kill Eva Nováková,' Jan said.

'He confessed,' Carver snapped. 'Why would you confess to a murder you didn't commit?'

Lane looked to Jan, then realised he already knew the answer. 'The Reid Technique.'

Lane himself had been trained in the Reid Technique. If he had gone ahead with his original plan of joining the police, he probably would have used it to torment confessions out of suspects, and would have thought he was using cutting-edge science to do it. But it was notorious for inducing false confessions from innocent people. Only a few years after Jan's arrest, Australia completely abandoned the Reid Technique in favour of the PEACE method. Too late for Jan.

Lane had seen the dates and times of Jan's arrest, and his confession. He'd been interrogated for hours, with the two police officers tagging in and out to have a rest while Jan was forced to go on and on. It was comforting to think that a confession was a capstone that closed a case without any uncomfortable, lingering questions, but there had been many cases of arrested suspects confessing only to be exonerated by the evidence. It happened more often than investigators liked to admit.

'What, that bullshit they pulled has a name?' Jan asked.

'Depends. Let me guess. Did they seem weirdly understanding? Like they were sure you had a really good reason for killing her, and if you just explained it they would be sympathetic?'

'One of them. The other one kept blowing his top.' Jan sighed. 'Fucking good cop, bad cop.'

'Classic. And the friendly one offered to get rid of the aggressive one, didn't he? Like you and him were a team against the other cop. How about strange, leading questions? Constantly circling back and asking the same question again and again? Accusing you of even worse, more outlandish crimes or motives?'

Jan nodded.

'Did they keep at you relentlessly until you cried and then acted like that was a confession?'

'I didn't cry,' Jan objected.

Lord. By the end of his grilling, Jan probably would have admitted to being Jack the Ripper too. A good lawyer could have had it thrown out, but not everyone got a good lawyer.

'This is ridiculous,' Carver muttered.

'It sounds like that farm needs to be investigated,' Lane said. What Jan had described, with Vincent picking up workers and bringing them to the outskirts of Rainier, was exactly the scenario Carver had proposed that could have brought Matilda into contact with Jan. Or into Rainier, anyway.

Carver looked like he wanted to argue, but whether he believed Jan was innocent or not, Lane was right on that point and he knew it. He threw his hands up in the air and walked out.

'What about Dean?' Lane asked, once the door had slammed closed behind the governor.

'Dean didn't believe me,' Jan said quietly. 'That I didn't kill her. He was so freaked out that I thought maybe she was someone he knew, but he swore he didn't. He wouldn't believe that I didn't know her either. Not after Vincent.'

'Why did you assume he knew her?'

'If anyone was going to, it was him. I don't think there was a single woman at the service centre that Dean didn't try it on with. His exes could have unionised. They actually iced him out for a bit after what he did to Ruthie, but turnover being what it was they forgot eventually.' He rubbed his arm, grimacing.

'Ruthie?'

'Yeah. She wasn't one of the working girls; she ran the register at the petrol station. She reckoned Dean got her pregnant, but he swore he was snipped. It caused a whole kerfuffle.'

'Could this Ruthie be Eva?'

'Nah, she was definitely still alive when they found the girl's body. Dean freaked out when that happened, wouldn't talk to me, then decided he couldn't handle it and was going to tell the police everything. I –' He rubbed his chest. 'I don't know. That whole time, it's like Swiss cheese. I don't think I was sober for more than two consecutive minutes from the night Vincent died to when I was arrested. I remember getting the text, and going off my brain, and I remember the cops hauling me off Tamara.'

'How was Tamara involved?'

'She wasn't, until I dragged her into it. I was a hopped-up, brain-dead idiot and thought I could offer her money to tell the cops I'd been with her the whole time. She spat in my face.'

'You gave a pretty detailed confession for someone who didn't remember anything and didn't even commit one of the murders.'

Jan shrugged. 'I coughed up the truth about Vincent within the first hour. But they wouldn't take "I don't know" for an answer on the others. It just went on and on and on. So long that I didn't just come down, I crashed, then went into withdrawal, and all while they kept firing questions at me. They wouldn't let me sleep. I just wanted it to be over, and I was going to prison anyway. So I told them what they needed to hear to let me out of that goddamn room.'

Lane's own interrogation, even with all of his experience and knowledge, had been a lonely and terrifying experience. He had been ready to confess, but there were some things he was determined to hold back. He had stayed silent until a lawyer arrived, and then gave every appearance of cooperating politely with the police. Even with all of that, it had been an ordeal, and he might have panicked and ruined more lives than his own if he'd been subjected to a Reid interrogation.

He didn't want to feel sympathy for the Rainier Ripper or anger at the police who'd brought him down.

He didn't want to have more in common with the Ripper than the police.

'Do you know anything at all about Eva?' he asked.

'Is that why you were sent here?' Jan sounded resigned, and exhausted, but not angry.

'Yes,' Lane admitted. 'How long have you known I was a plant?'

'It took me a good ten minutes to figure it out,' Jan said. Seeing Lane's expression, he explained, 'You move your "injured" arm all the damn time. Tell them to go with an ankle injury next time, eh?'

'You know,' Lane said, since he had nothing left to lose, 'from what Gemma told me about Tamara, I think it would mean a lot to her to know who Eva was, and that you didn't kill her.'

'Tamara wouldn't believe me,' Jan said. 'Besides, I can't give her a name. I don't know it.'

'Do you think Dean knew something?'

'Fucking Dean,' Jan mumbled, and then his heart monitor began to scream.

THIRTY

'WILL YOU ACCEPT a call from . . . *Lane Holland* . . . at the Special Purpose Centre?'

Gemma considered saying no. She wanted to crawl into bed with a bottle of Scotch and watch whatever medical drama Netflix offered her until the bottle was empty. She was regretting every choice she had made for the past week. Maybe the past seventeen years.

'Yes,' she said with a sigh.

'Gemma,' Lane said, sounding as wretched as she felt. 'Are you okay?'

'I'm fine. You?'

'Things are a mess here,' Lane admitted. 'Jan had a heart attack. They've had to take him to the hospital. He needs emergency surgery but he's refused it in the past, so I don't know –'

'Lane,' Gemma interrupted. 'I don't give a shit if the Rainier Ripper dies.'

Lane was silent for a moment, then laughed. 'I get that. But he knows something, Gemma.'

'About Eva Nováková?'

'No. He told me he didn't kill her.'

'Because serial killers are so well known for their honesty.'

'I know. But at this point it's a dying declaration. His second one, and the second time he's proclaimed innocence.'

'What do you want from me?' Gemma asked.

She suspected he just wanted someone he could talk to about this. She understood that, but she didn't have the bandwidth to be yet another man's emotional sponge.

'Do you know a Ruthie who worked at the service centre back around the time of the original murders?'

'Ruth Tanner? What's she got to do with the Ripper?'

'He thinks she might have had a child by Dean Shadwell, or at least been pregnant.'

'Nico Tanner is Dean Shadwell's son?' Gemma said, shocked.

'Maybe. Apparently he claimed he'd had a vasectomy. I don't know if this means anything, or if Jan was just confused and rambling. But if Dean had a history of reacting badly to finding out he was going to be a father . . .'

'And Eva Nováková was pregnant . . .'

'Murder is the number-one cause of death in pregnant women. Mostly at the hands of the baby's father.'

* * *

Gemma went for a walk, mostly to avoid running into Marcus before she had fully processed what Lane had told her. Maybe this was good news. Marcus seemed like a lonely guy. A previously unknown nephew might come as a wonderful surprise.

So why had Ruth never approached him? She hadn't begun to date Christian until her son was in high school. Before that she'd done it all alone. Another relative, especially such a wealthy one, would have been a godsend.

It didn't surprise her to realise that her feet had carried her to the footpath in front of Christian's pub. Through the open door she could see Nico standing behind the bar, talking to a customer.

She tried to find any sign of resemblance between him and what she remembered of Dean, or him and Marcus. Mostly he looked like his mother.

Her phone rang. She seriously considered ignoring it, given the calls she'd received lately, but she let that foolish idea go quickly.

'Hello, Mrs Guillory, this is Dr Ahmad. I'm calling to let you know that your husband is ready to be discharged.'

'Really? That seems awfully fast.'

'To reduce the risk of infection, we're releasing people as soon as is practical. Hugh is safer at home,' Dr Ahmad said, sounding apologetic.

* * *

The curtains around Hugh's bed were closed, which struck Gemma as odd. The room was a double, but the other bed was empty. Gemma heard the low murmur of voices as she approached. She pulled the curtain aside and found Hugh in intense conversation with a woman, only the back of her blonde head visible because she was leaning over the bed, right in Hugh's personal space.

The woman sprang back at the sound of the curtain being drawn, and Gemma realised it wasn't a woman at all. It was a girl. It was Fawn Nicholls.

Fawn and Hugh stared at her with such identical *caught* expressions that her entire world tilted sideways.

'What's going on?' she demanded.

The look on her face must have screamed what she was thinking, because they spoke over each other in their hurry to shut down her suspicions.

'She's a seventeen-year-old girl!' Hugh said, looking hurt that Gemma would even consider the possibility.

'He's my biological father,' Fawn said at the same time.

'*What?*' Gemma asked.

'*What?*' Hugh yelped.

'It's alright,' Fawn said, looking at Hugh. 'I figured it out on my own; Mum didn't spill the beans.'

'I have no idea what you're talking about, Fawn,' Hugh said. He looked at Gemma. 'I'm not.'

Gemma grabbed the back of the plastic visitor's chair for support. She believed Fawn – at least, she believed that Fawn believed it. She'd sat through a school production of *Macbeth* with Fawn playing Macduff; she did not have the acting skills to pull this off.

Hugh had seemed genuinely shocked, though. But if he hadn't known, why had he looked so damn guilty when Gemma walked in on them?

'Where are you getting this from, Fawn?' Gemma asked.

Fawn drew in a shaky breath. Gemma stepped back from the chair, and gestured that Fawn should have it.

'I've suspected for a while that my parents used a donor,' Fawn began. 'Mum has a speech ready to go anytime anyone mentions doing one of those genealogy DNA tests in my earshot. Apparently they're a menace ripping apart the fabric of society.'

'Yeah, I was there when she went on a tear at the memorial,' Gemma said. 'But that was about Eva Nováková, not genealogy. We all have our hobby horses.'

'I was still in earshot. Seriously, she's intense. "Those tests only check for a tiny fraction of the known BRCA mutations."' Fawn gave quite a good rendition of her mother's clipped voice. '"Women think they've been given the all clear when they are actually high risk. It needs to be a conversation between you and your doctor, not you and a website."' She switched back to her ordinary voice. 'On the topic of breast cancer, she once mentioned that I need to be extra careful about it, and my dad got really snippy with her. I don't know of anybody on either side who has had cancer, and when I asked them who it was they insisted she'd misspoken. When I found out Hugh's mother died of breast cancer, it all kind of clicked. And it's like you said about the right person asking the right questions. I realised I was never going to get an answer out of my parents, so I came to Hugh.'

Hugh shook his head. 'If your parents used a donor, it wasn't me.'

'Then why did you visit so often when I was a kid?' Fawn asked.

'What are you talking about?' This was news to Gemma. As far as she knew, they hadn't ever socialised with the Nicholls until their daughters became friends. 'Hugh?'

'I'm not your father,' Hugh said, not looking at Gemma.

'Will you take a DNA test then?' Fawn asked.

'No!' Hugh shouted, startling Gemma.

'Honestly, I think that sounds like a good idea,' she said. 'If it's negative, then we can all move past this.'

Something wasn't adding up. If Hugh had been friends with the Nicholls when Fawn was a child, why hadn't Gemma known about it? Why hadn't he taken her along? But if Hugh was Fawn's biological father, why keep that a secret from Gemma? Fawn was more than a year older than Violet; it would have happened long before she and Hugh were together.

But at the same time, so much of her life made more sense now. Of course Hugh didn't want to move away from Rainier. He would want to be close to *both* his daughters.

They must have got too loud, because the door opened to reveal a worried-looking nurse, trailed by Dr Nicholls.

'Fawn, what are you doing in here?' Dr Nicholls asked. 'I asked you to wait for me in the break room.'

Hugh and Fawn fell silent, and Gemma took matters into her own hands. 'Fawn is under the impression Hugh is her biological father.'

'Excuse me?' Dr Nicholls asked.

'I was just saying that if Fawn needs a DNA test to put her mind at rest, I think we should do it.'

'Fawn,' Dr Nicholls said, his voice gentle, 'I don't know where this has come from but –'

'You do know!' Fawn snapped. 'Stop gaslighting me.'

'*But*,' Dr Nicholls continued firmly, 'if you really want a DNA test to prove I'm your father, I'm happy to do one.'

Gemma let out a breath. She glanced sideways to see if that suggestion worried Hugh – perhaps his involvement in the Nicholls family gene pool had happened without Dr Nicholls' knowledge – but he also looked relieved.

'What, so the two of you can secretly swap out the samples?' Fawn asked.

'I don't know what kind of soap opera you think we're living in Fawn, but we should discuss it further away from poor Hugh and Gemma,' Dr Nicholls said.

'It doesn't matter what you do,' Fawn said. 'Violet and I already sent our samples off to 23andMe. If we're half-sisters, the results will say so.'

'I never approved of that!' Gemma said, glaring at Hugh. But Hugh was looking at Dr Nicholls with an expression of abject horror.

'We forged your signature,' Fawn said. 'Even if you cancel this order, it's only a matter of time until I'm eighteen and can approve it myself.'

Dr Nicholls's face went red. 'Fawn,' he said, his voice low and cold, 'after everything I went through to become your father, the least I deserve is a bit of trust.'

'Oh, fuck,' Hugh said.

The nurse slipped out, probably to go page security.

The pieces of an awful puzzle began to click together in Gemma's mind. Dr Nicholls telling her that they had been working with an adoption agency before suddenly having a miracle pregnancy. A picture of a five-month-old Fawn on his desk, meaning that her birthday was inside the window of dates for Eva Nováková's death, and the disappearance of her baby.

'Dr Nicholls,' Gemma said, bile rising in her throat, 'what is Eva Nováková's real name?'

'It's not what you think,' Dr Nicholls said.

'Daddy?' Fawn asked. 'What's happening?'

'What is her name?' Gemma asked again.

Dr Nicholls pressed his hands to his face. 'Petra,' he said. 'Petra Seifert.'

'Petra,' Fawn repeated. 'That's on my list.'

* * *

'Your mother and I struggled for years – nearly a decade,' Dr Nicholls explained. He held Fawn's hands in his own. She stared down at them like she had never seen a pair of hands before.

'Diets, temperature charts, fertility calendars, medication, round after round of IVF. When it was clear it wasn't going to happen, we looked at adoption. The year you were born there were only seventy domestic adoptions. Whether we went domestic or international, we were told to assume it would take five to eight years. So we put our names down, and we waited, and we hoped. And while we were waiting, I met Petra.'

Fawn made a hurt noise, and he shook his head. 'Not like that, love. Never like that. Petra was a backpacker from the Czech Republic who had overstayed her visa. She was working for cash under the table on the Dillon farm. I . . .' He sighed. 'The Dillons hired a lot of people like Petra. They liked illegal workers, because it felt safer. Less risk of a disgruntled worker blowing the whistle if doing that meant they risked getting deported. A bit of mutually assured destruction.'

'I think the term you're looking for is human trafficking,' Gemma said. She looked at Hugh, expecting him to agree. But there was no trace of surprise on his face. He was breathing in and out purposefully, the way he did when he was trying to stave off a panic attack.

She wanted to believe it was out of empathy, or horror, but that wouldn't explain how guilty he'd looked earlier.

'Nobody was getting lured in under false pretences or had their passport held hostage,' Dr Nicholls said. 'But it did mean they had a lot of staff not covered under Medicare. They were worried it would raise red flags if medical clinics were seeing an unusually large number of patients who were using travel insurance or paying out of pocket. So I did a bit of cash-in-hand work for them, just for minor medical issues. Patched up the odd injury, prescribed routine medications, gave flu shots. We were staring down the barrel of paying forty thousand dollars in adoption expenses, so every bit helped.'

'And that's how you met my mother?' Fawn asked.

'Lotte is your mother. But yes, I met Petra while working at the Dillon farm. And the second I saw her, it was like stepping back in time. She and your mother could have been twins.'

'So what, it was fine for you to sleep with her if she looked like Mum?'

'The most intimate contact I ever had with Petra was a hug, and your mother was there. Do you really want to know the nitty gritty details of how you came to exist?'

Fawn considered this for a moment, then shook her head.

'When I first met Petra, I just thought it was interesting she looked so much like your mother. I mentioned it to her, but we couldn't see any way they could be related – Petra was an only child, and her parents had never left Czechia. They had both passed away by the time she began travelling. Your mum's side of the family is from Norway and Australia, and no-one had ever lived in or travelled to Czechia. It was just a strange coincidence. I introduced the two of them, and it was your mother who suggested to me that we ask Petra to be a surrogate for us.'

'That's a pretty big ask for a near stranger,' Fawn said.

'Yes. But, well, we'd already resigned ourselves to the idea that becoming parents was going to cost us tens of thousands of dollars.'

Gemma frowned. 'Paid surrogacy isn't legal here,' she pointed out. She just wasn't sure she was buying this story.

'No. We were taking a big risk. We offered Petra a deal. She would carry a child for us; I would be the biological father, she would be the biological mother, and Lotte would adopt the child at birth. On the quiet, we would give Petra a significant amount of compensation, and sponsor her for a working visa as my practice's receptionist. If she wanted, she could be in your life like a big sister or aunt.'

'Wow, rainbows and unicorns all around,' Gemma said. She couldn't believe that a man she had always looked up to as a reliably wise and compassionate figure had treated a woman like a walking incubator. 'So how did she end up in an unmarked grave? Did she change her mind about signing her rights over to Lotte?'

'This is already a lot for Fawn,' Dr Nicholls said. 'Maybe we could –'

'It's a reasonable question,' Fawn said.

'Petra stopped working for the Dillons as soon as she fell pregnant. But when she was thirty-six weeks, a friend asked her to come back to the farm to help out. They had a shipment going out during the night, but couldn't get it done without another person. Petra was the kind of person who always wanted to pitch in when she was needed. I don't have all the details of what happened next, but they were rushing, and the mechanism on a tipping trailer malfunctioned and it dropped without warning, crushing Petra's hand and amputating it at the wrist.'

Gemma cringed.

'The friend –'

'It was Aubrey, wasn't it?' Gemma interjected. Aubrey had lived on her parents' farm at the time, and that would explain her unlikely friendship with Lotte.

Not to mention why she'd gone to talk to Hugh after Lochlan's murder.

Dr Nicholls sighed, and then nodded. So that was one more person who had known this the whole time while Gemma was left in the dark.

'Aubrey made a really bad decision. Instead of calling an ambulance, she called me. She told me Petra had injured her hand.'

'Because the shipment was illegal, right?' Gemma asked. Knowing that Rainier had once had a grow operation had always been spoken of as something funny, the not-so-gritty underbelly to contrast with the main street's Chantilly cream cakes and planters full of pansies. But apparently they had put vulnerable, desperate people's lives on the line to protect that secret. She could never look at the Dillons the same way again.

'I don't know. Maybe it was that, or maybe it was just that panic makes you dumb. I walked in expecting to stitch up a cut or splint a sprained finger. I found a literal bloodbath.' Dr Nicholls closed his eyes. 'I don't know if she would have survived if Aubrey had called emergency services right away. Frankly, probably not. The injury was catastrophic, and the hospital was forty-five minutes away. By the time I arrived, Petra was unconscious. She was in haemorrhagic shock, meaning that she wasn't getting enough oxygen – and neither were you, Fawn. Both options I had were terrible: we could try to transport Petra, who was on the edge of death, to hospital, and more likely than not lose both of you. Or I could deliver you by emergency caesarean section, and almost certainly kill Petra in the process.'

'Jesus.' Gemma put a hand to her own stomach. She could picture the scene, Fawn's frantic, brutal entry into the world on the floor of a farm shed.

'I've spent nearly eighteen years replaying it, thinking over the probabilities, the possible outcomes, what options there might have been that I didn't consider at the time. But I didn't have eighteen years to weigh up the options. In the heat of the moment, I did what seemed right.'

Dr Nicholls squeezed his eyes shut, and took a few moments to breathe. When he was ready, he continued. 'In medicine, sometimes awful decisions have to be made. So there is a framework, a hierarchy. Ideally, the next of kin makes the call: a mother, a father, a spouse, an adult child. If there isn't one, or they can't be contacted in time, the patient's doctors can make the decision. But I wasn't just Petra's doctor in that moment. I was your father, and I chose your life over hers. And I don't know if a court would have agreed that I had the right to make that decision.'

Fawn pulled her hands from her father's grasp to swipe at the tears that were running down her face. Gemma grabbed the box of tissues from Hugh's bedside table and offered it to her, but Fawn batted it away.

'I found myself there with you in my arms, and Petra dead, and I didn't know what would happen next. Was I going to lose

285

my medical licence? Would I be charged with murder? At best, I would be cleared legally, but it would be splashed all over the papers. You'd have lived in the shadow of the story.'

'I'd have lived knowing the truth,' Fawn said. And then she stood and walked out.

Dr Nicholls moved as if to follow her, but Hugh held up a hand. 'Give her a minute, mate,' he said, his voice shaking.

'Yeah. We're not done here,' Gemma said. She looked at Hugh. 'Where do you come in?' she asked, because it was clear that he was involved.

'I was on shift that night,' Hugh said. 'I got a call from a neighbour who thought they'd heard screaming. I walked into the shed just as Fawn was being born. Aubrey was screaming her head off. Petra was . . .' He faltered, like he couldn't find the words to describe what he'd seen. 'Then, suddenly, there was a baby crying.'

'Oh.' More pieces slotted into place. That was where Hugh's trauma had started, followed almost immediately by the murders of Vincent and Dean. His psyche had taken blow after blow, then less than a year later Violet had been born, and he'd lived with the sound of a baby crying round the clock. How often had she seen him zone out, completely unaware that mentally he was back in that shed?

'I know that it was wrong. I knew at the time it was wrong. But, Jesus, I wasn't even a full constable yet. I wouldn't even have been attending calls alone if our station had more than two officers. And it was Dr Nicholls. It was your best friend . . .'

'Don't put this on me,' Gemma said. 'You and I weren't even dating then. You did not look at Aubrey and see my best friend.'

'Oh for crying out loud, Gemma, I'd been in love with you for a good three years by that point. Of course I looked at Aubrey and saw your best friend.'

Of all the completely wild things she'd learned in the past half-hour, she didn't know why that was the one that pushed her over the edge. She sat down heavily on the end of the bed. 'What?'

'Can we not, please? You were with Vincent. I wasn't going to make a nuisance of myself over it. Then you guys broke up but, you know, the whole world went to complete shit. The one bright point was that we were together, and by the time I realised you saw our marriage as some kind of mutually convenient arrangement I was a little preoccupied having a nervous breakdown.'

'I'm going to . . .' Dr Nicholls took a step away.

'No,' Gemma said. They hadn't even scratched the surface of what Hugh had done, and she didn't trust him to tell the whole truth if it was just the two of them. 'Let's table this and go back to the night Petra died.'

'Fine,' said Hugh. 'Like I told you, I walked in and it was a complete nightmare. But it was obviously an accident, and it was two people I trusted. They begged me to let them handle it, and so . . . I walked away. I closed out the call and went on with my shift.'

Gemma let that sink in. 'That's not all you did, though.'

It would have been bad enough if that was all. But it wasn't. This went deeper.

'It was just a split second, a stupid fucking decision. I didn't realise all the implications at the time. I know it sounds ridiculous now, but part of me thought I was just giving them some breathing space to sort it out. But it started to sink in when Lotte announced she'd had a baby –'

'We'd always intended to keep our decision to use a surrogate private,' Dr Nicholls interjected.

Gemma had been wondering about that. She didn't remember any chatter amongst the teashop's regular ladies about the Nicholls using a surrogate. It was still unusual enough to be remarked on – back then, it would have been the talk of the town.

'We didn't run around telling people Lotte was pregnant, either. We didn't want to have to explain that away if Petra changed her mind. Lotte took some leave from work and we just . . . kept it private. Then when Fawn was born, the safest way to get her a birth certificate was to pretend Lotte gave birth at home, with me attending.'

'Well, as long as the paperwork was in order,' Hugh said bitterly. 'After that, I realised that Petra would never get a proper burial. I couldn't sleep. And when I could, I had nightmares about her. After a week, I broke down and confessed to my dad what I'd done.'

Gemma's throat constricted. One more person who'd known the whole time.

'I think I was hoping he would tell me to own up to it, to tell the sergeant the truth and deal with the consequences. But he said that I would ruin so many lives if I did that – the Dillons', the Nicholls', my own – to help no-one. But I couldn't stand the idea of Petra's final resting place being behind a shed somewhere, or worse. So my father offered to preside over a proper burial service for her.'

Gemma glanced over at Dr Nicholls, who was staring at Hugh with a stony expression. It was obvious this wasn't new information to him, but there was still a hint of anger in the set of his jaw.

'Dad could perform a funeral, but he couldn't consecrate ground. So I went back to Aubrey and insisted that we move the body. There used to be a fence between the cemetery and the park; it was removed in the eighties to open the space up. The spot we picked had once been part of the cemetery and so was consecrated ground. We wrapped her in a blanket and buried her there.'

Gemma remembered being shown that blanket by the police, stained with blood and dirt. She had even told Hugh the story, confided how difficult she had found it, and he had said nothing.

'We were able to cover up the grave with fallen leaves, and even moved around some small plants so it didn't look too obvious. By morning, it was like it had never happened.'

'But it didn't stay that way,' Gemma said.

'None of us could have predicted the Rainier Ripper. When her body was found we didn't know what to do, so we did nothing. It just snowballed.'

She could see it, a chain of bad decisions that, once made, couldn't be undone. Each one inevitably leading to a bigger, worse decision.

'You let the town live in terror for months thinking there was a psychopath stalking the streets,' Gemma said.

'There was!' Hugh said. 'Thank god the town was on high alert. If you didn't think that, would you have opened the door

289

to Dean Shadwell? Jan Henning-Klosner could have been right behind him, with a knife.'

'Maybe.' Gemma was reassessing the last eighteen years of her life. 'How far did you take it? Did you interfere with the medical examination? Wouldn't they have picked up on the fact that her stomach wound came from a surgical procedure?'

'I swear I didn't interfere. Maybe if the autopsy had been performed the day she died it would have been obvious, but after weeks of burial? I don't want to get too graphic, but no, they couldn't tell.'

'And Jan Henning-Klosner? What did you do to get him to confess?'

'I promise you I didn't coerce him into it. We had him dead to rights on murdering Vincent and Dean and attacking Tamara. Mick kept pressing him on Eva and the baby, and eventually he broke down and confessed to all three murders. It was like an answered prayer.'

Gemma had to force herself not to laugh at how ridiculous that was. If there was a God, he'd shown no interest in Rainier.

'I've tried my best to stop this from hurting anyone else. I monitored Missing Persons reports, and told Tim that the second someone came looking for Petra I would tell the truth. Same when families of other missing girls asked. I always put their minds at ease.'

'Like Matilda Carver's family,' Gemma said. 'You told them she'd been ruled out, and then put a fake note in the file.'

Hugh frowned. 'How did you know that?'

'None of your business,' Gemma said. 'That's how it works in our marriage, right?'

'That's fair.' Hugh sighed, twisting his wedding ring on his finger.

'So all this time, you've been protecting this secret. You've been running interference to make sure no-one looked closer at Eva Nováková. You've been conducting fake investigations to rule out possible identities like Matilda Carver.'

'Yes,' Hugh confessed. Out the corner of her eye she saw Dr Nicholls nod too – as the town's doctor, and with Lotte as the local magistrate and coroner, they were probably able to intervene sometimes.

'But to do that,' Gemma said slowly, 'you had to be a Rainier police officer. That's why you were so insistent on coming back once you were well enough. That's why you refuse to consider moving. Why you didn't want an outside detective working on Lochlan Lewis's murder.'

'Yes,' Hugh said again.

'I need to go,' Gemma said. 'Once the hospital is done with your discharge, I'm sure they can help organise a taxi to take you anywhere other than my house.'

THIRTY-ONE

ONE OF THE first things Vincent spent money on after starting his first trucking job was getting a UHF radio installed in his ageing but comfortable ute.

'I've got it in the rig, and now driving without it feels like there's something missing,' he'd explained in response to her baffled look.

The first time they took a road trip together, she understood what he meant. All her life, driving had been a lonesome activity, but it turned out there were conversations going on all around her; she just hadn't been on the right frequency to hear them. They would hum along through the dark, and every now and then the radio would crackle to life with the ephemera of the road. Holiday convoys losing track of each other. Truck drivers giving bulletins on petrol prices, or nuisance cars, or when the servo they'd just left had put a fresh batch of pies in the warmer. Kids playing at radio operator.

The first time she'd driven in her own car again, in the silence, she'd understood. There *was* something missing.

She had the same feeling now: it seemed that everyone in her life had been communicating with each other on a frequency she hadn't been able to hear.

Who else knew? Aubrey, obviously, and the Dillons. Was Mick in on it? Was there anyone she could safely take this to?

How far had Hugh gone to hide this secret? He'd been willing to bury Petra's body. To frame another man – an otherwise guilty man, admittedly.

He'd been willing to warp their entire life around it. To spend their entire marriage lying to her and hiding things. To let their relationship slowly collapse under the weight rather than tell her the truth.

Was Hugh capable of murdering Lochlan Lewis to keep it buried?

The idea struck her so hard she had to pull over onto the shoulder, afraid that she was too distracted to drive.

Hugh had the opportunity. He was no Antoine Tjibaou, but he was certainly strong enough to subdue Lochlan, and to lift his body into the fountain unassisted.

And he definitely had a motive.

This tour idea put their secret at risk. Lochlan had wanted to put up posters of Petra's face in two major cities. He wanted to tell her story to hundreds of people. He might have been willing to pay for her DNA testing.

But was Hugh really capable of murder? Could someone who was so broken up over all the hurt that he'd seen, deliberately cause more?

It was such an extreme step, when surely he had other options. Why not at least wait until he was sure the town would agree to the tour? Why deliberately pose the body in an outlandish, attention-grabbing way, if the goal was to prevent renewed interest in the case?

And there was still the question of who took the picture of Gemma and Marcus. Hugh was in a motel near the Special Purpose Centre at the time. Even if he had been able to take the photo, why would he? Why would he want to direct suspicion back towards his own household?

* * *

Her heart dropped when she pulled into her parking space behind the teashop. There was a navy blue Mazda SUV in Hugh's usual spot.

Aubrey's car.

Gemma tipped her head back, wanting to scream, but then she remembered that someone was stalking her, and the last thing she needed was a photograph of her having a meltdown.

Aubrey got out of the car when she saw Gemma emerge, and leaned against the door, her arms crossed.

'What the fuck is wrong with you?' Aubrey asked.

Oh. Apparently neither Hugh nor Dr Nicholls had called Aubrey yet to let them know they'd been rumbled.

'I asked myself the same question for a long time, but it's starting to become clearer lately,' Gemma said.

'You know that you're nothing to Jac, right? You're not their mother. You're not some kind of pseudo-stepmother. You're the girl their biological father dated twenty years ago.'

'I'm their friend,' Gemma said. 'And I'm their friend's mother. I'm the one they came to wanting help'

'Because you're a pushover. All the kids know that if they want something unreasonable, you're the weak link to go after.'

Gemma tried not to show how badly that stung. It was true, but it was still painful to hear. 'They knew they couldn't go to you for help.'

'Of course not! I would never have let them do this!'

'They were determined to, though. They'd have found a way, and at least I was there to support them.'

'It was a conversation with a serial killer, Gemma, not letting them try a glass of wine. I don't know what you were thinking!'

'You're hardly in a position to lecture me on thinking things through,' Gemma said.

Aubrey's face went white; Gemma couldn't tell if it was with fear or anger.

'If you're done yelling at me, I'd like to take my turn,' Gemma continued. 'Actually, I only have one thing to say. Petra Seifert.'

Aubrey's face crumpled. 'Oh god,' she said, pressing her hands to her eyes.

'You know what? I don't even want to talk about it. Just get back in your car and go away.'

'If it helps, I told Hugh he should tell you – a long time ago.'

That didn't make Gemma feel any better. It just confirmed to her that Hugh and Aubrey had been talking about this behind her back. All of them were in on this little secret together. Hugh and Aubrey and Tim and Lotte.

God, she was being ridiculous. There were so many worse things about what they'd done than her being left out. But she was replaying so many moments in her life that suddenly made more sense.

'Did you tell Mick?'

'That's different. Mick wouldn't have been able to accept it.'

'You think I would have?'

Gemma wasn't sure, actually. If she had found out because Hugh was honest with her, instead of being blindsided by it, would she have been able to see it his way? What she did know for sure was that if she'd had all the information she might have made different decisions. About marrying him. About taking on a huge debt with him. About moving back to Rainier. About even trying to forgive him for abandoning them.

Almost every decision she'd made in her life, all those wrong choices she'd been beating herself up over, had been made with only half the information she needed. How could she accept that?

'We're not bad people,' Aubrey said. 'We were all just trying to do our best in a fucked-up situation.'

Gemma scoffed, but before she could snap anything back, her phone buzzed. Grateful for an excuse to end the conversation with Aubrey, she fished it out of her bag.

A private number.

The station?

Could Fawn have blown the whistle? Or maybe even Hugh, trying to get ahead of it before she or Gemma turned him in?

But why would Mick call Gemma first, before his own wife?

She answered it on speaker. 'Gemma Guillory speaking.' She looked at Aubrey, a silent invitation to announce her presence, but Aubrey said nothing.

'Gemma.' It was Mick, his voice agitated. 'Are you at home?'

'I'm just outside. I'm about to go in.'

'Don't! Where's Violet?'

'She's inside. What's going on?' Her earlier anxiety was nothing compared to the terror that gripped her now.

'Don't go inside. A unit is on the way to your house.'

'What. Is. Happening?'

'We got a match on the fingerprint we found on the bloodied raincoat.'

'It was Marcus Shadwell?' She stared up at the dark windows of their home.

'No. The fingerprint belonged to Dean Shadwell.'

'*What?*' She locked eyes with Aubrey, who looked as mystified as Gemma felt. 'I don't understand.'

Gemma switched the call off speaker, and gestured for Aubrey to step in closer so she could still hear. She doubted that the sound from her cheap old phone would carry up to the second floor, but she didn't want to take any chances.

'We have a set of fingerprints on file from when Dean Shadwell was charged with possession of a controlled substance a few years before his death. The print on the raincoat is an extremely close match for those fingerprints.'

It took Gemma a moment to untangle that. 'You're telling me that Lochlan Lewis's killer was Dean Shadwell.'

'The evidence suggests that.'

'The Dean Shadwell who died right in front of me.'

'Either we need to fundamentally adjust our understanding of how life and death works, or the man who died in your shop was not Dean Shadwell.'

'Who identified the body?' Gemma asked, even as an icy certainty gripped her.

'A man who presented himself as Dean's brother Marcus.'

'Oh my god,' Gemma whispered. 'His last words. He said "Dean". We thought he was trying to tell us his name, when he was really trying to tell us who killed him.'

So much made sense now. The way Marcus had told his own life story like he was one of the villains and Dean was an innocent victim who deserved better.

'Violet is in there with him, Mick,' Gemma said. She felt hot all over, and cold at the same time. She'd left her baby alone with a monster.

'We're on our way, Gemma. She's going to be just fine.'

They ended the call, and Gemma turned to run through the gate. Aubrey grabbed her elbow, her fingers digging in even through the wool of her jumper.

'What the hell are you doing?' Aubrey hissed. 'The police will be here any minute.'

'Exactly!' Gemma snapped back. 'He killed Lochlan. He's up there, and so is my daughter. How do you think this is going to play out when the police knock on the door? I'm not going to let this turn into a hostage situation. What would you do if it was Jac up there?'

'Jac wouldn't be alone with him in the first place,' Aubrey said, but she relaxed her grip slightly.

'Twenty seconds, Aubs. He doesn't know what's going on yet. I'll go upstairs and get Violet, and we'll be back down here before the police have even turned the corner.'

* * *

She rapped on Violet's door.

'Holy shit, Mum, are you alright?' Violet asked as she opened it. 'Where's Dad? Weren't you going to pick him up?'

Gemma couldn't imagine how awful she looked right now. 'I need you to come for a walk with me,' she said. 'We're going to go calmly to the door. As soon as your feet hit the back stairs, I need you to run.'

'Mum?' Violet sounded scared.

'Everything alright?' Marcus – Dean – called.

Gemma turned slowly, trying to look natural. She could see him through the windows, on the front verandah with a cigarette in his hand. From where he was standing he would see the police cars pull up; they would lose the advantage of surprise.

'Hi, Marcus,' Gemma called, her voice high and thready. 'Don't mind us, we've had a bit of family drama.'

Gemma was practised at keeping her thoughts off her face. She could smile and chitchat with someone she felt nothing but contempt for, she could pretend she liked something she thought was hideous, she could glide through the day greasing every interaction with white lies and fakery.

But all week 'Marcus' had seen straight through that facade. And oh, she'd liked it, hadn't she? For the first time in a long while, she'd felt understood.

Through the window, he saw her. He understood.

She turned back to Violet and dropped her voice as low as she could. 'Never mind. Go inside your room and lock the door. Push your dresser in front of it. Don't open it for anyone except Mick Seabrooke or' – she racked her brain for the name of the female police officer she'd met recently – 'Panipak Seesondee. No-one else. Not even me.'

She liked to think that even under threat of violence, she would never let Shadwell use her to trick Violet into coming out, but better safe than sorry.

Violet looked like she was going to argue.

'Do it,' Gemma said, in the firmest mum voice she had ever used.

300

Violet eased the door closed, and part of Gemma relaxed as she heard the old-fashioned lock clunk shut.

Gemma had considered following her in and sheltering with her, but that gave Shadwell a single target. He was of average size, but he could still have the bedroom door down in minutes. Better to leave her daughter safe here, and draw his attention somewhere else.

She went out on to the verandah and shut the door behind her. The crime scene tent still stood, the white canvas flecked with fallen leaves and dirt. In her head she traced the line from the front door of the shop to the tent, then to the stormwater drain where the raincoat had been stashed, and then down the alley to her back gate. How had Shadwell done it?

'Sorted your drama, then?' Shadwell asked, leaning against the railing.

'Oh yeah,' Gemma said, too loud and too bright. 'Hugh has to stay in the hospital for a few days more. I wasted a trip.'

He knew she knew, and she knew he knew, but maybe if she just kept pretending everything was normal, he would too until the police showed up.

'Aw, shit,' Shadwell said. 'What gave me away?'

Or not.

'Fingerprints,' Gemma admitted.

He looked down at his hand, the one still wrapped in a bandage. Of course. What kind of idiot would grab a pot that had clearly just come out of the oven? The kind that wanted to

301

burn themselves. Thirty seconds of agony in exchange for a ready excuse not to be fingerprinted.

'Where? I was so careful.'

'On the poncho.'

His air of control wavered, just for a moment. 'What?'

'How did you do it?' she asked. Her only chance was to keep him talking, and you couldn't go wrong by stroking a man's ego. 'I've been driving myself mad trying to figure it out. You had barely any time; your plan must have been incredible.'

'I know you're trying to blow smoke up my arse, but it *was* a pretty great plan. It was simple, that's the trick.'

He reached inside his jacket, and pulled out a wooden-handled folding knife. An Opinel, like the one he said had been stolen from him.

'So you lied about that being stolen,' she said, her voice shaking. It made no sense. It seemed like a risky gambit – sure, it could create some doubt if the forensics proved his knife was the murder weapon, but why draw the police's attention to the fact he'd brought a knife to town?

'I didn't,' he said. He twisted the catch, unfolding the blade. Acid rose in her throat.

'Then how did you get it back?'

'The one that was stolen from me was Marcus's knife. This one is mine. Of course, I had to buy mine, while his was a gift from his dear old granddad. Story of my life.'

Gemma swallowed. It suddenly made a terrible sense why he carried them both with him. They were trophies. The knife he'd taken from his brother, and the knife he'd used to do it. He was completely depraved.

She wanted to take a step away from him, but was terrified of setting him off.

'My old buddy Jan bought one too, which came in damn handy when they found a weapon in his truck that matched the one I used to kill Marcus. Though the traces of Vincent Tjibaou's blood in the mechanism was all Jan.'

'You knew the Ripper?' That matched what Tamara had told her.

'We were in business together for a while. Small potatoes; a little ecstasy, a little oxy. Enough to make a good living, although nothing like what Marcus had handed to him by his bitch of a mother's family.' Shadwell shook his head sadly. 'Then Jan had to go and bring the heat down on us by killing Vincent – not to mention the girl and her baby. I had no idea I was in business with a psychopath.'

Gemma considered telling him that Jan hadn't killed Petra, and no-one had killed her baby, but decided to keep that card in her deck. He seemed happy to talk for the moment.

'Suddenly the area was crawling with cops, and it was only a matter of time before Jan got caught and dragged me into it. I wasn't doing another stint in prison; I barely survived the first time, and that was only sixty days. And that was the best-case scenario – I'm pretty sure he was planning to kill me next. I texted my dear old brother Marcus, and told him I needed help. I asked him to meet me in Rainier.'

'So when you asked him for help, he came through for you?'

'He could have really helped me if he'd wanted to,' Shadwell snarled. 'He could have changed my life with an amount of money that would have been pocket change to him. He came when I asked, but he wanted to shut me up with a token handout, not help me. Not the way he was capable of.'

'You're right,' Gemma said. 'It was your father who cheated, but you're the one who got punished. You were still Marcus's brother, but he let his family abandon you.'

'Shut up,' Shadwell snapped. 'I'm not stupid – that's not going to work.'

'Sorry.'

She thought she might have lost him but luckily, despite seeing through her clumsy attempt at sympathy, he was still eager to tell his story. It had probably driven him to distraction, knowing that he'd pulled off such an elaborate scheme but could never talk about it.

'I've lifted a few wallets in my time, so when Marcus met me in the park it was easy to take his wallet and slip my own into his jacket.'

'Why not wait until he was dead? Wouldn't that have been easier?'

'Maybe, but I figured if I did the switch after killing him, I could mess up the blood spatter or whatever, and screw myself. And it's a good thing I did it beforehand, since he turned out to have more fight in him than I expected. I was surprised he made it all the way to your door.' Shadwell's face lit up with an awful, cruel grin. 'You know the best part? How easy it was to slide into Marcus's life. I don't think my brother had any real friends. He had the sort of hangers-on who were happy to be ghosted rather than have to support him through his brother's death. I broke up with his girlfriend by text message. I went to ground for a few months, and when I started appearing in public as "Marcus", people just chalked up the physical changes to grief. I was about twenty kilograms lighter than him.' He laughed. 'One person complimented me on the weight loss.'

Gemma risked a glance down at the street below. It felt like it had been hours since Mick's call, but only a few minutes had passed, and there was still no sign of the car. There was no officer on tape duty at the crime scene, either. She didn't know what to make of that. Were they no longer guarding the scene? She'd had too much on her mind to notice the last few times she went past.

It was a weird feeling, desperately waiting for the police to arrive while also knowing that their arrival would shift the situation from tense to explosive.

'I do wish that I'd cleaned up a few more of the loose ends, though,' Shadwell continued. 'Maybe if I'd paid Ruthie off the first time she contacted me I wouldn't be in this mess now. But, then, if it worked once she would have just kept coming back. Maybe it was always going to end here.'

'So you are Nico's father,' Gemma said.

There was something off about this conversation. She didn't understand why he was so focused on the past, when she was more interested in knowing how he'd pulled off the murder of Lochlan.

Shadwell shrugged. 'Doubt it. I really did get the snip. With the shit I'd seen, the last thing I wanted was to inflict this world on more kids. But vasectomies can fail. The only way to be one hundred per cent safe is abstinence, as the nuns at school used to say.' He sighed. 'I certainly couldn't risk letting her have the DNA sample she wanted, since if the kid was mine, the test would show I was his father, not a paternal uncle. It'd blow my scam wide open.'

Surely the police should have arrived by now. Mick said a unit was on its way, and the station was only blocks away. Where were they?

Except, she realised, that had been the original plan. When Gemma and Violet didn't come right down as promised, Aubrey must have raised the alarm. It was no longer a matter of sending a couple of cops up to knock on the door and bring Shadwell in for questioning.

She took a steadying breath. That was fine. Maybe they were coming in more quietly, and wouldn't send a car. Officers might be getting into position already where she couldn't see them. They might have stopped to talk strategy, formulate a plan, maybe call in some off-duty officers from the motel. They just needed a little more time.

Shadwell seemed calm for now. She just had to keep him that way. Keep him talking.

'But why kill Lochlan? And how?'

She still couldn't get her head around that. Sure, Shadwell wouldn't want the extra attention that the tour would bring.

The last thing he needed was someone getting inspired to look closer at the circumstances of 'Dean' Shadwell's murder. But Lochlan's murder had immediately brought exactly the kind of scrutiny he'd been trying to avoid. And why had he just hung around waiting to get caught?

Shadwell stared at her. 'Lochlan?'

'Oh, don't even,' she snarled, a sudden surge of anger taking her by surprise. It was embarrassing enough that he'd been playing her all week. 'I told you: you left fingerprints on the poncho.'

'What poncho? I've never owned a poncho in my life.'

'The one covered in Lochlan Lewis's blood that they pulled out of that drain.' She pointed down the street.

Shadwell followed the line of her finger, staring down at the drain with a look of deep confusion. Then he shifted, his shoulders sinking into his chest. 'I don't suppose it was made of clear plastic?'

'Yeah.'

'I stopped in Gundagai to charge my car,' Shadwell said. 'It takes about fifteen minutes, so I went to use the bathroom and grab a coffee. When I came back, there was a plastic bag or something on my windshield. I figured it had blown out of one of the bins nearby. I pulled it off and chucked it back in.'

Gemma rolled her eyes. 'Sure.'

'I'm serious, Gemma. There's only two electric chargers between here and Sydney. The odds I would stop there on my way were pretty damn good. How hard would it have been to stake it out, and create a situation where I had to touch the poncho?'

'What if you hadn't stopped? What if you hadn't touched it, or wore gloves?'

'Then they probably had a plan B that they didn't need to use, because I did stop and I did touch it.'

'Why are you trying to convince me of this?'

'Because it's true.'

Gemma noticed movement at the edge of her vision, inside the house, and prayed it wasn't Violet opening her door. She couldn't turn to look, not without drawing Shadwell's attention to it.

If she had telepathy, she would scream at Violet to stay put. Don't open the door. Put her own safety first.

Against her will, she let out an odd, strangled laugh.

'What's funny about that?' Shadwell asked. 'I'm serious. You need to believe me.'

'I'm not laughing at you,' she said. 'There's nothing funny here. I just realised something . . .'

Her mother had told her, all those years ago, to do the same thing: put her own safety first. And she had, and then spent years hating herself for it. For not letting Dean – Marcus – in. For those wasted minutes that might have saved his life. She'd spent the last seventeen years desperate to please everyone around her. Taking care of them whether they wanted her to or not. Because she owed the world for her mistake.

'You were there,' she said. 'Watching. He got away from you, and you couldn't come up to the door to finish him off because you couldn't risk me seeing you. But you couldn't risk him surviving, either. So if I'd opened the door . . .'

Shadwell sighed, and flicked his cigarette aside. 'Yeah. I was watching. You were so fucking hot, Gemma. I mean, no offence, you're still pretty, but when I saw you through the window that night, all doe-eyed and pale . . . You wouldn't believe how many times I've jerked off picturing your face that night.'

'Fuck you,' Gemma whispered.

'It wasn't part of the plan, but god I was hoping you would open the door. But in a way it's cool that you didn't. Now Violet exists, because I didn't kill you that night. If you think about it, the two of you belong to me.' He leaned in close. 'Do you think the police will be able to get to me quicker than I can get to her? It'll be like a fun little race.'

Gemma screamed, and threw herself at him. She didn't care about the knife, she just cared about slowing him down. She would hold him back with her dead weight if she had to.

The force sent him stumbling back against the railing. She registered a strange cracking noise. She only realised it was the sound of the century-old mortar holding up the railing post when it collapsed under them and they crashed together to the pavement below.

THIRTY-TWO

GEMMA DREAMED OF clanging bells and squeaking wheels. She dreamed that a man climbed onto her chest, his knees grinding into her shoulders as he leaned over to press random buttons on the monitor beside her bed and yank at cables, grinning wider and wider as alarms began to scream one after the other. Sometimes his face was Dean Shadwell's, and sometimes he was Marcus Shadwell, and sometimes he was Hugh.

* * *

One time she woke up and Vincent Tjibaou was seated by her bedside, squeezing her hand. 'Wrong way, go back,' he whispered, and she closed her eyes again.

* * *

When she woke up for real, Violet was by her bed, reading a battered old copy of *The Handmaid's Tale*. When she noticed Gemma watching her she dropped the book on the floor and jumped to her feet, shouting for the nurse.

* * *

The next time it was still Violet, much further along in the book.

'Hey,' Gemma whispered. She tried to reach out to her, but her arms each weighed a hundred kilos.

'Mum,' Violet said.

'Are you okay?'

For some reason, that question made Violet laugh until suddenly she was crying in huge, wet gulps. 'Of course I'm not okay, Mum. None of us are okay. Everything is completely fucked up.'

'I know, I'm sorry,' Gemma said. 'I'm so glad to see you.'

'Me too.' Violet reached over and yanked a handful of tissues out of a box on the table next to Gemma's bed.

'Where's your dad?'

Violet's face fell. 'He's not allowed to visit. Nanna and Granddad got a court order, it was a whole mess.' She offered Gemma a shaky grin. 'I'm jealous that you got to sleep through it, honestly.'

'How long has it been?'

'Three weeks, nearly four.' Violet sniffed. 'You had a concussion, broke both legs and your left hip, and dislocated your left shoulder. But your spine is okay. You won't have any problems walking.'

'Sounds like my Olympic figure-skating dreams are over, then,' Gemma joked. Then she remembered. 'Shadwell?'

'Dead,' Violet said bluntly. 'He broke his skull and died a few days later. Apparently he absorbed most of the force of the fall. He hit the ground, you hit him.'

'Are they sure?' Gemma asked. 'There's definitely a body?'

'They're sure,' Violet said, squeezing her hand. 'That was a whole other mess, because of course when they called his wife in to identify the remains she identified him as her husband Marcus Shadwell. It's lucky they had Dean Shadwell's fingerprints on file to confirm it was really him or it would have been tricky. Especially since Mrs Nicholls resigned as the coroner, so the state coroner had to appoint someone new to make a ruling.'

Gemma closed her eyes. There was a lot to unpack there. 'His wife? Shadwell was a widower. Gabby Herald died.'

'Uh, no? She's very much alive, and pretty messed up by all this. She told *The Australian* they'd been trying for a baby.'

Had Marcus actually said that Gabby was dead? He'd definitely implied it, and Gemma had been more than eager to believe it, hadn't she? She hadn't pressed for any details.

'Then Shadwell was messing with her. He didn't want kids. He –' Gemma opened her eyes again. Something about that was trying to tug at her attention, but it wasn't important right now. 'Are you okay?'

Violet looked like she was working hard not to laugh. 'You already asked that. I'm fine.'

'I mean, are you and Dad okay at the house? It's a crime scene again, right?'

For some reason Violet didn't answer for a long time. Finally she said, 'Yeah. Yeah, it's a crime scene again. It's . . .' She swallowed. 'It's fine. I'm actually staying in the family accommodation here at the hospital. That's really good for putting things in perspective. It's hard to feel sorry for yourself when half the people you eat breakfast with are watching their kids die of cancer.'

'You're allowed to feel sorry for yourself,' Gemma said. 'I'm so sorry, Violet. I'd convinced myself that I was protecting you, and I really just put you in danger.'

'It is pretty creepy to think that we spent a whole week living with a psycho and didn't even know it,' Violet said. Gemma couldn't help noticing that she hadn't accepted the apology.

'I genuinely trusted him,' Gemma said. 'I was sure he couldn't have killed Lochlan and so thought he was a safe person. It was idiotic and I have absolutely no excuse.'

'You'd just seen something awful and terrifying that dragged up old, unresolved trauma. You were barely sleeping, and running on fight-or-flight mode. I can't blame you for not making rational decisions.'

Seeing Gemma's look, Violet smiled. 'I've had a couple of emergency sessions with a social worker here in the hospital. She's really good – you should talk to her.'

'I will,' Gemma said, meaning it. She yawned, and turned her face into the pillow.

'I'll let you sleep,' Violet said. 'And I'll let Nanna and Granddad know you're awake.'

'Please tell them I want them to let your dad in. I need to talk to him.'

* * *

According to the clock on the wall, Gemma had been asleep for either an hour or more than a day when she heard the familiar sound of Hugh's footsteps.

'Sorry,' he whispered. 'I was trying not to wake you.'

'You never did get the hang of that,' she muttered.

When she saw Hugh's face, it finally sunk in how much time had passed in her painkiller twilight. His bruises were gone, aside from a few traces of yellow where she knew to look. The scab above his eyebrow was now a patch of shiny pink skin.

'Thank you for coming,' she said.

'Thank you for letting me,' he said.

Gemma took a deep breath. 'So, first things first. What is Violet not telling me about the house?'

Hugh grimaced. 'That's on me. I told her not to say anything. She wanted to stay with you, but I didn't want her to have to break the news.'

'What?'

'It burned down. Our house, the shop, everything.'

After a moment of confusion, she understood. 'Shadwell's cigarette.'

Gemma didn't know if the painkillers were numbing her emotions, or if she really wasn't that upset. They were insured, and part of her was relieved to know that the building, with all of its messy history, had been wiped away. Still, there were irreplaceable things in there. Soft toys and artwork and old letters and photographs.

'I'm afraid so. The arson guys think it went through the open back door and hit the carpet.'

'That's unlucky.' She wondered if it really was down to luck. Perhaps it had been Shadwell's last-ditch effort to create some chaos he could use to slip away.

'We got a little lucky. No-one was hurt, and the fire didn't spread to any neighbours.'

'Thank heavens for that.'

'I'm so sorry. If I'd listened to you in the first place, I'd have been home. You and Violet shouldn't have been alone in the house with him.'

'It's not your fault,' she said. 'I think expecting you to protect and take care of me is where I went wrong in the first place.'

He winced. 'That's fair.'

'I didn't mean it like that,' she said. 'I'm talking about me, not you. I didn't want to be alone. I didn't want to be alone the night Dean died.' She tipped her head back and rolled her eyes up to the ceiling. 'The night Marcus died, I should say.'

Hugh huffed, an almost-laugh. 'It's tripping us all up.'

'I didn't want to finish raising Violet alone. I didn't want to be abandoned again. I was so afraid of it that I was running all over town like Miss fucking Marple, thinking I was saving you from yourself, when the real danger was in our house the whole time.'

'You couldn't have known. He kept up his ruse for nearly two decades; he'd had a lot of practice.'

'No, I could have known. But I wanted to fall for it.' The confession was painful, but if there was one thing she'd learned, the truth was better out than in. 'He was so concerned about me all the time. He was good-looking, and emotionally available, and recently widowed.'

'You were attracted to him,' Hugh said, his voice quiet with hurt.

'No. But I thought he was attracted to me, and I let that explain away any weirdness in his behaviour. Like the house purchase.' She groaned. 'It should have rung alarm bells that anyone, no matter how rich, would casually drop that much money. But I wanted it to be true.'

'There might be more to it than that. Obviously I don't have all the details of the investigation anymore, but one of the guys mentioned that he'd been moving a lot of money around, out of investment accounts into places he could access it without being tracked. Getting ready to make a big cash offer on a building was a good way to do that without raising red flags that he was getting ready to run. They think that's what he was doing all week – putting together an escape plan, not realising how close the police were to nabbing him.'

Especially if he'd been telling the truth, and had no idea there could be evidence linking him to the murder of Lochlan Lewis. But Gemma didn't believe him.

Right?

'Even so, he was trying to make himself as appealing to me as possible so he could fly under my radar, and I let him.'

'You're stretching very hard to blame yourself for the behaviour of a psychopath.'

'I'm not trying to blame myself; I'm just trying to explain something to you. Being stuck in here has given me a lot of time to think.' She forced herself to look at him properly for the first time. 'Aubrey told me that she tried to convince you to tell me the truth years ago.'

'I wish I had listened.'

Gemma shook her head. 'If you had told me before we got married? I'd love to tell you that I would have called it all off. But I honestly don't know. But I can tell you that if I had accepted it, if I had let you pull me into your little conspiracy, it wouldn't have been because I supported you or thought it was the right thing to do. I'd have done it because I was afraid to be alone. And that would have been just as poisonous as the marriage we did have.'

Hugh pressed his lips together and nodded, but stayed silent.

'If I had known before we were even together, then I would never have invited you in that day. And Violet wouldn't exist.' Her voice wavered. Maybe this could have, should have, waited until she was strong enough to feel so much. But she didn't think she could properly rest and recover until it was all out. 'That's the

317

hardest thing. Violet's very existence is so tangled up in the myth of the Ripper murders that I can't even wish it never happened.'

'Me neither,' he said.

'But that's so fucked up. So, I need to be done with this obsession with other ways life could have turned out. We've got this one. We need to live it.'

'Do you think you and I could . . . start over?' He shook his head. 'Not start over. Rebuild?'

She thought about it for a long time. Her sadness was a physical thing, hard and sharp inside her chest.

'No,' she said finally, and as painful as it was she felt better for getting it out. She'd spent so much of her time, so much of herself, trying to hold together something that was almost good enough, because the alternative was to have nothing at all. Now having nothing, needing to start from scratch, felt freeing.

'I understand,' he said. 'And for what it's worth, I promise I'll do everything I can not to make this any more difficult than it needs to be. I won't try to make any claim on the lot itself; that's Grey family land. You can take it and build on it, or sell it – whatever you want.'

'I don't want it,' she said. She didn't believe in ghosts, but she did believe in haunted houses, and their home had been one.

'I'll do all the wrangling with the insurance company. If the payout covers all our debt, we can split whatever's left over fifty-fifty.'

Gemma was hit with a wave of deja vu so strong that for a moment she couldn't breathe. Here was the bookend to the conversation they'd had all those years ago, when Hugh had convinced her to move back to Rainier. She couldn't believe how long she'd spent blaming herself, punishing herself, for saying yes. She wished she could wrap her arms around that poor, exhausted, frightened girl and whisper, 'Run.'

But that had never really been an option, had it? If she'd had all the information, if she'd understood Hugh's real motivation, then she might have been able to do that. But the choice at the time had been between a new start with her baby's father, or going it alone as a single mother.

With a pang, she thought of Ruth Tanner. Ruth had never even had the choice. Nico's father had ghosted her, and then before she could pin him down, he'd been 'murdered'. Then, from Ruth's perspective, his obscenely wealthy brother had refused to help her in any way, even with something that cost nothing – a DNA sample. Of course, it was obvious now why Shadwell wouldn't do it, but to Ruth it must have just looked like pointless cruelty. Contempt for a woman and child he thought were beneath him.

But what would it have helped? It wasn't like a dead man could pay child support. She wondered if Ruth would be able to get some now from Shadwell's estate. It would be nice if some little scrap of good came from this.

Something was niggling at her. 'Hugh,' she said. 'Children of murder victims get a pay out from the Victims Support Scheme, right?'

Hugh's face scrunched in confusion at the non sequitur. 'Thinking of murdering me to give Violet a leg-up?' he joked weakly.

'No, I'm trying to figure something out. It's on the tip of my tongue.'

'It's not the worst plan ever. It's about fifteen grand. Violet could use it for university. But I think she'd rather have two parents, instead of one dead and the other in jail.'

Fifteen thousand dollars wasn't that much money in exchange for a human life. But Gemma had done awful things when she was desperate for money. She'd sold a piece of her soul every time she listed a tea towel, and hadn't even made that much. It didn't take a lot of money to motivate a person when they were trying to bridge the gap between surviving and going completely broke.

'There's a time limit on when you can claim it, right?'

'Two years,' he confirmed. 'Unless it's a minor child; then they have until their twentieth birthday to claim.'

Nico Tanner was nineteen. They'd had less than a year left to prove that he was Dean Shadwell's son, or fifteen thousand dollars was about to evaporate. Ruth and Nico must have been frantic.

But they hadn't been. The man they thought was Dean Shadwell's brother had been in their town for days, and they'd avoided him like the plague.

Or had Nico tried to see him? He'd been headed towards Shadwell's door, the day Hugh and Gemma caught him at their house.

'You're freaking me out a little, Gem. What's going on?'

'Ruth Tanner,' Gemma said. 'It's driving me up the wall. Why did Shadwell come back to Rainier?'

'To kill Lochlan Lewis,' Hugh said. 'He couldn't let the tour go ahead. He couldn't risk the extra attention on the Rainier Ripper because someone might figure out who he really was. What really happened here that night.'

'Why do that in Rainier?' Gemma argued. 'It's so unnecessarily risky. If he was willing to kill to stop the tour, he could have done it quietly in Sydney. The police might not even have made a connection between the murder and the Rainier tour, given how many people Lochlan Lewis apparently owed money. Coming to Rainier and then triggering a murder investigation almost guaranteed Shadwell's secret would be exposed. Not to mention' – she was on a roll now – 'I still don't understand when he could have done it. I was with him upstairs when the body appeared in the fountain.'

'Shadwell had more than enough money to pay accomplices.'

'If he was going to pay someone to take care of it for him, wouldn't it have been more discreet? Why would he have been personally involved enough to get his fingerprints on the evidence? Especially given that he had to know his fingerprints would come up in the system as Dean Shadwell's.' She slammed a hand down on the railing of the bed. 'He was wearing gloves! When he got out of his car, he put gloves on. Why would he take them off again to commit a murder?'

'I don't know,' Hugh said, looking alarmed. 'But he must have, because he left the fingerprint.'

'Then he burned his hand,' Gemma said. Her head had begun to pound, but she couldn't stop. She knew she wasn't making any sense, but that was what she needed Hugh to understand. None of it made any sense. 'As an excuse not to have his fingerprints taken again. So the police would just use the ones they had on file for Marcus Shadwell. Because he couldn't risk them fingerprinting him and realising he was *Dean* Shadwell.'

'What does any of this have to do with Ruth Tanner?'

'That's what I'm trying to figure out!' Gemma almost shouted. She took a deep breath and forced herself back to a normal speaking voice, worried that the nurses would come boot Hugh out before she untangled this. 'Why would Shadwell risk coming back to Rainier, knowing that he would end up in a room with Ruth Tanner, the one person alive who could look him in the eyes and recognise that he was Dean, not Marcus? But she never went near him, even though she had every reason to confront him at the first opportunity. Why?'

'I think you need some rest, Gemma,' Hugh said. 'These are all good points, but I'm worried you're going to give yourself a stroke.'

'You're right,' she said, closing her eyes. 'I'm going to take a nap. But can you tell Mick I need to talk to him? Tell him that Christian Holst killed Lochlan Lewis.'

THIRTY-THREE

MICK WASN'T QUITE as quick as Hugh to answer her summons, which she supposed was fair. Two days passed, punctuated by other visitors, and dreadful meals, and meetings with doctors and specialists to discuss her condition and the plans for rehabilitation. She had a lot of physiotherapy appointments ahead of her. It was nice to know what her priorities were for the immediate future, at least, when everything beyond that was a great big question mark.

When Mick did arrive, he looked about ten years older than the last time she had seen him. When had that been? When she went in for an interview the day the photographs of her and Shadwell turned up? No, it was at the memorial.

He must have decided the upkeep on his dyed black hair was too much, because he'd buzzed it short and the stubble was steel grey. It suited him, in her opinion, but she understood why he was self-conscious about it. His face was grey too, and deeply lined, like he wasn't sleeping well.

She supposed that he had been processing the same feelings of betrayal she had, if the truth was out that Eva Nováková was Petra Seifert. Perhaps it was worse for him – not only had his wife been lying to him, but also Hugh, his partner of nearly twenty years.

'Hello, Gemma,' he said, more gentle than she'd ever heard him.

'Hi, Mick,' she said. Her voice was croaky, and she gestured for the jug of water on her side table. He filled a plastic cup for her, and helped her take a sip, then sat down in the visitor's chair.

'Thanks for coming,' she said. 'I probably could have just got Hugh to pass this on, but the theory I'm about to put to you is pretty wild, and I figure it would be an even harder sell coming from him. I assume he's not New South Wales Police's favourite person right now.'

'You could say that.'

'What's going to happen to him?'

'That's hard to say,' he said. 'His police career is done. He's tendered his resignation, which I've accepted.'

Hugh hadn't mentioned that, but she didn't blame him. He'd had a lot of heavy news to share already.

'I've advised him to get a good lawyer. We've retained one for Aubrey too.'

'Are you two . . .' she began cautiously, not sure she had any right to pry.

He nodded. 'We separated for a while. She went to stay with her parents, and Jac went to the Tjibaou house. Fawn too.'

He scrubbed a hand over his face. 'It's been like a game of three-card Monte with the kids. Fawn needed space from her parents, but if Jac was staying with Aubrey at the Dillon farm of course Fawn couldn't go there; it would have been too weird. So both she and Jac took themselves to live with Jaylene and Antoine.'

'Aubrey must have found that difficult.'

He shrugged. 'Maybe less than she would have before all this. With what came out about what really happened between Vincent and Henning-Klosner, there's been a lot of remarkably productive conversations between them. Which is not to say I agree with you putting Jac in contact with him.' He fixed her with a stern look. 'You might want to keep your head down around Jaylene for a while too; she was apoplectic.'

'I stand by it,' Gemma said, surprising herself. But she did. Yes, it was an impulsive decision made in the midst of sleep deprivation and paranoia, but she'd make it again now. Jac's parents and grandparents weren't going to support it, and Jac had been right – time was running out to get the answers they needed. Their means of getting the truth had been painful, but it was out, and now Jac could know their father as he really was, not the idealised version they'd been offered. The real Vincent Tjibaou was still a wonderful man worth loving.

'You were always way too permissive with those kids,' Mick grumbled. 'That's why they always wanted to be at your bloody house. Just because you had to grow up way too fast doesn't mean you can treat them like they're basically adults.'

'I don't want to fight with you,' Gemma said – mostly because she knew she was about to have a completely different fight with him, and wanted to save her energy.

'Fair enough; we'll put a pin in that. As far as Hugh goes, best-case scenario is he and Aubrey are charged with improper interference with a corpse, and it's dropped because the offence was so long ago. Worst-case scenario, there's a coronial inquest into Petra Seifert's death, which resets the clock, and they're convicted and spend up to two years in prison. If he is able to walk away, he'll need a new career, and I'll be happy to provide a reference stating that he's a damn good worker who made one incredibly stupid mistake.'

'What about Dr Nicholls?'

'He's been charged with failing to register a death, and has voluntarily surrendered his medical licence. There just isn't enough evidence to pursue it as a murder charge, or fully corroborate his story that Petra died through misadventure. The public discourse on the case is a complete mess; if I were you, I'd avoid the newspapers.' He drummed his fingers on the arm of the chair. 'Lotte has resigned as magistrate and coroner, and the Bar Association has launched an investigation.'

'Violet mentioned she'd resigned.'

'Yes, it's been a busy couple of weeks. Now, Hugh did pass on a message from you, which I'm assuming was the painkillers talking. You wanted to tell me that the actual killer of Lochlan Lewis was Christian Holst?'

'Yes. It's possible that it was Nico Tanner, but I think that's less likely.'

'Yes, that is pretty unlikely. Isn't it much more likely that he was killed by the man who had a history of using homicide to solve his problems, had an excellent motive to kill him, and was the owner of the knife that was used as the murder weapon?'

'So you did find Shadwell's knife at the scene,' she said, a little disturbed at how delighted she was at being right about that. 'I thought so.'

'We also found his fingerprint.'

'Which is compelling, I admit. But all that tells you is that at some point he touched that poncho, and he did try to offer me an explanation of how that happened.'

'And you believed him?'

'I didn't at the time, but I've been churning it over.' She tried to swallow, but her tongue was like a foreign object stuck in her mouth. She gestured for him to pass her the cup again. 'Did you find his fingerprints on the knife?'

Mick was silent for a long moment. 'No.'

'That's a bit weird, huh? Considering that he owns it. Was it perhaps wiped clean?'

'Yes. It makes sense he would do that, after he committed a murder with it.'

'So he killed Lochlan with his own very distinctive knife, wiped it clean of prints, then left it at the scene? Why not just take it with him? Why wipe the prints off when he had a very good excuse for having his prints all over it? For that matter, why take the risk of police noticing how similar it was to the one used in his brother's murder? He wouldn't risk that. But the real killer couldn't have known.'

'Do you read Sherlock fanfiction or something?' Mick snapped, then he took a deep breath. 'Sorry. But I think you need to remember that rule number one is: when you hear hoofbeats, think horses – not zebras.'

'Zebras do exist, though. And this is not adding up. Mick, please.'

'Okay,' Mick said. 'Tell me your theory.'

She cleared her throat. 'Let's start from the basics. Since Shadwell's death, have you been through his phone and email records?'

'Yes.'

'You found communication between Shadwell and Ruth Tanner, didn't you?'

Mick blinked. Score one for her. 'How did you know that?'

'Because Dean Shadwell – the real Dean Shadwell – was Nico's father.' Maybe. That wasn't completely proven, but it wasn't important right now. 'Ruth Tanner had every reason to bail up Shadwell in the teashop after the tour or in the days afterwards, but she didn't. And Shadwell didn't take any steps to avoid her. He was confident she would stay away from him, and the only way he could have been was if they'd communicated beforehand.'

'Hmm. I probably shouldn't tell you this, but we did interview Ruth Tanner about an email we found from her to Shadwell. She reached out to him two weeks before the tour demonstration, and told him that she wanted him to come for the demonstration and to vote in favour of the tour. If he did that for her, she would, I quote, "never bother you again". If he didn't, she would go to the media with "the truth" about Dean Shadwell. We questioned her about what she meant by "the truth", whether she knew Shadwell's real identity. She told us she was just referring to Dean's less-than-savoury history: the fact that he was in the Rainier area because he was running an illegal drug business with his friend Jan Henning-Klosner.'

A thrill ran through Gemma. That was one missing piece filled in. Of course Shadwell had come after that summons – the last thing he needed was anyone digging into the facts about Dean Shadwell. Perhaps he had even planned to shut Ruth up permanently, until Lochlan Lewis's murder put them all under a microscope. There was no way of knowing now.

'I was pretty shocked when I read the email, I can tell you. She can be a bit, um . . .'

'Fussy? Demanding?' Gemma suggested. She'd served Ruth enough times to know she could be difficult when she wanted to be.

'Sure, demanding. But she was mortified when I pointed out she'd essentially committed blackmail. She explained that she knew it was manipulative, but never considered it might be criminal.'

Gemma suppressed an eyeroll. 'So Ruth Tanner blackmails him into coming to town and attending an event, where he committed a murder?'

'Makes sense to me. Ruth wanted to support her fiancé's new business venture, and knew that "Marcus" Shadwell could be a make-or-break vote. She pushed him to help them, and unknowingly caused him to panic. He was trying to clean up loose ends.'

'Here's the piece that doesn't fit, no matter how hard you bash on it: he didn't have time. Aside from a few minutes, I was with him. I assume you believe me now, on that point?'

'He didn't have to commit the murder during that window, only move the body.'

'Because Lochlan was suffocated, then the body posed later.'

Mick looked annoyed. 'Did Hugh tell you that?'

'No.' She doubted Mick would believe her, but Hugh was in such deep shit that one more shovelful wouldn't do him any harm. She wasn't about to throw Jac under the bus. She went on: 'Even if he did have enough time to pose the body in the fountain – which I personally doubt – he had no opportunity to commit the murder. Lochlan Lewis was alive when Shadwell entered the teashop, and he did not leave again until I showed him upstairs. He was inside with us at the time of the murder. You know who wasn't?'

Mick looked up at the ceiling, like he was trying to recall who he had seen that night. 'I don't know. Who?'

'Christian Holst. Ruth came in on her own. A bit odd for a couple not to enter together. But I didn't think much of it at the time, and of course it didn't seem significant immediately after the murder, because I know Christian was inside the teashop before Lochlan's body was moved to the fountain. Because Ruth deliberately mentioned the fountain, so I would look out the window and see it was empty. To give Christian an alibi.'

Ruth had carefully chosen words that would stick in Gemma's head later, when everything went to shit again. 'There's ice in the fountain.'

'Ruth and Christian didn't come in together, because Christian stayed back to talk to Lochlan, his business partner. To walk him back to his motel. To kill him, quietly, as soon as they were out of the public eye.' She caught Mick's eyes and held them. 'Did he tell you that he was the last person to see Lochlan alive?'

'No,' Mick admitted. 'He told me he came in with the others. He voluntarily turned over the check-in data on his phone, which showed he was there.'

'Ruth could have checked in with his phone,' Gemma argued.

'Or you're just misremembering. Why would you even have noticed who came in when, let alone remembered it for this long?'

'Because it's what I do, Mick. I notice who's in the room with me, so I can run around like a headless chicken trying to keep them all happy. He. Was. Not. There.'

God, she hoped this was actually making sense. Maybe she was just babbling nonsense at him, still so full of painkillers that she was just imagining that she was presenting a logical case.

'Here's what I think their original plan was. Christian kills Lochlan, and leaves him in the alley behind where the poncho was found. Found by Nico Tanner, by the way. That was convenient, wasn't it? Christian returns to the teashop, and they take pains to establish he was in there before the body ended up in the fountain. Now, Shadwell was a smoker. That meant that they could bank on him leaving the teashop at least once to have a cigarette, making him the only person there without an alibi. Once he left, Christian or Ruth sent a signal to Nico to move the body. Christian deliberately caused a stir inside the teashop. I heard it from upstairs: a fight kicked off between him and Jaylene, and he was the instigator. Like a magic act – make everyone look at the back of the shop, then when they look back again the body is on display. Abracadabra.'

'There's a lot of moving parts there. Why risk it? What if something went wrong?'

'Something did go wrong. They saw Shadwell leave through the front door, and thought it was go time. They didn't realise I had gone to meet him at the back door, meaning he had an alibi after all.'

Mick nodded.

'So once that part of the plan fell apart, they had to destroy my credibility. Hence, stalking me until they got a dodgy-looking picture of the two of us together. I'm guessing the photographer was Nico Tanner. We saw Nico at our house the day after the murder. Hugh and I just thought it was funny that he was trying to get attention from the girls.'

'That doesn't answer the question of why they would risk such an elaborate scheme.'

'Because if they pulled it off, there would have been zero suspicion on them. It would have all tidily pointed to Shadwell, or at least created enough reasonable doubt to stop a conviction. Without that shield, Christian would have been the most obvious suspect. Because he has a life insurance policy on Lochlan, doesn't he?'

For the first time, Mick looked genuinely impressed. 'How did you figure that out?'

'I've run a business for nearly twenty years. I know that it's a common practice for business partners to have policies on each other. Our financial adviser strongly recommended it when we applied for the loans to take over the teashop. And Christian is the kind of person to take out event insurance on his own wedding. Of course his business was fully insured.'

'Gem, I've known Christian for years. You've known him all your life. He can be a jackass sometimes, but he's got a big heart. Are you suggesting that he went out, found a person to start a business with so he had an excuse to take out a life insurance policy, and then murdered him for the money? Not to mention framing a man he thought was an innocent bystander? That's psychopathic.'

'I don't think he thought of Shadwell as an innocent by-stander. I think he hated him intensely. Shadwell told me that Ruth wrote to him. From her perspective she was a struggling single mother, and he was her son's rich uncle who refused to offer any help. She wasn't even asking for money; she just wanted a DNA test to give her the confirmation she needed to get a victims of crime payout for Nico. And he wouldn't do it. She must have loathed him.'

'Seems tenuous to me.'

Gemma sighed. 'You know how I know you've never been broke? Raising a kid is hard. Doing it without the dad is even harder. Doing it with help you feel entitled to just out of reach?

Twenty years is a long time to let a head of steam build up. Christian loves Ruth and, like you said, he has a big heart.'

'Why not kill Shadwell then? Where does Lochlan come in?'

'I don't think Lochlan was on the up and up. Dig into him even a little, and you find a lot of disgruntled people. He presented himself to us as running tours in Melbourne and Sydney, but actually he had a habit of abruptly closing up shop and moving on to a new city, leaving behind a lot of debts. He was from London originally; what would have happened to Christian if Lochlan had flitted back there? He'd have been left holding the bag. I don't think Christian went out and found a mark – Lochlan did. Don't you think this tour idea has always been a little shaky?'

Mick shrugged. 'Christian certainly believed in it.'

'Exactly. Christian has spent years pouring drinks for everyone here. He, more than anyone, has seen the real face of the grief and trauma we all lived with. He thought he had an opportunity to turn it into something positive. He staked his reputation on it. If it turned out to be a scam? Well, I could see him killing over that.'

Mick let out a breath, long and slow. 'You're building a real house of cards here, Gem.'

'I'm not asking you to rush out and arrest them. Just ask some questions. Look at the evidence again.' She reached out, tentatively, and pressed a hand to his forearm. 'We've spent nearly twenty years under the weight of the so-called Rainier Ripper. That was the logical conclusion too, when something much more complicated was going on. Don't leave us back where we started. Please.'

THIRTY-FOUR

IN THE END, Lane learned how it all shook out through the newspaper. He tried calling Gemma once, but it didn't go through. He realised later, from piecing together clues in the news stories, that Gemma was the unidentified woman in critical condition. Whoever had charge of her phone must not have seen fit to answer a call from the Tin.

He was relieved to see a small story announcing that she had been released from the hospital. It was, however, a stark reminder that no matter how deeply involved he might have been for a brief point in time, life in here was separate. Prisoners only got what was given to them, especially when it came to information.

'*How they did it,*' Lane read aloud. '*Police allege audacious fountain murder plot.*'

Jan didn't seem interested in the article. After his heart attack he'd been successfully revived, but his outlook was dire. He spent several days in an induced coma, and now was rarely conscious and never particularly aware of his surroundings. Once the paperwork had ground its way slowly through the system, he would be transferred to the prison hospice for whatever time he had left.

Lane had no idea how he felt about any of that. Jan wasn't a good man. He might not be a serial killer, but he had murdered Vincent Tjibaou.

But Lane had murdered someone too. He hadn't pulled the trigger, but he had put someone else in a position where they had to, and in a way that was worse.

'*In explosive court proceedings, police alleged that Lochlan Lewis was murdered by Christian Holst, ending weeks of speculation as to which of the three adults charged in relation to the conspiracy to murder the young tour guide actually carried out the killing.*

'*The elaborate plot was intended to create an alibi for Holst, while falsely implicating another man who has not been named by police.*'

Lane folded the paper and threw it on the table beside Jan's bed. 'Well. Fun plan, but their big mistake was letting it get too complicated. There were about six hundred possible failure points that would have screwed them eventually. Not that I can talk. Neither of us knows how to get away with murder, do we?' He gazed at Jan's sleeping form. 'Can I tell you a secret? I never killed anyone. It wasn't me holding the gun. But I wasn't innocent.' He laughed. 'I spent so much time trying to find common ground with you, and it turns out we had something huge in common. We both belong in here, but not for everything written in our file.'

But there was still a huge gulf in their experiences – Lane was not going to die in here. There were three years behind him and three ahead. That was nothing, if he could just keep himself safe and play it smart.

THIRTY-FIVE

LANE HOLLAND WAS taller than Gemma had expected him to be. Perhaps because of the way he'd spoken on the phone, trying to sound as unthreatening as possible, she'd imagined someone slight. He wore a smart suit that was a little loose around the shoulders, and wasn't handcuffed, although there was a man hovering very close behind him with a Department of Corrective Services ID badge pinned to his pocket.

'It's lovely to meet you,' she said, holding out her hand for Lane to shake.

'If only it was under better circumstances,' he said. He shook her hand once, gently, before dropping it.

They'd both been called to give evidence at the Court of Criminal Appeal, although Gemma understood that it was largely a formality. Jan Henning-Klosner's convictions for the murders of Eva Nováková and Dean Shadwell – now identified as Petra

Seifert and Marcus Shadwell – would be vacated, but that would still leave him with his twenty-five-year sentence for the murder of Vincent Tjibaou. He had no chance of living to see release.

As she searched for an empty seat, Gemma felt an odd wave of deja vu as she observed the various groups and considered where she would be most welcome. Jaylene and Antoine had secured a seat at the front. Jac sat beside them, and then Aubrey and Mick. Their marriage had survived the revelations, and Gemma felt a twinge of envy at that.

Aubrey and Hugh had both been convicted of improper interference with a corpse under Section 81 of the Crimes Act and given good behaviour bonds. There had been a small outcry from some quarters that the sentence was inadequate and they were being given special treatment because of their association with the police, but it was a relief to Gemma that Hugh wouldn't serve any time. Violet had lost her home and the security of an intact family; she didn't need to lose her father for years as well.

Tamara Fleischer sat on the other side of the aisle. After Petra Seifert's identity was revealed, but no family came forward to claim her remains, Tamara had coordinated the effort to have a new headstone erected with her real name, and her date of birth and death. She took up a collection that quickly met and exceeded its goal. Lotte and Timothy Nicholls attempted to donate the full cost of the headstone, but their contribution was promptly returned.

Gabrielle Herald arranged for the body of Marcus Shadwell, previously buried in the Rainier cemetery under the name

Dean Shadwell, to be disinterred and reburied with the rest of the Shadwell family. She had her husband's body cremated. Nico Tanner asked her to first allow a DNA test to prove Dean Shadwell was his father, but she declined.

Christian, Ruth and Nico were absent, of course. Nico had confessed not only to moving Lochlan's body but to stalking 'Marcus' Shadwell on and off for months in hopes of getting a clandestine DNA sample. He was never successful, but learned enough about Shadwell's habits and routines to later hatch the plot to frame him. He and Ruth were awaiting sentencing for conspiracy to commit murder.

The ironic thing was that Nico's confession was the only solid piece of evidence against Christian Holst, who was still proclaiming his innocence. With this appeal making the science and psychology of false confessions front-page news, and so much contradictory evidence creating reasonable doubt, it had been a nailbiter right up to the moment the jury handed down a guilty verdict.

In the back row sat Hugh and Violet; Violet was staying with her father this week. She turned and offered Gemma an encouraging smile as she slid in beside them. Over her head, Hugh offered her a similar but much less certain look. Gemma smiled back, and then turned to the front as they waited for the justices to draw a line under the whole mess.

THIRTY-SIX

CARVER PULLED UP to the door of the Special Purpose Centre and cut the engine. Behind them the electric prison gates slid closed.

Lane stared down at his cuffed hands. He was still wearing his civilian clothes, his cheap grey court suit, but his day of almost-normalcy had ended as soon as Carver snapped the cuffs on him for transport.

'Can I ask you something?' Lane asked.

Carver stared at him in the rear-view mirror, but didn't say no.

Lane had been going to ask Carver how many strings he had pulled in the background in hopes of getting the truth out of Jan. Had he arranged for Jan to be transferred to the Special Purpose Centre?

Had he arranged for Lane to come here? Was he the reason those rumours had spread, making Lane's life in general population untenable?

Was he the reason Jan had mistakenly been brought to the showers at the same time the cleaning detail was in there, violating policy? Was he the reason a prisoner as dangerous as Ludwig had been on the cleaning detail, instead of under closer supervision?

Wasn't it a little too neat that Jan had been sent to the medical unit on the same night that a new murder was committed in Rainier?

But knowing the answer to any of those questions wouldn't help him.

Lane had given up on the idea of being a police officer decades ago. But for most of his life, it had been the safety net beneath him. Maybe not the high-flying career he could have had if he'd gone in straight from university, but a good, reliable union job.

That option was gone. So was any future as a licensed private investigator.

Carver had just been trying to manipulate him when he raised the spectre of Lane's future, but he was right. He did need to decide what he wanted to do next.

And calling Carver out wasn't going to get him there.

'I'm sorry that Jan wasn't able to tell you what happened to Matilda,' he said.

Carver smiled, but his eyes were flat. 'That's not a question.'

'No.' Lane looked around at the dusty grey car park, the ringlock fence, at the scruffy lawn and patch of trees beyond it.

Realistically, it could be another three years before the next time he was even this far away from the prison.

He looked back at Carver. 'Get me out of here, and I will find your daughter.'

ACKNOWLEDGEMENTS

I WOULD LIKE to acknowledge the traditional owners of the lands I lived and worked on while writing this book. At various times, this book was written on Ngunnawal, Wiradjuri, Wurundjuri and Waywurru country. I pay my respects to their elders past and present.

Rainier is a fictional town in a real part of Australia. Readers who tend to win at trivia night already know that the actual midpoint between Melbourne and Sydney is located in Tarcutta, which is in Wiradjuri country.

This book owes a great debt to the book *Duped: Why Innocent People Confess – and Why We Believe Their Confessions* by Saul Kassin PhD.

Thank you to:

My ever patient and supportive teams at Hachette Australia, Hodder & Stoughton and William Morrow.

My editors, Rebecca Saunders, Emma Rafferty, Ali Lavau and Rebecca Hamilton.

My lovely agent Sarah McKenzie.

My 2022 Book Gang: Warren Ward, Al Campbell, Fiona Robertson, Dinuka McKenzie, Andrew Roff, Scott-Patrick Mitchell, Natasha Sholl, Jonathan Butler, Michael Grey, Sally Bothroyd, Maggie Jankuloska, Nikky Lee, Kate Murray, Karen Ginnane, Brendan Colley, Roz Bellamy, Denise Picton and Kylie Orr. I would not have enjoyed this year half as much without you all.

Freya Marske, and the tireless sprinters of the Word Camp.

Everyone in my team at DAWE. Nick, yes, I named a murderer after your cat. Sorry.

My friends and family. Any characters named after you are either an accident or intended as a compliment.

My love and my joy for making the space I needed to get the work done. Thank you.